Keith Bradbury studied English and Drama in Manchester before going into the world of education. He now lives in Madrid and spends his time writing, reading, walking, playing guitar and cooking. He also writes poetry. This is his first novel.

To Nicky

Love & Best Wishes

Keith x

April 2022

To my wife, Jane, who sowed the seeds many moons ago of my love for Spain, and without whose belief in me this book could not have been written.

Keith Bradbury

LET THE DEAD HOLD YOUR HAND

AUSTIN MACAULEY PUBLISHERS™

LONDON ★ CAMBRIDGE ★ NEW YORK ★ SHARJAH

A CIP catalogue record for this title is available from the British Library.

ISBN 9781398448278 (Paperback)
ISBN 9781398448285 (ePub e-book)

www.austinmacauley.com

First Published 2022
Austin Macauley Publishers Ltd®
1 Canada Square
Canary Wharf
London
E14 5AA

Chapter 1

Everything reveals a mood of infinite woe, an oriental curse that has befallen these streets. All that is tranquil and majestic in the Vega and the town, is rife with angst and tragedy in this Moorish district.

Federico Garcia Lorca - Impresiones y paisajes - 1918

A Street in the Albayzin, Granada
1503

Lowering the worn black hood of his dust and dirt encrusted riding cape, the weary traveller gazes tentatively at his surroundings. This area of Granada is a labyrinth of winding paths, dark alleyways and sinister looking streets whose cobbled stones are uneven and treacherous once the light fades. The houses to him are built in a seemingly random pattern. Many look identical, many are whitewashed, many little more than hovels. Occasionally, he had passed several Carmen on his way here; high walled free-standing houses which, judging by the scents wafting from them, contained lemon and orange trees. But they were exceptions.

In the area in which he now stands the odours are not so inviting. This particular narrow street is one of the worst he has passed through; filled with a vile cocktail of rubble, mud and waste both animal and human. Black flies of an abnormal size are the only things moving now as they circle the filth at his feet. He swats them away with the hem of his cloak but they will be back all too soon. Keeping himself upright has been a challenge thus far and, given what lies festering on the ground, a necessity.

It is no place for a horse and he has left his, at the cost of a *real*, under the watchful gaze of a street child with cracked black teeth and frightening swathes of open red sores on his arms. He knows his mount will be safe. The child though will no doubt haggle for a second coin on his return.

He is less sure about the safety of the building that is just about standing in front of him. Could this really be the right place? After so many years within the walls of the red palace could the woman he sought now be reduced to living in such dire circumstances? The low arched door looks to be ajar and seems to beckon him, as if whoever awaits within is expecting his company. Yet no light escapes from the gloom beyond. Part of him wonders if he is doing the right thing, he could be back safely ensconced behind his desk at home many leagues to the north, writing, studying and reading.

But something had been driving him now for quite some time, leading him to this moment, something he realised some years ago that was fashioning his destiny. Only his father had known of his quest to find this woman and to record what she knows. It had been a long journey and one visited many times by near misses, dead ends and false trails. His father had been worried so much that in the end he had forbidden him to go but he had taken the difficult decision to slip away nonetheless, whilst his father was out one day. He regretted not saying farewell but he had known that if he did not find this woman then much of his people's heritage and history would be lost for eternity. He hoped his father would one day understand, one day be proud of his work.

And so here he now stands, his breathing shallow, as he tries hard to not inhale too much of the rank air pervading this small, squalid neighbourhood, deep within the Albayzin. Stepping forward he gently coaxes the door further open, enough to enable him to pass through. Surprisingly, it does not creak as he had expected. For some reason the lack of sound disturbs him further.

He calls gently into the void.

'Assalamu alaikum!'

If he has made a mistake, then these words could well cost him his life.

But there is no return of his greeting. Nor indeed any sound of life.

Only a cold draft of air answers him like a sigh and brushes past his face gently, like the phantom hand of a long dead lover.

He steps over the threshold and finds himself in a small vestibule. He pushes aside a heavy hessian curtain and carefully steps out of the stygian gloom into the heavy atmosphere of an incense laden room, semi-lit by a host of tallow candles. He can just make out several low tables crammed to teetering fullness with books and scrolls. Despite the best efforts of the incense which emanates from where he knows not, there is an overriding smell of old age and decay. Just for the moment it is significantly preferable to the rancid air of the street.

He glances at the low vaulted ceiling from which hang ropes of fat garlic and assorted dried herbs, thyme, rosemary, some bundles of cinnamon and a net of what looks like nutmeg. The thought of food blindsides him just for an instant and his mind flicks back to his mother's cooking. He realises he has not eaten well for several days. He surveys the rest of the room. Apart from the low tables there is no other furniture, although around the room he notices several large bundles which he assumes to be rags and discarded cloth, though he is puzzled as to why there is so much.

A doorway looms in the far-right corner, partially curtained off by more hessian sacking. He wonders whether to call out again. He wishes now he had more than just his dagger to protect him. He considers whether to look at the books which stand in small stacks on the table like mini mountain ranges, when his eyes are drawn once again to the bundles lining the far wall.

And to one in particular, larger than the others.

And now he could swear it just moved. And then he suddenly sees.

The eyes.

And they are staring at him.

He takes an involuntary step back, startled and scared more than he dare admit.

Startled by these eyes that seem to penetrate deep, deep into his soul. He swallows his fear, picks up a candle and tentatively draws nearer. He places his free hand over his heart and bows. Then he kneels at the feet of the living bundle whose gaze has not left him for one iota of a second, nor, seemingly, blinked.

By the light of the candle, he realises that he is in the presence of a dauntingly large woman dressed in thick swathes of heavy dark blue-black cloth. He places the candle carefully and reverently next to him.

There is something about her size which intimidates him. As she slowly lifts her arms to lower her veil down to her shoulders, he notices more clearly the immensity of her limbs. Her hands are twice the size of his; gnarled walnut forms that one time could no doubt have swatted him away like a gnat. Her hair is a tight matted bun of silver, white and grey streaks. In places she has bald patches and he tries not to stare. She rests her hands on her vast thighs and moves her feet apart slightly and he notices her footwear is the esparto grass sandals normally worn by peasants. Aye, he thinks, that she should be reduced to this.

9

'Am I, by Allah's will, I trust I am, in the presence of the one known as La Mora of Ubeda?'

Silence hangs heavy between them as her eyes continue to judge him.

He starts to speak again, 'I am—'

'I know exactly who you are, scholar,' she interrupts. 'You are from the town of Arevalo in the land of Avila in Castile.'

Her breath comes in a rattle. It does not sound good.

'I have sensed your arrival for several months.'

Her voice crackles like autumnal twigs on a fire. He flinches at her words, amazed that she knows of him and part of him wants to ask *how* she knows of him *or* of his journey, though no doubt she has her spies far and wide amongst the poor of Granada and beyond.

'Yes. I am he. And yes, I have indeed travelled far to kneel at your feet this day. I am here to bathe in your wisdom, to hear your words and to record them so others may know of you and what you have done for our people. I am…'

'Do not tell me your name. If I do not know I cannot tell. It is enough that you are here.'

The candlelight suddenly flickers violently around the room as a skinny white cat leaps from somewhere high above him, sending disturbing, distorted shadows up the red clay walls. The creature looks at him with complete disdain, stretches and settles into the folds of La Mora's lap. He has never been sure about cats. He has never yet met one that seemed to like him.

La Mora coughs up phlegm and spits to one side. The scholar tries to hide his shock at an act he never thought a woman such as she would perform. But I am not here to judge how she should behave, he thinks to himself; after all she has lived through, all she has had to see and suffer, it is not my place. She looks at him as if judging his strength of purpose but possibly that it is just his interpretation and his usual insecurities surfacing.

'Tell me what I think you seek first then perhaps…perhaps we can help each other.'

Hesitantly and in a timorous voice he speaks.

'I am writing a treatise on the Qur'an.'

'Speak up, man.'

He clears his throat and inwardly chides himself to speak more assuredly.

'It is my way of helping to keep our world alive and to help in teaching, preserving and spreading the Prophet's words, praise be unto him. And I also wish to make a record of the last days of our last king, Muhammed, known to the Christians as Boabdil, may Allah bless his soul.'

She stares at him with no sign of emotion. He feels uneasy and sharp pains shoot through his already tired legs folded under him as he tries hard to sit still.

'I am told that you often discussed the finer points of the Book with him. I wish to show the world how he was not, is not, the coward portrayed by the Christians. Not only a learned man but a brave man.'

'No doubt you play your part well as a Morisco,' she replies, ignoring his words.

The scholar hesitates before replying, thrown slightly by the question.

'I do. And yet I and my brothers and sisters continue to practise Islam in the shadows and shades. If I can record your words, record what you have witnessed, it will not be lost to history. And our faith can be strengthened by your wisdom.'

'Ah!' she says and a cynical smile creeps across her heavily jowled jaw line.

'What I have witnessed.' A hard unfriendly smile crawls across her mouth like a slash.

Outside in the middle distance, a dog emits what sounds like his last sad farewell bark to the world and a welcome smell of jasmine wafts into the room from the far door, almost as if summoned from the distant Carmen to alleviate the rankness of this squalid corner.

La Mora now begins to speak once more and her words rattle out of her mouth like walnuts cracking open.

'I have more than 90 winters. I should have passed from this life a long, long time ago but Allah is keeping breath in my body for a reason of which only he knows. Perhaps it is a penance, so that I continually relive the horrors I witnessed in those days, weeks, months, years after we left the Alhambra. Someone indeed needs to record those scenes; none must ever forget what blasphemies and evil took place once that devil's whore Isabella and her bastard husband tore the heart out of our world.'

She pauses, tries to moisten her tomb-dry lips with a tongue that seems unnaturally large and alarmingly pale. The scholar again inwardly shudders. The only other sound now is the steady thrum of the crickets outside. La Mora turns as if to spit again but instead seems to think twice and swallows. The scholar is no less repulsed but in the gloom he can once more, fortunately, hide his reaction.

Without moving a muscle, she continues.

'I no longer leave these walls. One day either they, or I, will collapse. But I neither seek nor wish help from anyone, nor do I want to live out there, it is no longer a place I recognise, nor do I want to be reminded of who now lives in the palace. For me to have to see the land I love swallowed and spat out by Isabella's greedy brood is too much for these ancient eyes. I have withdrawn into the shadows of my grief. I weep each night over the fall of the Nasiri.

I have seen such horrors and pain, Scholar, such nightmare scenes, that one as young as you could not imagine; scenes and indeed sounds, that haunt me each night and no doubt will follow me beyond the shores of time. To witness such cruelty, such humiliation, it has broken my heart, but not yet my spirit. No one *ever* in the long-told tales of this world wept over such misfortune as that of the sons of Granada.'

She slowly begins to rock backward and forward, closing her eyes.

'Remember my words. I saw noble ladies—widows and married alike—subjected to the cruellest mockery and degradations. I watched hundreds of young women sold at public auction. I lost all of what little family I had. All died defending our faith, our home, our land. And,'

She pauses as nightmare scenes of death and worse, are played out once again in her mind.

'And I witnessed the terrible violation and destruction of Arabic books in the Bib-Rambla.'

She stops her tale once again and this time does spit into the dust of the floor and with such venom, that to the Scholar, it is as if she is spitting into the face of some invisible enemy.

'You would not have been able to believe that such an act could be carried out. An act of such vandalism against culture. Ancient manuscripts, papers, copies of holy writings piled high. A funeral pyre of knowledge, wisdom and faith. Once I even saw a man take a copy of the Qur'an which he then tore up and used as paper for his children to play with.

I later watched from a hiding place in one of the towers as that dog son of a whore, Cardinal Cisneros, set light himself to a pyramid of books, smiling as he did so. May Allah make him suffer in hell. They say more than 5000 works perished that night. And for what? To wipe out everything that we are? Does he think by such a vile act he can eradicate our people, our history, our soul? I hope he burns in perpetual flames of damnation for the whole of eternity.'

La Mora spits more fiercely, this time to either side but now it is clearly a sign of hate towards the Cardinal rather than the need to expel phlegm. The Scholar is mesmerised by her words. He has heard of the burning of the books but to hear it from one who was there makes him feel an even deeper sadness and sense of loss. Such senseless, mindless actions. A bronze moth flickers around the dancing flames of the candles as La Mora continues.

'Later that night I ran around gathering up any pieces of paper that had escaped the blaze. They were strewn all everywhere. I felt hurt so deep in my heart, I thought I would stop breathing.'

She is now squeezing the cat so hard that it suddenly leaps from her lap with a venomous yowl. La Mora opens her rheumy eyes and calls after the cat with words he does not understand. The room seems to have suddenly grown smaller and the atmosphere more intense. It is as if her words have come to life and are crawling before the young man's eyes. For a terrifying second he thinks he smells burning paper. But then the moment passes and he stares at the woman in front of him and wonders about her powers.

He knows that for a short while in the early years after Boabdil's departure abroad, the Christians searched high and low for her, branding her a witch, but she seemed to have just vanished into thin air. He knows from those who told him where to find her that she has not been in this house for more than a year, he is not even sure whose house it actually is. He also now realises that it is clear that all along she knew that he was coming, that she had been waiting for him.

The scholar turns and gazes into the deep dark shadows of the room, feeling her pain. All this, he knows, must be recorded. He must consign the pictures and details of the abominable acts she has related to his memory. He looks back at La Mora, who now seems shrunken by the sharing of the experiences. Head bowed, she speaks again, her words rattling from her throat like verbal motes.

'Enough. On that table behind you, lie some books and papers from the Alhambra. Most are unimportant. I have already hidden the most valuable books belonging to Boabdil and his ministers. They are safe. The top two smaller scrolls, however, contain writings which tell in far more horrific detail of the events that I and others witnessed in the years after 1492. They will serve you well in spreading the truth of what really happened.'

The Scholar carefully places the scrolls in a deep inner pocket of his cloak. 'I will look after them and keep them safe.'

'You must, as if you were to be found with them, your life would be forfeit, your head removed and perched on a stake and your heart flung on a pyre.' The Scholar flinches at the unwanted imagery and tries to remind himself that he could be brave if he tried.

'But I have something else to give you. Something far more precious and at the same time far more dangerous. Something which needs guarding with your very soul. It contains a secret that one day might bring our people together again and be a reason for Allah to watch over our return to Granada. Now though is not the time. Our people are weak, our enemy strong and cruel. So, this secret must be guarded and passed on, until it is one day in the hands of people who know that the time is right and of what should be done. It is the key to what truly took place once we left the palace.'

The scholar's mind now careers in all different directions as to what this might be.

'Do not be afraid.' She reaches into the folds of her cloak and produces a small, beautifully engraved silver pouch. She offers it to him and he takes it as if handling an injured bird in his gloved hands. It is decorated with the Nasrid shield and motto, '*There is no Victor but God*'.

La Mora continues.

'It once held a section of a small Qur'an. It belonged to someone very special. Someone truly great. Someone for whom I not only worked but whom I worshipped and would lay down my life for.'

'Is this…did this belong to whom I think it did?' the Scholar whispers into the gloom. La Mora raises her head and sits up as straight as she is physically capable.

'Indeed. The last sultan of Granada, Abu Abdallah Muhammad bin Ali.'

'Boabdil! This is his?'

'Lower your voice,' La Mora commands.

'This is far more than what you see. Open it.'

He does as he is told. He looks up.

'It…it is empty.'

'Ah! So it seems. But sewn into its lining is a piece of paper carrying information that would bring the whole Christian army bearing down on us, were its existence to be revealed to them.

All I ask of you is to keep it close and hidden as I have these past eleven winters. And, one day, when you are old and your stars are about to go out, pass it on to someone you trust, as I have, someone with whom you would trust your mother's life and someone who will continue to guard it until the planets are aligned in our favour once again and the time is right.'

'Of course. I will. It is a great honour,' he replies, thinking at the same time that it is also an enormous burden; one of which he hopes he is worthy. 'But why me?'

'Do you think for one moment I would choose someone I did not know about?'

'No, I just. I am just… just honoured.'

'That is as maybe. There are precious few options left to me, but what I know of you, I know that you will not let our people down, nor let our king down. We have been watching you for many years and I know that you are the one to carry this treasure.'

The Scholar is desperate to ask her who the 'We' are. He at least now knows he was right. He had been chosen. Thinking back, he realised he had been fed information over the years by other scholars and wise men and had hints poured his way until he came up with the idea of searching out La Mora. All along she had known he would come because she had sought him out. He feels awfully small and unworthy. He trembles as he holds the pouch. If only he were a soldier, good at wielding a sword and not just a writer who would struggle to defend himself in combat of any sort.

'How will I know to whom I should pass it?' He cannot seem to stop staring at the pouch.

'Trust your judgement, Scholar. When the time comes, you will do the right thing. Look for someone who reminds you of yourself, who has the same virtues, the same passion for our people. And fear not, I know what you think, had I wanted a soldier to guard it I would have chosen one but I have chosen you and I am rarely wrong in my judgement of people.'

The scholar almost gasps as he realises that La Mora has just read his mind.

'Now, hush. Let me share with you a little of those last days inside the Alhambra. For you have said you wish to record what passed. So, record these words. Then you may learn a little more of why what you now carry is so important.'

She glances over his shoulder at the doorway.

'I do not have long.'

She lets out a deep sigh and closes her eyes.

'It was early January 1492. We were all gathered in the Sala de Barca.'

As he listens to La Mora's tale, he cannot help thinking of the silver pouch now hidden deep in the folds of his cloak and the secret it contains, which he now must carry and guard. He has no idea of what the secret might be, what the message the paper hidden inside contains. Better to be ignorant of God's ways, he thinks to himself.

He drifts slowly back to La Mora's words. She is recalling the day they left the Alhambra for the last time and she paints a vivid picture of the grief, the sadness, the characters present as Boabdil's days as ruler of Granada drew to an end. The Scholar cannot help but be mesmerised by her words. The Alhambra, the place he has dreamed of so many times. To walk within its walls, through its scented gardens with the sound of running water everywhere, the fountains providing the background music of calm and tranquillity. How he wished he could have been alive at that time when the Nasrid dynasty was at its height.

An hour passes and the scholar has sat so still he has almost become unaware of his body, of his breathing, of his very being. La Mora has finished her tale and has lowered her head, almost as if she has dozed off. The detail that La Mora went in to was unreal. So much for him to later recall and record. But his auditory memory had always served him well in the past. A skill developed over centuries passed down to him from storytellers in his family and the teachers he has spent so much of his short life with.

Then she shares with him Boabdil's last words to her and the task he set her. All at once the importance of the pouch he now bears hits him hard. And all he had once been told about, all he had once believed had occurred between those fateful years of 1492 and 1493 is blown apart in a moment. He wants to ask questions. But La Mora does not move. He is afraid to disturb her. The telling seems to have worn her out.

Now he has been passed this pouch to carry and guard. Yet he is still not sure exactly why he of all people has been asked to guard it, to preserve the secret it contains. Deep down he now understands what that secret might be and he certainly now possesses a much clearer idea of the danger he would be in were he to be caught with it.

Quietly he murmurs to himself, 'I pray Allah feels I am worthy. Watch over me.'

'I hear your concerns, Scholar.'

Her eyes remain shut as if she is once again reading his mind. This woman scares him at the same time that she enthrals him and he hopes to Allah that she does not read his fear.

'I have looked into the shifting sands of the future and I know that there will come a day when our people will be reunited with this Al-Andalus of ours. It is not lost forever. We have, God willing, a foothold in it for always, one we must not lose. Only if that pouch falls into the wrong hands will our enemy truly win but with your strength, your patience and your belief, I know that one day thanks to you and all future guardians of this information, the spirit of Boabdil will rise again.'

Suddenly, before he can speak one more syllable to La Mora, there comes the thumping sound of boots careering up the street towards the house, men shouting wildly and an explosion of dogs barking.

La Mora does not hesitate.

'Go! Through the back! Hurry!'

'What about you! They will kill you!'

'I have died many times. I am not afraid.'

La Mora covers her face and slips back among the bundles before he can protest. He has a good idea who is hurtling towards them and he does not want to be caught; cowardice and self-preservation get the better of him. He takes a swift glance at the books on the table, grabs one and heads out through the hessian covered doorway.

Just in time.

Chapter 2

Madrid, 2017

The Caixa Forum is a short walk from the Prado, the Thyssen and the Reina - Sofia art galleries. It stands almost adjacent to the Retiro Park in the area known as the Paseo del Arte. Visitors cannot miss it, right outside its entrance is a remarkable vertical garden which at this early autumnal time of year was a magnificent array of greens, ambers, reds, yellows and gold. Any Madrileño will tell you it is a sight not to be missed.

The Forum is well known for opening its doors to a wide range of the arts, from exhibitions, to concerts, to talks and conferences, on everything and anything. The work of Andy Warhol, much of it on loan from the Warhol Museum in New York, occupied the main gallery and was attracting a wide audience from all corners of the world. Posters around the place announced that later in the year, there would be one on Albrecht Dürer and following that, one on the life and times of Walt Disney, this is a place where art is for all.

This particular morning its main auditorium was hosting a lecture entitled,

'Boabdil, The Last Moor−Fact and Fiction in Art.'

The speaker was a woman in her late 20s, expert on all things to do with the 800-year Arabic rule of Al-Andalus, a writer and self-styled history detective. She was currently undertaking a new study of Boabdil's last days and in particular trying to ascertain the whereabouts of his final resting place, a mystery which had now endured for well over 500 years.

Eventually, she hoped to write a book which traced his movements from the time he left the shores of Spain for North Africa, to his death. Her photo adorned a poster at the entrance to the auditorium. An equally young woman, dressed head to foot in black, was studying the blurb closely. She pushed her fake Ray Ban sunglasses up onto her head.

In truth there was not much she did not already know about the speaker, Lucy E. Hawksmoor. But she read anyway. It was mostly a basic overview of a woman who was known far more for her feisty temperament and keen desire to push the female cause in the staid world of historical academia. None of that got a mention here.

Educated privately in England. Read History at University. First class honours degree. Followed by a Master's degree in Islamic Studies. Now attached to the University of Granada but on a sabbatical. Gives lectures all over Europe. Home is in Cordoba when not working in Granada. This latest lecture highlights the overtly westernised image of Boabdil and seeks to re-evaluate the man and his ultimate place in history.

She popped a piece of gum through her ruby lipsticked lips into her mouth and looked at some of the people milling in through the entrance. She hoped she was on the right lines and had read the situation, and Lucy, correctly. Lucy *E.* Hawksmoor. She had always been puzzled by the 'E', no one knew what it actually stood for. I pray to God I've judged you right, she thought, or else I am going to look very stupid.

She lowered her sunglasses back over her eyes and headed through the doorway, then up the stunning white central staircase towards the main auditorium, where Lucy Hawksmoor was in full flow, unaware of what was about to happen to her life.

***

If we rewind half an hour, another young woman, dressed in deep red, had also perused the poster with similar interest. She too read the blurb but it was nothing new to her either. But she was not here as an admirer, though she had a similar desire to ensure she had got her opinion of the woman correct. She also knew a lot about Lucy E. Hawksmoor, possibly more than Lucy E. Hawksmoor would want her to know. The young woman looked around and, seeing no one was looking, she made a gesture as if pointing a gun at the picture of Lucy, pulled the imaginary trigger, whispered, '*Bang,*' then smiled to herself and she too walked into the Caixa Forum.

***

The young woman in black had slipped quietly into a seat at the back and scanned the audience. No one there to worry her as far as she could tell. Everyone generally seemed transfixed by the speaker. There seemed to be an eclectic mix of academics, always instantly identifiable by their attire, a distinctive odd mix of tweed jackets and rose or bizarrely vibrant yellow-coloured corduroys, students dressed in baggy t shirts and equally baggy, multi-coloured Arabic style pants scribbling notes and a smattering of tourists who had wandered in no doubt without a clue who Lucy was but nonetheless were hanging on her every word.

At the front, on the podium, stood the slight figure of Lucy E. Hawksmoor. Although she was 28 years old, she looked little more than a teenager, but looks, as her observer well knew, could be very deceptive. This girl, this woman, had proved time and again that she could stand up for herself, both in interviews and when dealing with arrogant sexist professors who thought they knew more.

Today she was dressed in black leggings, white Nike trainers and a plain baggy white t-shirt that reached almost to her knees. Her long, darkish blonde hair was tied up in a high ponytail with a chequered blue scrunch. She blew apart the traditional image of the dull and crusty history lecturer. Her infectious enthusiasm for her subject, allied with the way she dressed, a casual relaxed nature and her disregard for convention made her very popular with her students, though less so with some of her colleagues. Oh and the fact that she occasionally popped up on history documentaries laughing and joking her way through history, which made her even more fans on the street but again, fewer in the halls of academia but the jealousy had never bothered her, indeed she seemed to thrive on upsetting the traditionalists.

She spoke in a casual yet confident southern English accent and the girl in the fake Ray Bans could not help but be captivated by both her looks and her mannerisms. She was entranced for a moment but then quickly made herself focus on listening rather than just staring at this most different of lecturers.

Lucy took a sip of bottled water as a new slide appeared on the white wall screen.

'So, let's look at the final two slides, the topic of which in both cases is the final days of Boabdil in Granada.'

'This work is entitled, '*La Salida de la Familia de Boabdil de la Alhambra*' by the Granadan artist, Manuel Gómez Moreno González, a miniature poem of a name, I love it! And I love this scene. It was painted in Rome in 1880. So, it's no Polaroid snapshot of the event!'

A gentle ripple of laughter played around the room.

'For some, this is a more sympathetic and human painting and it captures the emotions of the family well.'

Lucy flicked on her laser pointer to pick out characters and detail.

'Here we see Boabdil's mother, Aixa, wrapped in a glorious white cloak, she is certainly the standout figure–so still, so serene, so proud and upright, in stark contrast to the distraught figure of Boabdil's wife, Moraima, who appears to be weeping profusely. To the left, we see two people embrace and it is surmised that the figure with his back to us is that of Boabdil himself.

It's certainly one of the few paintings where we do not see the sultan's features or his expression. It is as if the artist is unable to portray accurately such hurt, such sadness. What we cannot see, what we can't make out, is to whom he's talking. And of course, we would all love to know what he is saying and to whom he is saying it! Oh! For Sky TV in the 15th century!'

A few giggles filtered through the room.

'It appears that the scene is set in the room known as the Sala de Barca, near the doorway leading out to the Comares courtyard, also known as the Court of Myrtles. The room either gets its name from the Spanish for 'boat' or from the Arabic word for 'blessing', which is 'Baraka'. This latter interpretation gets my vote, especially as there is a lengthy inscription above the portico as you enter the room which reads:

'*Blessed be He who has entrusted you with the command of his servants.*'

So there!

The next room is the Hall of Ambassadors or throne room, where Boabdil, within a few moments of this scene, would meet the emissary of Isabella and Ferdinand, the commander of León, Gutiere de Cárdemas, to hand over the keys of the Alhambra and effectively of Granada itself.'

Lucy paused for a moment to take another sip of water then took a piece of chewing gum from her pocket, unwrapped it and popped it into her mouth.

The watching young lady in the back row couldn't help but smile at this woman's nonchalance.

'Next slide, please. Ah yep. Right. Possibly, *the* most written about theme—El Suspiro del Moro, The Moor's Last Sigh. Quite a few artists over the centuries have endeavoured to depict this event. This version, possibly the most famous, was painted by Francisco Padilla y Ortiz in 1892. As Elizabeth Drayson remarks in her excellent and highly recommended book, '*The Moor's Last Stand*' published just recently, the viewer is left in no doubt of the sympathy of the depiction of the vanquished Moorish king.

Here he is stopping on his journey into exile to take one last look back at his beloved city, his Granada. There is something very human about the man in this picture. The way he is positioned in the scene makes it almost seem as if he is about to walk back towards the city; as if he has to return one more time. But return, sadly, he did not.'

In her chair at the back of the auditorium the watching girl in black shifted a little uncomfortably.

'There have been several versions of this apocryphal event.' Lucy continued to chew as she spoke.

'Aixa, his mother, can clearly be seen gesticulating towards Boabdil. No doubt uttering those words which have gone down almost as fact.'

Lucy broke into Arabic.

'Ibki l-yawma buka 'a n-nisa'i 'ala mulkin lam tahfadhu hifdha r-rijal.'

She paused and turned to the audience.

'Thou dost weep like a woman, for what thou couldst not defend as a man.'

'Harsh? Yes, possibly, but only if it ever happened, if it was ever said. No Arabic chroniclers of the time mention this event and they were by no means sympathetic towards Boabdil. Mr Washington Irving, of course, in his rather fanciful 1829 account entitled '*Conquest of Granada*' also retold the same tale thus perpetuating the myth for more modern audiences. Hey, but the Christian chroniclers had a field day with it! It was without doubt intended to discredit Boabdil.

The paintings we have seen this morning and the stories written by the conquerors, who always write the best histories, all serve to create an erroneous image of Boabdil as a weak man doomed to failure. Christian chroniclers took no time at all to rip up the 800 years of Muslim rule in Spain. We need to remember that Islamic Spain was a tremendously fertile ground for learning, producing a long line of intellectual, aesthetic and scientific advances, all attributable to Muslim, Christian and Jewish thinkers and the atmosphere they created. This blossoming was due in part to the spirit of tolerance that prevailed for much, though it has to be said, not all, of the history of Al-Andalus, a tolerance extended not only just to other religious groups but at work within Muslim society as well.

Despite the passage of over 500 years since its fall, Al-Andalus continues to cast its spell. As the birthplace of some of the world's outstanding scholars and artisans, home of dazzling architectural masterpieces and the setting of a brilliant society notable for both the height of its achievements and the depths of its decadence, Al-Andalus retains its emotional impact and its privileged place in Muslim historical memory.

And part of this spell that keeps me constantly intrigued is the legend of this man, Boabdil. Muhammad, last king of the Moors. A Spaniard—yes, I repeat, a Spaniard—he was born in Spain along with his ancestors of the Nasrid dynasty, a family tree that stretched back 500 years. I know I have made flippant comparisons in the past, though believe me, I am often misquoted by those who do not wish to really listen to what I say but what Isabella and Ferdinand perpetrated was for power and greed. Whereas the Moors intention was to spread the word of Islam, not to force it on others and, by so doing, extinguish all other beliefs. Ferdinand, in particular, used religion as a battering ram and eventually a scourge, to rid Spain of all Muslims and Jews. OK. Enough politics. For now at any rate.' She smiled to herself.

'So, yes, what of Boabdil post the *reconquista* as the Christians term it?

We know he remained in the Alpujarras for a short while. We know his wife and youngest son died, whilst they were there. It is written in some sources that he then crossed the sea to Fez in October 1493, via the port of Melilla. Some historians have written that he died there in 1553. Other writers have him dying in battle. Others that he died of plague or famine or just sheer exhaustion not long after landing in North Africa, which, frankly, wouldn't surprise me as he must have been completely knackered after all he had been through.

Some have him buried in Fez and a team of archaeologists are, as I speak, investigating this possibility, though bureaucracy is doing its best as always to stall the project. But personally I feel that Fez is an unlikely location. Still, they have found two unidentified bodies in a less than salubrious spot and some research points to it as a place where someone famous was at some point buried, so we await DNA. I'm not holding my breath on that one though, but it naturally tickles my curiosity and I look forward to discovering who the two people are. I do find it odd though that there is no writing, no inscriptions extant.

Anyway, the other favoured spot is Tlemcen and indeed there is a tombstone with an onyx plaque, which *does* have an epitaph. It was discovered in the 19th century by workmen building a road. It's now in the town's museum.'

A new slide flashed up on the screen.

'This is the inscription:

'This tomb is that of the just, magnanimous, generous king, defender of religion, emir of the Muslims, victorious by the grace of Allah.' It then goes on to mention the name Abu-Abdullha and his arrival in Tlemcen, one hundred miles down the road from Melilla and his great reception there.

So, interesting. But we do not know where the stone *originally* lay and Abu Abdullha was also the first name of Boabdil's uncle, who for a time was indeed the Sultan of Granada and was exiled to North Africa too. Mystery upon mystery!

So, this is the journey I am on, to find the last resting place of this man. A man much maligned and much wronged by history. And his exile divested him of any significant identity. I wish to return it to him.

I do hope this talk will encourage you to find out more about Boabdil and the magnificence of pre 15th century Al-Andalus.

Anyway, enough. I am sure you are all dying for a drink, I know I am, there are some laid on I believe after the talk. All that remains is for me to thank you so much for listening!'

She gave a semi theatrical bow.

The crowd broke into a loud round of applause, many standing to acknowledge the presentation.

Lucy now scanned the audience for the first time, she rarely liked to make eye contact during a presentation. It was a method of hers to imagine she was only talking to her father and not a whole crowded room. Several people caught her eye in particular. One was a rather good-looking young girl in the back row, all in black, who seemed to be smiling very directly at her, then there was the Forum Director who dressed very badly and seemed unsure whether she should continue clapping or stop and the third was a woman in the front row, who was neither smiling, nor clapping; she was just staring at Lucy, making her feel more than a little uncomfortable. It was not, she knew instinctively, a stare of admiration.

She was dressed in a plain red tee with jeans ripped rather excessively at both knees. Above her right ankle she wore what appeared to be a bandage of some sort. She had blonde hair that looked as if it had been dyed by someone unsure about what they were doing, it was oddly patchy and slightly discoloured and it hung in rather curiously Nordic plaits. She wore startling black eye liner but no other makeup on her pale skin. Lucy took all this in in no more than a few seconds but she felt the image would remain with her for quite some time and for all the wrong reasons.

As the applause died down, the rather hesitant Forum Director—a lady who clearly did not relish standing up in front of anyone to say anything it seemed—finally let her own clapping tail off and stood to speak. She seemed to stand and smile for a little too long before speaking as if gathering her thoughts and Lucy stood staring back at her smiling, a little amused that the woman had perhaps forgotten who she was.

'Thank you once again, er… Señora Hawksmoor, for your time and… and… for your most fascinating talk. We wish you well with your research.'

At last, thought Lucy. The Director beg to clap again a little too enthusiastically and people joined in though some had already begun to head for the exit. Lucy took a final slug of water, wiped her mouth and began to place her notes in her bag. She felt that the talk had gone well but was never sure how engaged people were. Still, the place had been full so that was a positive. Despite her outward confidence, inwardly Lucy could still worry that what she was doing was not as interesting to others as it was to herself and was often still genuinely surprised at her popularity or that frankly anyone turned up at all.

She felt a light tap on her shoulder and turned around to find herself confronted by the young woman in red and behind her, no more than a few metres, stood the back-row beauty in black. Lucy quickly refocused her attention on the curious woman in red, who was smiling at her in a way that could only be described as unnerving. Lucy was expecting a question or maybe a compliment, so when she spoke, Lucy initially did not quite take it all in. Her voice was low and a little croaky, the product, Lucy thought, of a good few years of chain-smoking Ducados.

'Señora Hawksmoor, I hope you do not think everyone in this country is behind your work?'

'Sorry?'

'There are many who believe that idolising these people and the period in which they infected Spain is not helpful to the future of our country. Please be careful. I would not like your research to in anyway cause you trouble. I think it best if you turn your attention elsewhere, preferably outside our country. I hope you understand and that we do not need to meet again.'

She paused for a second then added, with an overly ingratiating smile, 'Nice meeting you. Love the shoes!'

Lucy had no time to reply as the woman turned abruptly on her heels and headed toward the exit, bumping, on purpose it seemed, into the girl dressed in black as she passed, with no apology offered. Lucy stood still, rather taken aback by the woman's words as they began to sink in.

The girl in black approached. Lucy spoke first looking over the newcomer's shoulder at the woman in red as she disappeared up the stairway and into the crowds.

'Wow, what the fuck. I am not sure she was too keen on me. That was seriously *so* not nice.'

She now looked at the girl in front of her. 'And are you here to give me advice too?'

'Not at all. Far from it. I loved your talk. I am a big fan of your work.'

'Oh! Really? How nice! Thank you.'

'I just wondered if by any chance I could take you for a drink, Miss Hawksmoor. I have something that I think could be of great value in your current research.'

'Well,' Lucy replied, 'that sounds a much better proposition than the previous lady's.'

She checked the time on her iPhone. 'Yep, I'm good for an hour or so. And I guess it would be very rude to refuse such a politely phrased offer. Gracias!'

Lucy picked up her linen bag and slung it over her shoulder. It sported a silhouette of a black cat and the words,

'*Como Mola Ser Gato En Madrid.*'

'Nice to see you like cats, me too.'

'Oh yes, I do. Love them. Got this bag from a seriously cool book shop in Malasaña. Cats everywhere. Real ones.'

'I must go sometime.'

'You should.'

They walked towards the exit, Lucy accepting several handshakes from people as she went.

As they exited the Caixa Forum, their departure together was noted and a phone call was made. Lucy and the girl in black were oblivious to the hard stare aimed their way by the lady in red standing in the shadows.

***

Within five minutes they were sat on two high stools in the Tinto y Tapas bar, a short stroll from the Caixa Forum. The walls were peppered with tiles depicting different scenes, real or imaginary, from Spanish history and literature. The obligatory leg of Iberico ham stood to one side of the counter and Lucy eyed it hungrily.

'Here, try this. Tinto Verano.'

'Cheers,' said Lucy. 'I don't normally accept drinks from strangers. But in this case, I think I can make an exception.'

'Oh, sorry, how stupid, I haven't introduced myself.'

Lucy just smiled in reply and took an olive from the bowl that came with their drinks. Nice and garlicky, just how she liked them. Lucy had never been one for being worried about eating garlic so much, in any form, although she often used the lame joke that her love of the stuff was what kept her single. But Lucy had always been happy in her own skin and had no desire to change her ways for anyone, she took the 'take me as I am or don't bother' approach. Though having said that, she had no shortage of offers from both sexes.

She was just too wrapped up in her world to give time to others at present. Still, looking at Gloria, she was teetering towards a willingness to forego her self-imposed celibacy, at least for the afternoon.

'My name is Gloria Sarmiyento Ruiz.'

'Now that's a name! Sounds like an author. I'm so jealous of Spanish names, one of my favourite authors is Carlos Ruiz Zafon, you've got to be a writer with a name like that.'

Gloria pushed her sunglasses onto the top of her head, a little disconcerted by Lucy's over enthusiasm but continued.

'I've been following you for some time, Miss Hawksmoor.' A pause.

'Not metaphorically I assume?'

Gloria looked up at Lucy. 'Sorry?'

'I'm joking.'

She smiled and Gloria smiled back and then looked down, realising she'd lost her train of thought, not knowing for a second what else to say. The smile made Lucy feel another distinct twinge of attraction; this girl, she thought, is just too like something out of a Dior advert for her own good.

In the brief silence, Lucy assessed Gloria over the top of her glass as she took a long cold draft of the refreshing drink. Long blue-black shining hair swept back in a ponytail, with which she was now distractedly fiddling. Dark hazel eyes, beautifully bronzed skin, lips that looked like doors to a velvet heaven. She liked what she saw, but as so often in the past, mentally told herself off. This was no time to be getting involved with any girl, not even one quite so bewitching as Gloria.

Gloria decided to play for time whilst she gathered her thoughts.

'Going back to names, I like yours too. I think English people don't always realise how their names can sound fascinating too. If I might ask, what does the E stand for, Miss Hawksmoor?'

'Please, just call me, Lucy. The E, yes, well it's interesting, well, not really, just quirky, bit of a family thing, having odd middle names, my father's fault in my case I'm afraid. So, *Gloria,* where do you work?'

Gloria realised Lucy was not going to tell her, so she refocused, ordered two more drinks and continued.

'I work part-time at Salamanca University, Arabic Studies department. I write for a web site too on the history of the Muslims in Spain and issues affecting the Muslim population of Spain today.'

'Hmm, impressive,' Lucy replied. 'I haven't been to Salamanca in a while. Good people to work for?'

'Yes, they give me space and I'd say they were always encouraging new thought, new ideas.'

'And what new ideas fascinate *you*, Gloria?' Lucy was now leaning forward, her elbows on the table, her head resting on her hands gazing at Gloria in a way that made her shift in her chair.

'Well,' she was lost for words and was beginning to wonder if this was a good idea after all.

Lucy sat back up straight.

'Don't worry, I'm teasing. So, come on, any chance you can enlighten me as to who the nasty lady in red with no fucking dress sense is?'

'Yes. Unfortunately, I can.' She looked momentarily distracted as she felt her elbow,

'I think actually she bruised my arm as she bumped into me. She is really not someone you want to cross. Nasty is correct and well known for all of the wrong reasons. Her name is Ximena Martinez. Except, she changes her first name from time to time, just to confuse people. What you really need to know is she is the leader of a very unpleasant Neo-Fascist group called Casa Social.

They have been responsible for attacks on mosques around the country from time to time, some occasional harassment of immigrants and general shit-stirring, posting anti-Muslim propaganda, etcetera, though it is always extremely cleverly worded and hard to counter. She even has lawyers working for them, ensuring they do not overstep the mark legally in print. She's a student of anthropology and a fully paid up racist, although she's very clever not to ever say anything so direct that it will get her into prison.

Her group's slogan is 'Spaniards first'. She wants Spain to be for the Spanish and by that she doesn't care if it says you're Spanish on your passport. Because if you are black or Muslim or Jewish then she wants you out but her argument is wrapped in euphemisms. She was interviewed last year and went on record as saying just that, that to be Spanish it is not enough to have the Spanish DNI, that's our identity card, as I'm sure you know.' Lucy nodded.

'And then she said, *If you have a paper that says you are a cat, are you a cat?*'

'Bit tough on cats,' Lucy interjected, 'and, unless I'm stupid, a bit bonkers.'

'Bonkers, I like that, great word. Yes, exactly, she plays with words, but the message is clear under all the shit. She said that a person is not Spanish because they were born in Spain, that being Spanish is a way of looking at life, it is a lineage, it is a story, one that a DNI cannot confer upon you.'

Lucy was now starting to pay more attention and not only to just Gloria's looks.

'Jesus. You know I *have* heard of Casa Social come to think of it but never really paid much attention to them. I haven't come across them in my work in any way though. Well, until today's car crash.'

Lucy lowered her voice to a whisper. 'So, let's get this straight, in short she is a full blown racist but doing a very good job of not being so overt as to get herself into serious trouble?'

'Exactly,' she took a sip of her drink and stirred the ice and orange slice round the glass like a child with a milkshake that's running out.

'So, tell me what she said to you exactly.

Lucy gave her a brief summary of their brief encounter.

'Hm, So…OK, she was there to make the point to you that she doesn't like you being so supportive of the Moorish history of Spain and ergo being so critical of the Christian victors.'

'I guess so. Sounds lame, doesn't it. Can't really see why what I'm doing is of any interest to her or her group, other than she clearly doesn't like Muslims. This is history I'm talking about after all.'

She sensed Gloria wanted to say something but Gloria just finished her drink, so Lucy continued.

'I do remember that attack on the mosque in Granada a few years back. A lecturer friend of mine who attended prayers there was quite shaken by it.'

Lucy looked across the table at Gloria who seemed to have clammed up. 'So, come on, what do you think? Should I be worried?'

'Well, it seems odd that she made the effort to actually attend your lecture in person and sit through the whole of the talk without saying anything but that's her style. I guess it's just as well to be careful. You know, just be aware that you have appeared on this woman's radar, so to speak. And clearly that was an implicit threat, basically, move on to something else.'

'Very strange and slightly creepy. Right, fancy another? And then, of far more importance than my fascist stalker friend, you can tell me why you were at my talk. OK?'

Gloria realised she was staring at Lucy. She had never been attracted to any woman before but there was something about Lucy that made her feel, well, different. It had thrown her slightly. Lucy pushed back her hair and adjusted her scrunch. Then Gloria snapped out of her mini trance.

'Yes. Of course. But how about we change bar, somewhere quieter.'

Gloria paid the bill and followed Lucy out of the bar, wondering how to broach what she had come here to tell her. Lucy meanwhile was wondering why Gloria wanted to take her out for a drink and what she wanted. She quite fancied Gloria but also knew she had a lot of work on and once again reminded herself she had no time for relationships and anyway she was fairly sure Gloria was straight, but hey, what the heck. For the first time in a while, Lucy switched her phone off and breathed deeply.

Just go with the moment, she said to herself, just for once.

Chapter 3

'Since the good things of the past were not constant, present misfortune can also change in a similar way.'

Count of Cabra to Boabdil

The Alhambra, Granada. January 1492

In the far distance, the jagged snow-tinged peaks of the Alpujarras, gently kissed the wintery blue skies as the season continued to progress as time had ordained. Kites soared high up in the atmosphere and little sound could be heard other than their occasional distinctive whistling cry. Down within the walls of the Alhambra Palace the scene was also uncommonly quiet. No cats mewled; no dogs barked. It was as if the world knew that there was about to be a seismic shift in the balance of power and Allah himself had called for silence.

The normally bustling Comares courtyard was occupied not by the usual myriad of servants, merchants, councillors and family members but solely by ten fine Arabian horses; five black, four brown, one white. There were also two sullen mules, one of which was so laden with bags it was surprising it could stand at all. A group of men dressed ready for the road stood holding the reins of the horses. Each beast seemed to sense the tension in the air and from time to time they emitted a low, nervous whinny and stamped their hooves impatiently, as if desperate to be away from the place as soon as possible.

A man suddenly appeared from an arched doorway across the yard, dressed in a crimson riding cloak with fine gold threaded patterns woven throughout, which swirled around him like shifting sand. He approached the tall bronze studded doors that led into the room known as the Sala de Barca. Like so many in this heavenly palace it was decorated with the most beautiful tiles of every hue and colour. Around the ceiling, carved into the stone with exquisite craftsmanship, were the words

لا يوجد منتصر ولكن الله – 'There is no victor but Allah'—repeated over and over again, so that whichever way one looked the words caught the eye, ensuring the statement stayed with the reader for some time.

As the new arrival in the room once more cast his gaze upwards and saw these words, he suddenly felt shameful and tried to dismiss from his mind the thought that they had all let Allah down and, more worryingly, the fear that *He* had deserted them. He exchanged glances with a man known as Al-Aben Comixa, a member of the Ulama, the scholars of Muslim religious learning and law. The look they exchanged was momentary, yet long enough for a deep, overpowering sense of sadness to flow swiftly between them. Aben spoke gently.

'Al-Mulih, can you believe this is really happening? That what we feared has finally come to pass?'

Al-Mulih, vizier and chief advisor to the Sultan, did not reply. There were no words adequate in his vocabulary to frame his feelings, fears and regrets. He nodded almost imperceptibly to Al-Aben and stared at the cast of figures gathered within the sumptuous room.

By the far wall, gazing through a lattice window stood the erect and proud figure of Aixa, mother to the Sultan, dressed head to foot in a shimmering white silk robe and headdress. She was so still it was as if she had turned to marble and Al-Mulih thought for a moment that she would be a fitting statue to leave behind. It was almost as if what was happening around her was none of her business but Al-Mulih knew, had seen at first hand, how distressed this force of a woman was and knew how much she had wept over the course of the last few days.

In the centre of the room the diminutive and beautiful figure of Moraima, wife to the Sultan, knelt to comfort her young son, whispering no doubt, words of hope and encouragement. Her robes were a startling blue, so deep a blue that it seemed as if they had been made from the ocean itself. Several of her servant girls huddled together close by, not speaking but all staring at Moraima and pondering, he thought, their uncertain future in a life beyond the walls of the only home they had ever known.

Finally, his eyes rested on the figure of the Sultan himself, Abu Abdallah Muhammad. Better known to the Castilians as Boabdil, a Christian corruption of his first two names. Here he stood, the last Moorish King of Granada, head of the Nasrid dynasty. Within the next hour, in the adjoining chamber, almost 300 years of Nasrid rule would come to an end and, Al-Mulih inwardly quailed at the thought, almost 800 years of Muslim tenure of the magnificent lands of Al-Andalus.

This was a burden no one would wish on any man. But the shoulders of the one who stood before him, a man of some 30 winters, were still broad and, despite his world slowly crumbling around him, he gave off the air of one not bowed. Not yet humiliated. Not yet humbled. Something about his manner made Al-Mulih feel he was up to something. Something to which, unusually, he was not privy.

Even more curious, was with whom he was choosing to spend seemingly a large portion of his remaining time in the Alhambra. He was locked in quiet yet earnest conversation with a mountain of a woman. She stood almost two hands taller than the Sultan and was having to stoop slightly to hear his words. She was shrouded from head to foot in funereal black, which to Al-Mulih caught perfectly the mood of the moment. This woman was known as La Mora of Ubeda, the keeper of the King's books.

She was also a renowned expert on the Qur'an and he knew that the Sultan often consulted her on matters of faith and conscience. He apparently enjoyed her company, something Al-Mulih certainly did not, she always made him feel uncomfortable, both intellectually and physically. It was hard to place an age on this creature but she could not be far off 60 winters. And yet she was in no way a feeble old woman.

Al-Mulih had heard of her famed arm-wrestling competitions with the guards, bouts she rarely lost. Her shoulders were the width of most doorways in the palace and many men were quietly in awe of her, others simply avoided her through fear, as some believed her to be some kind of sorceress, not that any would have ever voiced such ideas in front of the Sultan. Her loyalty to her master was rivalled only possibly by Al-Mulih himself.

He wondered to himself now what was passing between them. By the look on their faces it was clearly of great importance. At the conclusion of their conversation, the Sultan appeared to give La Mora a small parcel. She then bent further to kiss his raised hand. Her face as she drew away was one of grave seriousness and yet there seemed to be a sense of relief in her expression. As Al-Mulih moved closer, believing the conversation to be at an end, he caught the Sultan's final words to her,

'May the peace of God be with you and may your life be long and may Allah almighty watch over you in your quest. I am relying on you.'

La Mora nodded slightly as if indicating the vizier's presence and stepped back into the shadows.

As the Sultan turned towards him, Al-Mulih could not help wondering what quest La Mora had been set and why he had not been consulted. No doubt something to do with his books. Al-Mulih could not let the thought distract him further. Time was of the essence.

The King spoke. 'Al-Mulih. Pardon me. My mind is everywhere. So many to bid farewell to. So many to reassure. What is the latest news?'

Reassure, he thought? A little late for that he feared.

'Your Majesty, the time is upon us.' Boabdil stared at Al-Mulih as if his mind was still somewhere else. He nodded slowly and then spoke calmly, aware no doubt of the effect his behaviour would have on all those around him.

'Is everything as it should be? Have they kept their word?'

'Yes. Gutierre de Cárdenas, Commander of León, awaits with a small party of his men at the Alixares Gate. They arrived moments ago as dawn broke. The city still sleeps. As agreed, he is here on behalf of Queen Isabella and King Ferdinand of Castille and Aragon, who are camped outside the walls on the hill of Armilla.'

Boabdil was for a fleeting moment amused at how Al-Mulih still insisted on giving everyone their full title as if Boabdil did not already have these names burned into his soul.

Al-Mulih continued, 'Once you have handed over the keys of the Alhambra to the commander, you, my lord, your family and entourage are to leave for your estate in Andarax in the Alpujarra, as stated in the terms laid down between your majesty and the Christians.'

Out of the corner of his eye, Al-Mulih caught a flash of white light and realised Aixa had finally moved.

'The terms laid down!' she spat. 'That it comes to this. Everything is in favour of that demon son of a whore, Ferdinand and his poisonous wife. I shall not be here when you hand over our world, my son. I shall wait with the horses. Come!' she barked to her maids and in a flurry of silk and seething, she left the room.

For an instant no one moved.

Boabdil had closed his eyes but when he spoke his voice was as calm and collected as before.

'Show the lord commander to the throne room, Al-Mulih. Let us finish this business quickly and then to horse. I have much to discuss with you and my council regarding my plans for the coming days and months.'

Al-Mulih saw La Mora turn at these words and leave the room, though unlike Aixa, he didn't think anyone else noticed. She was clearly not accompanying them to Andarax, he surmised.

As he bowed and turned to leave in order to escort the Christians into the Alhambra, Al-Mulih could not help feeling that Boabdil was once again plotting something. He certainly did not give the impression of a man about to relinquish his home, his life, his world.

Along the dark passageway to the Alixares gate, Al-Mulih almost collided with La Mora as she came swiftly out of a side door. In her arms were several books and two scrolls and in the collision some fell to the floor.

'Allow me, madam,' said Al-Mulih and he bent to recover the books. He sensed her tense as he did so. Only two books had been dropped from those she carried; the other item which had fallen was a small silver pouch, designed to carry words from the Qur'an.

He looked at them briefly then handed them back to the towering and rather intimidating figure of La Mora.

'Yours?'

She took them with her free hand and slipped the pouch deep inside the folds of her robes.

'As you know all I possess belongs to the Sultan and Allah. I am merely a guardian.'

'May I ask what it was you and his majesty were discussing back there?'

She stared at him in such a way that he felt an uneasy swirl deep in his stomach.

'You may ask, my lord, but it is not my place to tell you. You can always ask his highness.'

Al-Mulih ignored the insolent response. This was no time for argument.

He bowed and turned to resume his errand.

La Mora called after him. 'Fear not, Al-Mulih. Allah is with us within these walls, as shall our king be, for all time.'

He turned to speak, but she had gone.

Her words rang in his head as he walked.

If only, he thought, if only.

I fear Allah today has deserted us, he mused.

But Boabdil?

Here?

For all time? He shook his head and dismissed her words as mere ramblings.

As he reached the gate, overhead the red sky darkened over the fiery red palace; he felt a chill run through his ageing bones.

'So,' he murmured, 'the end begins. The end begins.'

Chapter 4

Madrid 2017

Lucy and Gloria had made the short walk to a nearby bar called Santa Rita. Gloria said it was a little more out of the way and a better place to talk. Indeed, when Lucy saw it, she was bowled over. A gem of a place with artsy decor, books on shelves and a warm feeling to it.

She particularly liked the mural on one whole wall, a rather voluptuous version of Santa Rita holding a knife and fork and looking heavenward as if waiting for heavenly table service. Gloria had described the owner, Fernando, as warm, friendly and welcoming and he did not disappoint. And more importantly, Gloria had added, Fernando was discreet.

They sat at a table that could not be seen from the window and Lucy noted it was also a spot from which clearly Gloria could keep an eye on the door. For the first time since her encounter with Ximena Martinez, she felt a little uneasy. Nonetheless when Gloria ordered two glasses of Albariño, Lucy switched off her inner alarm.

As the waiter poured their wine at the table, Gloria began with generalities. Lucy was keen to get to why Gloria had invited her for a drink in the first place but for the moment she was happy to play along.

'So, Lucy, where did you get your love of history from?'

'Ooh, the easy ones first. I inherited it from my dad, like so many things, including my sarcasm, a general mistrust of my fellow beings and my taste in food and wine. He's a history teacher, well, he was, he's retired now. He's fun to be with for a while but he is also a cynic of the most annoying kind. He can irritate the balls off me sometimes.

He lives here in Madrid, at least for the moment, but he has gypsy blood and loves to travel widely. Fun to be with, but as I say, not for too long and he's quirky. You either get him or you think he's mad as a hatter. Probably a bit like me. We get on like a house on fire, most of the time but we do have our moments when we clash, we're too similar in many ways I guess. But I love him to bits notwithstanding. And, to get back to your question, I am prone to rambling too, like my dad by the way.'

Yes, so whilst other kids were being read fairy stories, he regaled me with tales, myths and legends from history. Then, later as my love of the subject grew at school, we spent many a night discussing characters from the past, arguing our take on particular events, playing what if and I got to learn how to look at things from a different angle and, most importantly, to not always believe the accepted version of events.'

Gloria couldn't help but be amused by Lucy's flurry of words. She was a natural speaker, which she knew was something that did not come easy to herself.

'He sounds quite a guy, your father. It's James Hawksmoor right, he's mentioned in your bio on Wikipedia.'

'Hmm. Don't believe all that you read there. About either of us! No idea who the fuck wrote it. My Mum gets only a fleeting mention which is wrong, I sometimes think she's a saint for putting up with us both, especially my dad. She is the anchor in the family. But hey, they're besotted with each other really, though they give each other a lot of space, which no doubt keeps them both sane and keeps the passion alive I guess, so to speak.'

Lucy took a large glug of wine, almost draining the glass in one which amazed Gloria.

'Is he really related to Nicholas Hawksmoor, the famous architect?'

'Well, we have reason to believe that is the case. My Dad is convinced, though there are some mysterious moments in our family tree where things go vague, a bit weird. Hey, could you ask for some more olives or maybe some…'

Just at that moment the waiter placed a dish containing chunks of chorizo and slices of cecina on their table. 'Wo, the guy reads minds, nice tapas!'

'Another glass to accompany it?'

Without waiting for Lucy's reply, Gloria called over to the barman, 'Dos mas!' Gloria had noted how adept Lucy was at changing the subject seamlessly. No point in stalling anymore anyway. Lucy realised as she chewed a delicious piece of strong chorizo that Gloria was staring at her again.

She needed to move this all on a step.

'Hey. Look, sorry. You must think I'm here just to sponge a drink off you. Well, I am *but* I also do want to know your story and why we are really here.'

Lucy had to stop herself from taking another slice of cecina.

Gloria knew it was indeed time to tell her story.

After several minutes of more background blurb on her life and times, not all of which Lucy took in if she was honest, Gloria finally got to the point.

'I have something for you. Something that has been in my family for generations. It has always been passed onto someone to look after, to guard, to protect. Look, this is going to sound strange but we have been waiting. Each keeper, each one to whom it has been given has been told to wait until the time is right, until they find the right person who comes along in their life who they think will guard it the same way. Eventually, it has always been foretold, there will come a day when a person will appear who will be able to use the information within and the time will be deemed right for it to be revealed.'

Lucy couldn't help herself.

'How would the person know?'

'There are no instructions as such, no guidelines. It's all down to intuition. Apparently. But so far that's not happened. It has just been passed on from generation to generation. The one who will understand and unlock all it holds has, at least not up until this point, materialised.'

Lucy cut in again. 'You mean they have now?'

Gloria ignored her.

'My father is the present keeper. He lives in Cordoba. I told him, after I read about you a while ago that I believed you were, you are, the one. You are the key. You will be able to bring it into the light. It is just a feeling I have had since watching you for the first time on YouTube, reading your work, especially the work in which you are now engaged. And the time politically is right.'

Now Lucy was feeling a little sceptical and unsure where all this was leading. A thought crossed her mind that she may be a little mad.

'OK, so, you have '*a feeling*', just a feeling.'

'Yes, nothing more, nothing less. Now I have met you and heard you, I am more convinced than ever.'

Lucy was by nature not someone who instantly warmed to people and her fear now was that she had been sucked in by Gloria's looks and that perhaps she was indeed deranged.

But she snapped back at her inner doubting Thomas and decided, just for the moment, to keep her council and humour Gloria. So for the next 20 minutes she listened intently as Gloria told her all that she knew about the mysterious woman known as La Mora of Ubeda and her meeting over 500 years ago with a young scholar, the first chosen keeper; a man chosen by La Mora herself. Lucy listened intently, nodding at intervals, particularly when she knew some of the history already. Slowly, Lucy found herself becoming more and more fascinated.

Gloria kept her voice low and clear and although Lucy felt it was unnecessarily clandestine, she played along.

'When he left La Mora, the scholar journeyed back to Cordoba and met a man who she had recommended he should visit. His name was Yuse Vanegas, a teacher of Islam who gave classes on the Qur'an, though, obviously given the time and situation, they were held in the strictest secrecy. The scholar attended these classes and they became good friends.

According to the story handed down, the scholar eventually became seriously ill and on his death bed he called for Vanegas and passed on that which La Mora had given him; so Vanegas became the second keeper.'

'Does this young scholar have a name?'

'Sadly, the scholar's name has been lost in the mists of time.'

Lucy inwardly quailed at the naff expression but chose not to comment.

'However, Vanegas was a good man and clearly the right man and it remained in his family for hundreds of years, eventually being passed on to one of my distant relatives, an Imam called Ali ben Sarmiyento. Our family was originally from Granada and it ended up back there with this man for a while until my great grand parents moved to Cordoba.'

'So, you're Muslim?' Lucy interrupted, regretting how unnecessary the question was.

'Yes. Not practising. Not really. My father is certainly not a strict Muslim. He was quite a character in his youth and I seem to have inherited his lack of religious verve, zeal, whatever you want to call it. But his faith still matters to him even so and it means a lot to me.' Lucy registered the pause.

'And it is a good faith; my people are not the terrorists many westerners would have one believe.'

'Obviously, that goes without saying,' Lucy replied. 'It's a sad world. We seem totally unable to live together. It's all the same God to my mind. Not that I'm a great religious believer either—I'm what my father calls a 'collapsed catholic'—don't ask. You go on. Tell me where you think I fit into all this and, without being rude, what the hell this 'thing' actually is. You've got me hooked.'

She smiled and tried to hide her tiredness, hoped she wasn't sounding sarcastic. Part of her now just wanted Gloria to get to the point then she could get back to her hotel and lie down.

'Well, it's *what* you do and *because* of what you're doing, who you are looking for. And the way you speak about it and write so passionately, that is what has led me to believe for sure, that you are the one with whom we can share what my family guards. I just know. And that is the way it has always been. Part of its magic, if you like.'

Lucy feared they were now going round in circles and tried hard not to show her impatience.

'So, to cut to the chase, what is it?'

Gloria stared at her and Lucy thought she'd upset her by sounding too much in a hurry.

'Gloria? Are you OK?'

'Let's go.'

'What?' Gloria was already out of her seat.

'OK, why?' Lucy felt a rush of annoyance but quelled it.

Gloria took Lucy's arm and ushered her from the bar, leaving a few euro notes on a small silver tray as she passed by.

'I think we're being watched,' she whispered without looking at Lucy. 'Do not look round but the guy at the very end of the bar, I am sure has been watching us.'

'What, like staring at us?'

'No. But he has not moved since we came in. I think he was trying very hard to listen to what we were saying. He hasn't touched his drink either. Call it sixth sense.'

Lucy couldn't help but think the whole thing over dramatic. The guy probably just fancied Gloria. Of course, the thought that she could have been the object of his attention never crossed her mind, it tended not to these days.

Twenty minutes later after a brisk walk during which neither spoke, they arrived at a bench in the Retiro Park by the fountain of the fallen angel. Lucy had wanted to ask Gloria *why* she thought the guy at the bar was watching them but when she set eyes on the remarkable black statue of Lucifer, she lost her train of thought. Writhing snakes pinioned his arms and legs as he fell from heaven into the depths of hell. It invoked a shiver in most people, even on the warmest of days.

Gloria was staring at it too.

'The Angel Caído. It's one of my favourite statues in the whole of Spain. Created by Ricardo Bellver in the late 19th century. Inspired by John Milton's *Paradise Lost*. Though I'm sure you know that.'

Lucy continued to study it. 'Yes, I know of it but seeing it for real, wow, it's an incredible piece, quite haunting. All the times I've been to Madrid and never visited this spot before.'

'And guess what? It stands at exactly 666 meters above sea level.'

'You're joking!'

'No! Spooky or what? Some say that this spot is a gateway to hell itself.'

Lucy sat back on the bench.

'Hmm, not a bad front entrance then.'

Gloria smiled. 'I can't help feeling that the bad guy is often only the bad guy because we are told by those in charge who is good and who is not.'

'Oh, for sure. History is always written by the victors, Gloria. History books can be unreliable teachers. Which brings us back to your story. I'm hoping what you have to tell me, now we are *alone* alone as it were, is in some way related to Boabdil.'

Gloria, put her hand in her small shoulder bag and drew out two pieces of paper, one white, one red. She looked round, a tad over dramatic for Lucy's liking but seeing no one in sight, Gloria handed them to her. As Lucy unfolded the white sheet, her eyes were met with a picture of a small leather pouch, embroidered with beautiful silver patterns of geometric shapes.

'Wow, interesting.'

A lot of thoughts raced through Lucy's brain simultaneously. She was suppressing her excitement, just. So, her first question was rather mundane.

'How big is this in real life?'

'It's about 10 by 12 centimetres.'

That was enough for her.

'Ah,' Lucy smiled. 'A pouch. I'm guessing a pouch made to carry a small section of the Qur'an?'

'Yes, that's it. But, well, this one contains no part of the Qur'an.'

'Go on.'

'Sewn into its lining was what you have in your other hand, well, a photocopy. I couldn't risk bringing the real thing.'

'The real thing, my interest is hotting up.'

Lucy unfolded the red single sheet of paper which had been rolled like a cigarette. On it were a few lines of writing. She peered closely. The handwriting was small and the words tightly packed together.

Lucy looked up at Gloria, staring at her as if waiting for enlightenment.

'Gloria, do you actually know what this is?'

Gloria bit her lip. 'No. Well, yes, in that I have an idea what it might be about, but it is written in an archaic language and I cannot decipher it, well to be honest, I've never tried, nor have I ever wanted to. My father said it is not the role of the carrier to understand what is written. But of course, I do know who the pouch belonged to.'

Lucy looked up. 'You are kidding me?'

'No.'

'Jesus Christ alive and all the fucking saints, Gloria!'

'Yes. the last Muslim ruler of Granada, Boabdil himself.'

Lucy felt her breath sucked out of her lungs.

'Are you saying that this is what La Mora passed on to the scholar and has been guarded all this time?'

'I am.'

Lucy was now feeling as if she was floating slightly and had anyone asked her at that moment to close her eyes and say where she was, she wouldn't have had a clue. She looked again at the paper.

'The original, it's this same colour paper?' An urgency had come into Lucy's voice, which made Gloria a little nervous. She knew that now she had her hooked she needed to carefully reel her in. Lucy though was already leaping on the bait.

'Well, it's more a deeper red, a scarlet maybe, no lighter than that, but anyway, I couldn't find such a coloured paper to copy it on to.'

Lucy breathed deeply and exhaled whilst gathering her thoughts which were currently charging around like wild horses inside her head.

'OK, well, my guess is, it will be the crimson paper of the Chancellery of Granada. The Nasrid dynasty used this colour for all their most official documents. Not quite blood red, but the symbolism of the colour no doubt had its effect on the reader. It had meaning to them; if it was on this colour paper then it had power. Only serious stuff was put down on red. And Boabdil himself was known to write his diary on the same-coloured paper. Doesn't make it easy to read though. Shit, if this is real, then this is incredible.'

Gloria bit back an 'of course it's real.' She knew it was Lucy's job to question evidence.

Lucy looked at it again then from her white linen shoulder bag she produced her iPhone and with three taps of the home button switched on its magnifying glass tool.

'I know it's not as sexy as carrying a real magnifying glass,' noticing Gloria's expression. 'I think every self-respecting historian is a budding Sherlock at heart and should have one.'

'Sorry?'

'Ignore me.' Lucy smiled as she peered at the writing, suddenly noting her tiredness had vanished. She felt electric and alive as if someone was phoning her inner brain cells and they had all started ringing at once.

Gloria watched her closely. There was something about Lucy that struck a chord in her deep down, producing a feeling she had never really experienced before. Was it attraction? This was very new to her and a little scary. Could this be right? She realised she was in danger of losing focus. Lucy thankfully interrupted her thoughts.

'This, as you quite rightly already figured, is not Arabic. So, the question is, what is it? And the answer I am *fairly* positive is, that it's a version of Aljamiado.'

'Ah, I've read about that. Wasn't that some kind of secret language?'

'Yep, it was invented by crypto-Muslims and it uses the Castilian language but with a mixture of Arabic and Greek letters. Meant that if ever anything got into the wrong hands it would look like gobbledygook to the uninitiated. I've only ever seen short examples of it for real, never a whole page of writing like this.

It's quite something. Well, it's more than that. It's fucking amazing, Gloria, the given proviso being, as with every artefact, that it is kosher. And I'm not doubting your belief that it is one bit. I just have to say it, keeps my feet on the ground, though in this case I am metaphorically a good 6 inches off planet earth as we speak.'

Gloria noticed she wasn't looking at her. Lucy couldn't take her eyes off the paper and, as she stared at it, an odd feeling swept over her, as if the paper was staring back at her. She looked up to the sky and closed her eyes. The feeling went.

'So, can you translate it, Lucy?' Gloria looked round once more as she spoke to ensure no one was watching.

'Well, no, but as they say, I know a man who can. Or to be more precise, I know a man who knows a man who can.'

Gloria liked the way Lucy always seemed to be able to inject a light-hearted note into serious moments. It was a feature of her lecture style.

Lucy now held the paper right up close to her eyes.

'Gloria, I'm not sure how closely you've looked at this but, rather curiously, just near the end of the piece is a figure that is definitely not a word. It looks like, well, you tell me. See if you agree. Third line from the end, near the centre.' She handed the paper and iPhone over to her.

Gloria had taken her sunglasses from her head and hung them from the 'v' of her black top; her hair cascaded forward around the paper like a velvet waterfall and Lucy tried hard to ignore the desire to reach out and push it back over her ears for her.

Gloria studied the paper and the figure Lucy had indicated.

'Oh yes, I see it. It's, it's a Hand of Fatima. Wow!'

'And the question is, what is it doing there? It's very elaborate, almost too much so for the magnifying glass to pick out all the detail.'

Gloria looked at Lucy, handed her back the iPhone then rolled up the paper once more. She stretched out across the bench and took Lucy's free hand in hers and enfolded Lucy's fingers around the paper.

Then she spoke. Now she had to get really serious and hoped Lucy would not make light of her.

'What I do know, Lucy, is that I believe this piece of paper will help in your journey to find Boabdil's last resting place. It is possibly the last thing he wrote before he left the Alhambra or before.'

Her words tailed off as if she had changed her mind on saying anything further. Letting go of Lucy's hand, Gloria sat back.

'The point is, it has to be something that matters. Something of great importance. From what has been passed down to us orally over the centuries it almost certainly contains information about Boabdil's plans, of what he intended to do once he left for the Alpujarras.'

A kid on a skateboard suddenly whizzed past so close he nearly clipped Lucy's arm.

She shouted a few choice obscenities after him which drew attention from an elderly couple coming the other way who stared at her as if she had just come up from hell with Lucifer. She smiled back and waved.

Gloria shook her head. 'You've made two good friends there.'

Lucy continued to stare at them until they had gone past. Gloria waited till she was sure all was quiet again and that she had Lucy's full attention once more.

'So, my big question is, will you look into it, find out what it says? And of course, at the same time, I know it goes without saying, keep it to yourself until the time is right?'

Lucy wanted to freeze this moment. She had felt a serious tingling race up her arm when Gloria had taken her hand. She almost hadn't heard what the girl had said.

'Well, according to the blurb you've read on Wikipedia, I am apparently a historical detective, so of course, I want to know what it says. It normally takes a lot to excite me when it comes to supposedly new finds, but believe me, this excites me.'

Lucy looked up at the statue as if Lucifer was going to chip in. She looked back at Gloria's expectant gaze.

'I have to admit for a brief moment when you first began talking back there I thought this would all be some kind of a hoax but this looks very genuine and for it to have been passed down for so long it clearly must be of some significance. I guess it was something seriously important back when—question now is—is whatever it refers to still in existence.'

Gloria seemed a little hurt by the reference to it all possibly being a hoax but carried on regardless.

'What do you mean by still in existence?'

'Well, sometimes we come across writings about places that no longer exist or they refer to people who no one now knows about. But that's a worry for the future.'

'OK, well, keep the paper until you see the original. Who is it you need to show it to? It must be someone you really trust, Lucy. The fewer people who know about this the better.'

'Oh, I trust this guy alright. There are only two men I trust completely in this world, my brother Lance and my dad. And my dad is the 'trusted guy' in question and he knows a guy, whose name escapes me at the moment but will come back any second, who is into all this mystical writing of ages past and until recently was working on translating Kufic script all around the Alhambra walls.'

Gloria's face lit up. 'Alvaro Castilla! Your Dad knows Alvaro Castilla?'

'That's the guy!'

'Qué guay!'

'Wow, Gloria, you know your historians. My Dad will love you.'

'I've followed Señor Castilla's work translating the walls of the Alhambra in the news. He's some guy.'

A group of Chinese tourists emerged as if from nowhere, clearly in a gregarious mood, pointing and gesticulating, fascinated by everything, especially the statue and snapping copious photos of it. Lucy and Gloria fell silent and observed the human shoal as it passed.

Gloria made a rather unpleasant comment about them all wearing face masks, which Lucy chose to ignore. She stood, slinging her bag over her shoulder, all in one graceful flourish.

'Right, time to go.'

Gloria looked a little surprised but then glanced at her watch.

'Yes, of course. Right. Look, Lucy, thank you so much for listening.'

'No, thank you, Gloria. Glad you chose me to share this with.'

'So, what next?'

'We go our separate ways and I get in touch with my dad.'

They set off together towards the exit and for the first time spoke about things other than history.

***

Fifteen minutes later they were stood at the top of the metro steps. Lucy turned to Gloria.

'Actually, I've been thinking if I'm going to do this, it might make sense for you to tag along. How do you fancy packing a bag and coming with me to Cordoba that's where my dad lives at the moment. Well, lives as in staying in my flat. You get to help me and meet my dad and, all being well, Alvaro.'

'Really?'

'Yes, really. I can't promise much in the way of pay but your knowledge of Arabic will come in handy and you might learn something, if that doesn't sound too arrogant. And you know things about some of the not very nice people in Spain that I do not.'

She smiled as she spoke and Gloria knew this was a road she had to go down, the chance she had been hoping for, waiting for. An offer she couldn't refuse. Her plans were falling into place more easily than she could have imagined.

'I don't need paying, Lucy. And I'm not sure I would be much of a bodyguard.'

'Christ, do you think I'll need one!'

'Not if we're careful. I'm joking!' she said, as she noticed the look of mock horror on Lucy's face.

'Lucy, just let me double check I can get away. Give me your mobile number and I'll message you this evening to confirm.'

'OK, of course, then if it's all fine with you, I'll book the rail tickets online. We can meet in the morning outside my hotel, the 7 Islas, on Calle Valverde. We can do breakfast before we go then grab a taxi to Atocha.'

'Sounds fabulous. OK. I'll also call my father, maybe we can drop in and see him while we're there. I can't wait to meet your father too.'

'Well, he's never dull and, as I say, he'd love to meet you.'

'What does he do all day? Sorry, that sounds rude.'

'No, it's fine. He spends most of his time on the roof terrace with my cat, drinking wine, reading or writing poetry. And when he's not there he'll be found sampling tapas at one of several bars or wandering round the Mezquita; my place is literally a two-minute walk from it.'

'Sounds a good life to me. My father's place is a bit further out, near the Jewish quarter. Anyway, must go, I'm keeping you.' Gloria had noticed Lucy checking the time on a clock above a nearby pharmacy store.

'Where are you staying? Far?' Now Lucy realised it she who was prolonging the good-bye.

'I'm staying with a friend from uni, she has a flat in La Latina. If you fancy it, we could have supper this evening?'

Lucy liked the idea but knew she had to make a move and get on with her workload.

'Tempting, very tempting, Gloria, but I need to make some phone calls and do some reading up on this text. And to be honest, I'm knackered.'

They embraced lightly and kissed each other on both cheeks.

'Adios y hasta mañana!' Gloria called over her shoulder as she walked down the stairs and into the bowels of the metro system. Lucy smiled to herself.

As she turned away an elderly man sitting on a blanket with a ragged looking dog winked at her as she passed. She handed him a 10 euro note and his eyes lit up like beacons. Nice to see I've made someone's day, she thought as she headed for her hotel, pondering on the way about all that had happened in a remarkably short space of time.

In fact, had they known it, both their heads were whirring and mulling over all they had discussed and, indeed, thinking about each other. Lucy was holding on tightly to the slip of red paper. She didn't want to get her hopes up and not in front of Gloria, just in case. But she had a strong feeling that this sheet of paper might well hold the key to her search for Boabdil's last resting place; she hadn't wanted to say it at the time, not until she had it confirmed but she could actually read a little Aljamiado. And the few words she *had* understood had sent ripples of excitement down her spine.

Gloria meanwhile was thinking that she had definitely done the right thing. Lucy had been without doubt the right person to reveal the writing too. Her father would be relieved when she told him. Her friends in the Party would also be happy. She had chosen not to mention them to Lucy, there would be plenty of time for the politics. She felt Lucy would not understand, well not yet. She had sensed mentioning it was not what Lucy would want to hear, especially after her meeting with Ximena Martinez.

She was also thinking about the effect Lucy had had on her. She knew Lucy was gay; she had come out a long time ago at university. But until now Gloria had never felt anything for any other girl. The ripples of excitement that ran down her spine were of a different kind. And also not part of the plan, so she knew she would have to be careful.

As they both disappeared from view, a kilometre away, leaning on a shop front by a newspaper kiosk on Gran Via, a woman with a bandaged ankle answered her mobile phone.

Across the city a man sitting outside the Bar Retiro spoke into his. The woman said nothing, just listened.

He spoke in a low voice, stubbing out his cigarette in his saucer as he did so.

'I saw enough. There might be a problem. The girl is clearly looking to get the professor involved. I'll let the others know,'

Ximena Martinez propped her phone under her chin and lit up a cigarette

Then she inhaled deeply with her eyes shut.

'Boss?'

'I'm here. I need a little space, a little time to think what to do next. In the meantime, worry the girl. Enough to put her off our professor friend for a while.'

'Consider it done. The guys are already on it.' He rang off and sent several texts pinging across the Madrid ether.

Ximena stubbed out her cigarette and coughed.

Now, she thought, we have to ruffle some feathers a little harder. Some, very hard.

Chapter 5

'The servant, soon, will slaughter his master,
The handmaidens turn on their mistress and queen.
Slime to slime returns.
Soul-ascends to soul.'

Ibn Ezra 11th c.

A Street in the Albayzin, Granada. 1530

Two of Queen Isabella's soldiers stood in the dimness of the room, each bearing on his chest the black winged eagle clasping the shield of Castille, the much-feared Royal emblem. One carried a vicious looking pike, the other a smouldering torch. Their morions glimmered in the half light.

'There was no one out the back,' one said. 'The whole damned place is a hovel; rotten food and chicken shit and entrails everywhere on the kitchen floor. It stinks like a Moor's latrine.'

'Ah, entrails!' cried the other soldier. 'The sure signs of a witch. The fat old bitch will have been using them in black magic no doubt.'

He forced a laugh but he felt distinctly uncomfortable here.

The one with the pike bent down to look at the books on the low table.

'Looks all fucking Arabic to me.'

'How would you know you can't even fucking read!'

'It's not Spanish, I know that much you moron, so it must be Arabic.'

'Well, this is her place, no doubt about it. But where in God's name is she? They said she can't have been here long but maybe she's caught wind of our visit and fled.'

'Well, the old pig daughter of a whore can't have gone far. Not at her age.'

'Let's turn this shit pile of a place upside down then burn it to the ground. At least then we can prove we finished the job.'

The pike bearer walked toward the pile of rags along the far wall. The other turned toward the front door.

The sharp cry of intense pain which ripped through the room stopped him dead in his tracks. He turned rapidly to see his companion falling to the floor holding his right boot which had a long dagger protruding from it.

'Hija de puta! Ostia! Kill it! Fuck, fuck, fuck! Jesus!' These brief fierce exaltations turned out to be his final words on this earth.

His companion sprang towards the pile of rags but he was too keen and therefore, sadly for him, too late to realise that the largest ball of rags was an alarmingly huge hulk of a creature that now held the pike between its legs and it was pointing straight at him. As he lunged, the sharp tip of it was thrust into his right eye socket, accompanied by a fleeting whooshing sound, followed by a sharp crack as it connected with the back of his skull.

For a moment he seemed to freeze as if giving time for his last few thoughts to assemble in his now punctured brain. Whatever they were, he had no chance to voice them as he fell first to his knees then onto his side taking the imbedded pike with him. His torch rolled from his grasp and the flames licked and spat, catching hold of the rush matting covering the floor and igniting it all too quickly.

La Mora had already risen as the soldier hit the floor and now stood over the two bodies. Then, bending careful amongst the gathering flames extracted the pike from the soldier's skull and rammed it with all her might into the chest of the moaning soldier holding his foot.

She stared at him with empty eyes.

'Die, bastard,' she whispered.

Then she spat on both their bodies. There was commotion at the doorway, more soldiers had arrived. But the fire had already reached that point and no entry was possible for them.

La Mora turned to move towards the back door but that way too was blocked by flames that now licked at her feet. This was it. Her time on earth was at an end. She held her hands up in prayer and closed her eyes.

'Allah, I can now leave in peace.' She looked to the heavens as the flames licked at the hem of her garments. Then she knelt into the all-consuming fire without fear or regret.

She silently mouthed her final words. 'Boabdil, my lord. Remember me.'
And into the burning shadows, La Mora of Ubeda committed her soul.

Chapter 6

Madrid 2017

Gloria was aware she was being followed. She was almost certain she'd just seen the same man who'd been at the earlier bar that day, the one who had creeped her out so much they changed location. He had been buying a ticket from a machine near the barrier when she went through into the metro to catch the train to La Latina. She glanced along the platform, scanning the crowds and there he was again, about 100 meters away, speaking on his mobile. Now Gloria was beginning to feel more nervous, imagining everyone who glanced at her was working with him and was watching her.

The train arrived and she got on, well pushed her way on; it was as packed as ever and like most metros in the world people seemed to think their need to get somewhere was more urgent than anyone else's. The carriage was full but after the second stop she managed to grab a seat.

She took a small bottle of water from her bag. It had been given to her by a rep at the station concourse, some new company promoting its brand by dispensing freebies. She'd been hoping it was a fizzy drink but nonetheless she was grateful as she hadn't had time to stop and buy a drink and after all the wine she realised she was a little dehydrated. It didn't take much with her. She took a sip and stared into the middle distance thinking again about her meeting with Lucy and what had happened at the lecture; the fact that Ximena Martinez was there worried her more than she had let on to Lucy.

Her father had warned her as soon as she drew anyone else into their secret he said she could become a target. It was only because of who Gloria had decided to share their knowledge with that he had agreed she should go and test the water but it had not prevented him from worrying and warning her to be extremely careful and vigilant. Her father had a natural mistrust of most people and although Gloria had pushed Lucy E. Hawksmoor's case as the one to tell, he was still worried that she was too well known and could attract attention from the radicals and racists who did not want any Muslims in Spain, full stop.

Gloria was now questioning what she felt was possibly her own stupidity in revealing the information to Lucy in the open. She should have been more patient and waited until they were alone in a room some place, away from any chance of prying eyes. But getting to meet Lucy E. Hawksmoor was a difficult task (she made few public appearances and her P.R. team had rejected several requests for meetings in the past few months) and it would not have been acceptable to have simply asked her to meet with a stranger in a private room somewhere. That would have seemed seriously odd and there was no doubt in Gloria's mind that Lucy would have said no.

The train stopped and, like some peculiarly choreographed ballet, people swept on and off, the majority managing to avoid any serious bodily contact with consummate skill. One of the newly arrived passengers, a man of some 40 years or so, was a busker carrying a trumpet that looked as if it had seen better days, rather like its owner.

He slipped a small haversack off his back and took out a mini amplifier which he placed at his feet only a metre or so away from Gloria's seat. He looked up and down the carriage and smiled in general at the assembled captive audience, though few returned it and even fewer made any eye contact at all. Regardless, he soldiered on, put the trumpet to his mouth and began to play gentle jazz accompanied by a backing track from the amp. Such buskers were frequent sights around Madrid, especially on the Metro.

On her visits to the capital Gloria had witnessed saxophonists, accordion players, would-be opera singers and even once, on an admittedly less crowded train, a woman playing a full-size harp. A friend of hers, who lived near Callao, had introduced her a few months ago to a band called Ataca Paca who regularly busked on the streets of the capital. She'd bought their CD and loved the blend of flamenco style music and traditional songs.

On trains, Gloria was always one of the few who applauded the music whatever it was like and later popped a few coins when the canister came round before the performer moved to the next carriage. As usual most passengers seemed to pretend he was not there and continued to stare at whatever type of screen they were holding: Kindle, mobile, iPad, the odd laptop. Few, she noticed, were reading an actual book or newspaper. Sign of the times, she mused as she finished her bottle of water.

The automated voice announced the next stop. Tirso De Molina. She would get off here and after a ten-minute walk to her friend's flat in the heart of the La Latina barrio she would be able to relax and plan the next stage.

Just as she was standing to press her way towards the door, the busker turned and bumped into her. For a moment it seemed as if the man was going to fall and he caught at Gloria's left arm, almost pulling her to the ground too. Fortunately, a young guy on the other side sporting a neat goatee and wearing Doctor Dre headphones managed to supporter her whilst the busker at the same time regained his balance.

Gloria felt her bag drop from her shoulder to the floor and as she stumbled to retrieve it the young man caught her arm, possibly thinking she too was going to take a tumble as the carriage lurched to a halt. She turned to him with a quizzical look.

'I'm sorry,' the young man said, 'I hope I didn't hurt you. I didn't mean to grab you. I thought you were going to fall.'

'No, no, of course, thank you. I'm fine. Just a bit of a shock,' Gloria replied, which sounded daft as soon as she had spoken the words. The shock was that the guy had grabbed her at all. As she turned round she saw the busker holding out her bag.

'Ah, that's kind, thank you.'

More apologies and thank-you's were dispensed all-round and Gloria stepped onto the platform. Something though, a pin prick of doubt, of suspicion, made her turn back to look at the train as it began to pull away from the station. She could not be certain, but she was fairly sure that both the young man with the headphones and the busker were staring at her.

The train slipped out of sight and the moment was gone. Gloria hurried towards the exit. As she approached the barrier, she checked in her jacket pocket for her public transport card then remembered she had put it in her purse. She opened up her bag and rifled through it. No purse. Fuck!

She felt panic begin to rise in her stomach like a geyser about to burst and the feeling spread up towards her chest. She started to look around for a member of the metro staff or someone, anyone, to help her. She needed to get through the barrier and up to street level, find a policeman quickly. She'd been robbed. Who though? When? Her mind raced. No! Not the busker? Surely not. The young guy? No! Yes? But.

'Bastards!' she muttered to herself. 'Fuck, fuck. fuck!'

This was serious. She was not feeling well. Maybe she could get a signal on her mobile down here. Maybe she could call the police, yes, call now. But as she searched further through her bag she saw with a gut-wrenching stab of painful realisation that her phone was missing too.

The panic was now liquid. And it swirled around her brain like a gyroscope. Something was wrong. She knew it. Felt it whirling in her. What was happening to her? She couldn't think straight. The people pushing past her did not seem to even acknowledge her existence. Gloria's world was now a kaleidoscope of colours curling and flowing around her misty inner eye.

Reality was beginning to slip away from her. She could sense her legs buckling as she held on to the wrong side of the barrier. She felt as if she was going to be violently sick and, as she raised her head towards the ceiling, the whole place began to revolve around her like a manic merry-go-round. She crumpled to the floor in an ungainly heap. It was then and sadly only then, that she was noticed. The last thing she heard as the lights in her head were extinguished was a cry for help.

'Yes, Lucy. Help me,' she whispered.

Then the blackness consumed her.

Chapter 7

Islas Hotel, Malasaña, Madrid

Lucy lay on her bed, flipped open her laptop and powered it up. She went straight to her email. Nothing out of the ordinary. One from her brother Lance, asking if she was free anytime in the next few months as he had holiday to take and fancied popping over for a visit. She scanned his reasoning quickly. 'Need a break from this mad fucking job as everyone in this office is increasingly stressed with the state of the world economy, the money merry go rounds,' etc. etc. so on and so forth. Lucy scanned further on. 'And if I don't get away soon I'm going to explode or maim someone with a biro.'

That's Lance, ever the dramatist but she always loved seeing him. He was the proverbial breath of fresh air and one thing he could never ever be accused of was being dull. She sent a swift reply saying he should just suggest some dates, she'd sort something.

There was one from her Mum asking how she was getting along with Dad and that if he was being a pain to send him home. She did however finish by saying she hoped the lecture went well. That was a collector's item. Her mum could have whole conversations with her or write epic emails without ever mentioning Lucy's work. She herself had been a translator for some famous dictionary firm or other and now ran her own translation business from home.

There was a part of her which clearly wished Lucy had never moved away and the majority of her conversational topics revolved around how well Lance was doing in banking and loving life in London. Lucy often had the distinct impression that her mum thought that what Lucy did in comparison was not a 'proper job'.

But despite all that Lucy had a strong love and admiration for her; she had always been her own person and had instilled in her daughter the importance of standing up for herself and that self-belief for a woman was of paramount importance in what, despite it being the 21st-century, still seemed to be very much a man's world. Indeed, Lucy had recalled her mum's advice often and put it to use in more than her fair share of verbal battles with her male colleagues in the world of academia.

Until now, at least, it had stood her in good stead and despite appearing to be a lot younger than she looked, her colleagues now knew she was not one to cross and her wisdom and straight talking had won her more friends than enemies on the circuit. Lucy typed a short reply saying all was well—whatever that meant—and added that she hoped that like her dad, she might want to visit one day too. She knew that was never going to happen but she liked to ask her every now and then anyway.

There was an update from a colleague on the archaeological dig in Fez that caught her attention, saying they'd got no further with local authorities on whether DNA samples could be taken from the remains of the two bodies which they knew were down there beneath the tomb thanks to geo radar. The Moroccan authority had apparently got the hump because the Andalus Memories Association who were co-sponsoring the search, had called the state of the tomb at Bab-al Mahruq, 'abysmal'; her colleague had concurred that the mausoleum, a square dome structure with four horseshoe shaped arched openings had indeed become a shelter for drunks, tramps and drug addicts and was in a poor state of repair.

If people had thought that was Boabdil's last resting place at any point, no one clearly cared very much. But the impasse had now reached childish proportions, he noted and someone was going to have to apologise if the thing was to get back on track. This annoyed Lucy, as the first thing you ensure in anyone else's backyard is that whatever you do, you treat them with respect; not start harking on about how badly they've let things slip.

Lucy emailed him back and told him to contact a guy called Mohammad Abdul Rahman, an anthropologist, currently working in Morocco at the Université Mohammed V in Rabat, whom she knew reasonably well and ask him to intervene as he had contacts in the Fez town council. She gave him his contact details and said he could remind Mohammad that he owes Lucy Hawksmoor a favour.'

She had indeed helped him out a year back when he needed someone to vouch for him at a hotel in London. They were staying there for a conference when the doorman, a 'bloody racist' according to Mohammad, would not let him in. She smiled at the memory though, at the time it had been unpleasant, well certainly for poor Mohammad. He was not one for dressing for the occasion and had actually, Lucy recalled, looked like a down and out, but that was no excuse for the appalling behaviour of the doorman. The doorman for sure would not forget Lucy Hawksmoor in a hurry now; she had certainly put him in his place during an almost two-minute 'briefing'; as she described it, on racism and how he may be, just possibly, in the wrong line of work.

The rest of her e-mails were either invitations to give lectures or requests for advice on a range of topics. One or two she noticed were from a girl at a restaurant in Cordoba whom she knew fancied her. She decided to ignore those for the moment.

She was just about to close her inbox and ring her father when a new message pinged in.

The subject was *Request*, but the email address was not one she was familiar with. She knew she should ignore it, consign it to her Spam mailbox, but for some reason the word request triggered her weaker side and without really thinking she opened it.

'Oh fuck! No!'

It was a photograph.

A gruesome, graphic, photograph. One that made Lucy catch her breath and put her hand over her mouth. It was a close up of a young man's face. His skin was a grotesque purple and white. Saliva ran from his mouth and his eyes, bulging and blood shot, had almost popped out of their sockets. Lucy could make out a rope around his neck, almost embedded in the skin of his throat. He was clearly very dead.

Superimposed at the foot of the photo was a curt and chilling message,

'THE ONLY GOOD MUSLIM IS A DEAD ONE. BE CAREFUL WHO YOU HELP.'

Lucy slammed her laptop shut and ran to the bathroom. She wretched at first for a moment or two bringing up bile and then she threw up some remains of the tapas she had eaten that afternoon. She let her body collapse and she sat on the floor by the toilet. Death that close-up made it all too horrible. She could not ever recall being that shocked before. Most of the dead people she had ever encountered had passed away centuries ago and looked nothing like a real person anymore. She wiped her forehead on her sleeve and then her mouth on several sheets of loo roll.

'Get a grip, girl.' She pulled herself up, gripping onto the sink and ran the tap, throwing cold water on her face. She looked at herself in the mirror and steeled herself to go back to her laptop.

'OK, who the fuck sent this.' But when she looked at the message again, the picture had gone, all that remained was a message left blinking in its place:

'FILE HAS SELF-DESTRUCTED'

'Shit!' She scrolled down and looked closely at the details at the foot of the email, whoever they were had used a platform called Digification to send it. She googled it—attachments sent via this platform disappear after being opened. 'Jesus! Bastards!'

Someone was clearly trying to scare her and, she mused, they'd done a fucking good job. But who was the guy in the photo? Had it been real?

'Christ, Lucy, of course it was real.'

He had looked young, maybe in his early 20s. Lucy sat and thought back to her meeting today with Ximena whatever her name was and somehow she knew for certain that this woman had something to do with this email and clearly the implied threat to Lucy herself.

Be careful who you help—what the hell does that mean? Who am I helping? Ximena had made it clear and obvious that she had not wanted Lucy to continue her quest to find the last resting place of Boabdil. But helping? How the hell was this helping anyone other than posterity? Lucy poured herself a large glass of white wine from the mini bar and drank it almost in one.

'Well, fuck you, Ximena!' and she toasted her reflection in the full-length mirror by her bed.

She poured herself a second glass. She had stopped shaking.

Time to call her father.

***

'Christ, Lucy, that sounds awful. You poor thing! Are you sure you're alright?'

'Yes, Dad. I'm fine. Wine, as you well know, seems to frame everything in a better light. And never mind poor me, what about the poor bastard in the photograph.'

'I know, sorry. Just worried for you.' A silence. 'Lucy?'

'Yeah, I'm still here, Dad. It's just been a crazy day. One minute, I'm enjoying doing my stuff in a lecture hall, the next some racist cow is threatening me to back off looking for Boabdil's grave. I mean, that is a first, a historian being asked to stop looking into the past, it's not like I'm digging up roads or anything.

Then I meet this girl who has some, well, possibly, some amazing evidence that could really help. I mean, I think it's a genuine lead but I need second opinions. And then to round off the super weirdness of this day I get this hate mail, blows me away on my laptop.'

'Just hold on darling, let me turn the tele down completely, it's not a great line, there that's better. OK, so what's the plan now?'

Her Dad could be exasperating sometimes. Was he listening even?

'Well, completely off and out of left field I know but any chance you can get in touch with Alvaro Castilla? He could really seriously help me with this lead.'

'Alvaro? Yes, I can give him a call, see what he's up to. Can't promise anything, like all you lot he's always out and about somewhere different.'

'Great, thanks, Dad.'

'I'll let you know how I get on when you get here. What time are you arriving?'

'Aiming for late afternoon.' Lucy eyed the wine bottle and decided she may as well finish it.

'OK, let's do supper at El Rincon. Maria has been asking after you.'

'Has she now, well there's a surprise.'

Maria owned the El Rincon de Carmen, a beautiful restaurant in a beautiful location only a five-minute walk from Lucy's flat. Her eyes always lit up whenever Lucy came for lunch. They were good friends but nothing more and that's how Lucy intended it to stay. It was Maria who had sent the e mails that Lucy had ignored. Maybe she was being mean. She made a mental note to reply to them later.

'You know she's got a soft spot for you.'

'Dad, I'm 28, I do not need you acting as Cupid, thanks. Yes, she's a lovely girl but not my type. End, once again, of conversation.'

'OK, fine! I'm backing off as we speak.'

'Let's go to Casa Mazal instead. I'll call ahead and book. And, oh, this Gloria girl is coming too.'

She paused for a reaction, a suggestive comment, nothing good.

'Her family live in Cordoba and she's agreed to come and help me for a while. See what we can see.'

'Has she now.'

'Daaaaad! Please! She is rather gorgeous I'll give you that but she's *also* got brains and I know you'll like her and she deserves to be in on whatever we find. She brought it to me after all.'

'I'm looking forward to meeting her already. But you really can't tell me anything more about what you have?'

'No, not over the phone. But believe me, it is potentially Olympic gold standard.'

'And your exaggerated euphemisms, thankfully, you get from your mother. I just hope it's not all a waste of time. You are sure this Gloria is genuine?'

'I often wonder if anyone in this world is completely 'genuine' whatever that means. I'm always wary of most people, I meet at first, which by the way is definitely a trait I get from you. Yes, I reckon she's pretty kosher. And I don't think it's a waste of time either. I have the feeling that today's events are all somehow tied up. I don't think it's all coincidence.'

'And are you sure you don't think you should call the police about the email?'

'What would I say? It's now just a blank email. Whoever sent it is bound to be clever enough to ensure the address is not traceable.'

A pause. Lucy yawned. 'Right, Dad, I really do need to get to bed. I'll text you tomorrow when we're an hour away. I need to try and forget about all this for the night.'

A silence on the line.

'Dad? Are you still there?'

'Lucy, turn your TV on, now.'

'What, now?'

'Yes, for Christ's sake, now!'

Lucy turned the speakerphone on, threw the receiver on the bedside table then quickly flicked on the TV with the remote.

'What am I looking for?' she shouted.

'Go to any news channel, quick!'

Lucy flicked to the first news channel she could fine.

Then she froze.

'Oh, Jesus.'

There, on the screen, was the face of the young man she had just seen strangled in the email. According to the rolling sub text he was a young Muslim student, 21 years of age from Granada.

'Are you there, Lucy?' She heard her father's voice on the handset but couldn't get any words out.

'Lucy! Are you OK? Lucy?' But she still couldn't take her eyes off the TV She slowly picked up the handset.

'Oh God, Dad. Shit!'

'Lucy, listen. They're reporting it as a suicide, saying there's a note, but from what I can make out his mother is saying he's been murdered.'

'What do I do now?'

'Get yourself here as soon as you can tomorrow. We'll decide then.'

Lucy turned off her phone without saying goodbye. She stared at her laptop lying shut on the bed. For the first time in many a long year, she felt afraid.

The email had not been a hoax.

It had not been staged.

It was real.

And Lucy now knew that the danger to her was also exactly that.

Chapter 8

Andarax Late Summer 1492

'The very stars have lost their way
Oh Flower withered all too soon
Could the heavens not have been generous
Could the very breeze not stir?'

Ibn – al - Hammara

Facing the arid Sierra de Gádor in the Sierra Nevada foothills, Andarax occupies a hillside position almost a thousand meters above sea level. It is backed by rocky peaks and dense pine forest, with sweeping views over the fertile river plain of the Río Andarax.

It is high summer and deep within a dark and cool chamber in the small palace perched seemingly impossibly on this stark hillside, sits Boabdil on the edge of his wife's bed. She is gravely ill. Her skin is pallid and she has, for the past week, suffered night fevers. Her brow has to be constantly bathed to remove the beads of sweat.

Maryam bint Ibrahim al-'Attar, known simply as Moraima, the love of his life, mother to his three children, holds Boabdil's hands in hers but there is little strength in her grip. She has seen and suffered more than she should have, witnessed the death of her youngest child, a daughter, from a fever when only months old and, just two months ago, their youngest son, Yusuf, who passed away after a short illness.

And she had had to endure eight years apart from her eldest son. Ahmed, who had been held hostage by Ferdinand and Isabella as insurance against Boabdil not fulfilling his promise to hand over the Alhambra to the Christian monarchs. They had not been reunited a year. Now, at hardly 28 summers old, she lies locked in a fever that no medical man in the court can cure.

Aixa, Boabdil's mother, sits in the far corner of the room.

'I fear she is dying of a broken heart. The last years have been agony for all of us, but, for her, it has been too much, losing her children, losing her home–these have each taken their toll.'

Boabdil sighs heavily. He tries hard not to listen to his mother's words, though each one stabs home through his guilt.

He whispers gently. 'Of all the people I have let down, it is you, Moraima, you on whom I have inflicted the most pain. Forgive me. Please. Please do not leave me.'

His eyes well with tears.

Her eyes are now closed.

Her grip feels looser. Boabdil squeezes her hand hard as if by this single act he can hold on to her for all time.

Aixa's voice seems to echo outside his consciousness but he catches her last words.

'I will leave you together.' She stands and slips out of the room like a ghost.

Boabdil does not turn his head but continues to stare like a lost child at the love of his life.

He lays his head on Moraima's chest and, after a brief few minutes, feels the last few heart beats pulse through her silk shawl.

Then she is gone.

Boabdil's cry rips the air apart and filters through the walls of the palace to all who live there.

Time stands still.

Several hours later, Boabdil stands on a balcony overlooking the sun beaten slopes which fall away from the palace.

His vizier appears almost instantly from within to stand beside his Sultan.

'Has her body been prepared?'

'Yes, your majesty.' They both gaze silently into the middle distance.

Unspoken is the fact that Boabdil himself should have overseen the preparation of the body of his wife but he could not, though he did sit by her for the first few minutes or so whilst the women washed and prepared her for her final journey. His mother had been surprisingly supportive and took her place too amongst those gathered there for the solemn ritual cleansing.

'It is not my place, your highness, but I must ask even so, are you certain that this is what you wish to do? It is a dangerous course of action and I fear we may struggle in the time we have remaining to get her body there safely.'

'You have known for several months and yet said nothing of your concerns. Why now?'

'Because deep in my heart, I felt that you might still change your mind and cross the sea. Well, I prayed that you might do so. That you might realise that you could have a life there.'

An awkward pause ensues, which Al-Mulih decides to quickly fill.

'But now with your tragic loss, may Allah watch over her, I see it has made you even more determined and, well, therefore we must hasten your plans and, of course, I will do whatever I can to ensure they come to pass.'

Boabdil reaches out and places a hand on Al-Mulih's shoulder.

'Dear friend, you are rambling! I know your intentions are true. And yes, indeed, crossing to Melilla, was something I did once consider. But to where then? To the people in Fez? To them, I am a nobody. What life would I have were I to stay there?'

Al-Mulih lowers his head and closes his eyes. He knows Boabdil's words have truth.

'And now, with Moraima taken from me, I have no life anymore anyway. I am a shell. I am the King who could not keep Granada, who could not keep the Alhambra, who could not keep his wife.'

Overhead, an eagle circles, then falls to earth so swiftly its prey has no time to move and Boabdil watches as it rises into the sky carrying some small animal in its jaws, the imagery not lost on him.

Boabdil smiles wanly. 'See, even nature mocks me.'

He sighs deeply. 'This is my land. The land of my ancestors. We are of this land. I know nothing of the northern shores of Africa. That is not my home. This is.' He gestures with both his arms outstretched to the wide horizon.

'Our Granada.' Tears well in Al-Mulih's eye, probably for the first time in many a long year. Boabdil continues.

'My Granada. We have breathed its air for over 500 years. My ancestors bones make up its dust. I shall keep my promise to my wife.'

Al-Mulih knows now no argument will change Boabdil's mind. His course is set.

'Who else knows of your plan, sire?'

'Just you. I have no one else I can truly trust. And of course, La Mora, as you now know. She holds the key to it all. I must send word that we now have to bring the plan forward.'

'Will she have time?'

'She now has perhaps less than she expected, but she is resourceful. Moraima must go to her within the next two days and I will follow in the early days of next year. It will be impossible for us both to go. Too dangerous also.'

'Your majesty, I have been with you a long time. I believe now though that Allah calls to me, that he is parting our ways. I will be of more use being the one who escorts your beloved wife's body to her final resting place.'

Boabdil turns to his old and trusted friend. He smiles gently and he touches his own heart with both his hands.

Al-Mulih's heavily lined eyes and furrowed brow show his slow realisation.

'You knew, you knew all along I would offer?'

'Yes, my friend. But I never would have asked. I have trusted you with our lives and now in death, I trust you even more.'

Al-Mulih wonders if this is all folly. Whether he and La Mora truly can fulfil Boabdil's last wishes. And whether indeed he will ever see his master again. The days ahead will no doubt be fraught with danger but what else is there left for them in this world?

He knows in his head that in all likelihood they will fail.

But in his heart, he knows there is more honour in them meeting their deaths trying, than running any further away. The Nasrid are no cowards. Boabdil and he then begin to discuss detail and timings, routes and precautions. Al-Mulih knows that despite everything, this is their chance, their moment, to change the course of history, even if no one will know it for many, many moons.

But Allah will know.

And one day, the world will know too.

Chapter 9

National Police Central District Offices, Granada 2017

'My son was murdered. I know it.'

The policeman stared at her sympathetically from across the table, wondering how he would react if this had been his son. He ran his hand through his thick black hair, now starting to show early signs of grey at the temples. He sighed inwardly and thought of what Andrés was doing at this moment.

He and his wife had heard nothing from him for a week now. Contact was becoming less and less frequent as he immersed himself more and more in his work at the National Museum of Archaeology in Madrid. He said a quiet prayer for him, despite not being religious, then looked out of the window at the late afternoon sun casting shadows across the blocks of offices opposite. What the hell was this all about?

Murders were rare in Granada; well, rare, relative to Europe and to anywhere in Spain come to that. They had only recently had a lecture from a so-called expert on world crime. Spain apparently came out as having the second lowest death by murder rate in Europe. Those of the 300 or so that occurred the previous year were usually as a result of alcohol fuelled domestic violence. And yet suicides were even rarer. Or so he thought.

'You do not think that he left this note stating his intentions to take his own life then, señora?'

'No,' she replied quietly but firmly.

Miguel Gomez flicked back through his notes. He tried to avoid the photo once again that was mixed amongst the papers on his knee. The look on the young man's face was haunting. He didn't have to look at it again to recall the agony. It was photoshopped into his sub conscious.

'But you did agree with my colleague at the time that it was his handwriting on the suicide note?'

Yamina al-Jayyani stopped ringing her hands for a moment and looked up. She cast a hollow glance towards the faltering spin of the rather ancient ceiling fan as if searching for strength but only finding uncertainty. She was probably no more than 45 or 46 but the death of her son had aged her considerably over the last few days since Gomez had first set eyes on her. He registered the bloodshot eyes and the deepening dark circles around them that gave her countenance a harrowing aspect and he averted his eyes once more toward the window.

'It is very like his handwriting indeed, sir. I agree. But he was always so neat. The handwriting on the note is a mess. Most of his communication was always on his computer or his mobile phone. But when he did write, his script was fair and pleasing, sir. And, if... if it is his then he must have been made to write it.'

She swallowed hard as if drowning in the stale atmosphere of the room. 'Reda had no reason to end his life, he was happy, had so much to achieve, so much to live for. Was loving University life. He had friends everywhere. Ask them. Ask them all if they think he would do this. I tell you once again, he was a happy, happy boy.'

She looked down again at her hands clenching them then wringing them as if unable to control her movements, almost tearing her handkerchief.

'My boy.'

The tears tried to come again but she was so exhausted and had shed so many already that her eyes now began to sting instead, as if only the salt of her grief remained. She squeezed them tight shut and took a deep breath.

'I understand. And my colleagues are indeed out now at this very moment speaking to as many of his friends as they can. All I can do at this stage is to promise you we will do all we can to get to the bottom of what happened. At the moment, there's so little to go on. But hopefully soon we will have the results back from the forensic investigation of his room. Maybe that will tell us if anyone else was present at the time of your son's death.'

She opened her eyes, glanced at him momentarily then lowered her head once more and began to speak in a low barely audible voice.

'I told your colleague, the one with the long black ponytail. I told her that Reda had said a week ago that he thought he was being followed, but when I quizzed him further, he just laughed it off, saying he was probably just being paranoid. Well, that's what he called it. He had been getting involved with a local political group. I told him he should just concentrate on his studies and leave politics to others.

But he argued that Muslims needed a voice in government. I said I thought we were fine just as we were. No need to upset the apple cart. He got cross sometimes, saying I should not just accept the crumbs, that we deserved more say in our future, that I was too passive, too meek. Much of what he talked about I often didn't understand to be honest. I can't see what the problem is. But...'

Her voice trailed off, as if lost in her thoughts.

Gomez took his pen out.

'What was the name of this group he was involved with, señora?'

She put her head in her hands, summoning up the information from her memories.

'He just called them PRUNE.'

He scribbled the word on his pad.

'Yes, I've heard of them.' PRUNE he knew was their acronym. The Partido Renacimiento y Unión de España. The Party for Revival and Union in Spain.

'I believe they are a harmless group, señora. We have had no issues with them but I will look into it anyway.'

'Could his involvement have got him into trouble, trouble with others?'

'I really can't say but I doubt it. Though, as I said, of course, I will look into it and see what I can find.'

The door to the interview room opened quietly and a female officer with a jet-black ponytail and a livid scar above her left eye poked her head in. The sound of distant muffled voices and keyboards being prodded filled the room.

'Sir, you are needed. Room B.'

She made a face toward the seated mother, indicating that whatever it was, it was to do with her.

'Señora. Please excuse me. You have already met Officer Carrasco; she will see you out. She can also arrange for a car to drive you home. I will be in touch as soon as possible. You have my word. And if you think of anything further that may help us, please do not hesitate to get in touch. You have my card.'

Yamina al-Jayyani stooped to pick up her handbag then rose unsteadily to her feet, with one hand using the table to support her.

'My brother-in-law is waiting in the car park. Thank you anyway.'

She followed Officer Carrasco out through the door then turned to look Gomez straight in the eye.

'I do not presume to tell you your job, sir. But I will not rest until I have justice for my Reda. And my family will not rest, nor the people of the Albayzin, until we know the truth. Someone did this to him.'

Gomez bowed slightly.

'Nor will we rest until the truth is out. I give you my word, señora.'

Carrasco took her arm gently and led her away.

Two minutes later he was seated with two other officers around a table in Room B.

'Well?' Gomez looked from one to the other. 'What is it?'

Of the two men in from of him, the first to speak was the oldest and most experienced, José Rueda.

'We have Intel from one of our undercover officers regarding the movements of several key players in Casa Social. Something is stirring, boss. All has been relatively quiet since the firecracker attack on the mosque up at San Nicolas last year, but they are casting their net further and teaming up, if reports are to be believed, with some nasty sounding far right thugs from Italy and Germany. Long and short is, they look like they're going to step up their levels of violence.'

Gomez sat with his arms folded staring at the floor. 'And what has this to do with the death of Reda al-Jayanni?'

Matias Rodriguez, the young computer wizard of the force, spoke next. He switched on his iPad screen and popped on his bright red Gucci glasses. Gomez was still trying to get used to having such a flamboyant member on his team, but the lad was good, very good.

'Well, it seems that an image of al-Jayyani, of him deceased, was sent to at least five leading Muslim supporters with a superimposed message along the lines of 'only good Muslim is a dead one' etc, etc. Nasty stuff. But, anyway, the image was sent on a platform that self-deletes once the e-mail is opened. More sophisticated than we've seen from Casa before it has to be said. So, we know of two people to whom it was sent and both have raised the matter with the police in their locale—one in Malaga, one here in Granada.'

'Shit.' Gomez sighed and leant across the table, his head in his hands.

'I could do without these bastards sticking their heads above the parapet.'

The whole community of Andalusia was working in relative harmony; across the area relationships between the various communities had been generally peaceful and Gomez was proud of how the social climate in Granada in particular, given its history, was, on the whole, one of happy acceptance and toleration.

Gomez, leant back in his chair, hands now behind his head.

'Anything else, Rodriguez?'

'Well, yes.' He pushed his glasses rather ostentatiously back up his nose. 'Oddly, one of those who received the message was not Muslim themselves. Not sure how relevant that is, other than I believe it's unusual for Casa to target non-Muslims. I'm trying to see if I can trace the source or to see if it was sent to other people who haven't come forward yet. A long, long shot.

And I've asked the guy here in Granada to whom it was sent to bring his laptop in today. There may be a trace I can find. I am contacting the guys who developed the platform to see if they can help in anyway. Though it has to be said, I think they're a bit dodgy themselves.'

'Hmm…OK. Good work. Thank you. I have a bad feeling about this whole thing. Sounds fairly clear that it wasn't suicide. Unless somehow they got to snap a photo of him dead after the event but that seems highly unlikely if not just simply bloody odd. Fuck's sake!'

Gomez ruffled his hands through his hair and slapped both his cheeks as if trying to snap himself out of his bad mood.

'Anything from forensics, Rueda?'

'Well, there are definite traces of a struggle in the room that weren't picked up initially. There were tiny specks of blood on the door frame and some prints that we can't as yet match up. Looks like someone had a cut on his or her hand, maybe. We're taking samples from all known colleagues, friends of the victim to eliminate them. But there's something else the team found. It had probably blown under the bed but when they moved it they found this.'

José Rueda offered Gomez an evidence bag, inside of which was a leaflet advertising the loathsome Casa Social−it was one of their, on the face of it, innocuous requests for food bank donations, but everyone knew the intended recipients had to be Spanish only and no needy Muslims would ever get a handout from them for certain.

'OK. But he could have picked this up from anywhere, had it pushed through his letterbox even. I doubt it's a calling card from a would-be murderer.'

'True,' Rueda replied. 'But, from our interviews in the area it turns out that a group of Muslims from a local political party were threatened a week ago or so after an evening meeting in the Albaicin. Not reported at the time. Just verbal and a bit of pushing and shoving apparently but a noose was drawn on the door of one of the members.

He said he was fairly sure he'd been followed home by a couple of guys who no doubt were the culprits. Sadly, he said there was no point reporting it at the time as he felt nothing would've been done. And he wasn't frightened by it. Anyway, it turns out that Reda Al-Jayanni attended the meetings the night they were all jostled and abused.'

Gomez flicked a fly off his trouser leg and rubbed his blood shot eyes. 'This is beginning to fall into place. But, Christ, it's a hell of a step up from firecrackers and graffiti to actually hanging someone.'

Rodriguez nodded.

'However, this morning we also got a call from the Guardia who have a female undercover agent in the Madrid branch of Casa Social. She reckons that their leader, er…'

'Yes, Ximena Martinez. I know of her all too well sadly,' Gomez interrupted.

'Well, boss, it seems that she has put the word out to beef up the scare tactics on Muslims. Apparently she's going after several intellectuals in particular who give support to the Muslim community.'

Rueda spoke up. 'But how would the murder of this guy and let's face it, it looks more and more likely it was murder, figure in their plans then? Why him? Why now?'

'I guess,' answered Gomez, 'those e mails with the warning message were designed to frighten would-be sympathisers off. If they think their support leads to Muslims dying maybe they'll think twice. Were they big wigs?'

'One was a banker who is helping fund the new party in Granada, he's the non-Muslim. The other a leading civil rights campaigner, works with Amnesty and Muslim groups, both here in Spain and abroad,' replied Rueda, flicking back through his notepad.

'When are you going to join the 21st century, José and start using an iPad?' quipped Rodriguez.

'When hell freezes over and when you start wearing normal clothes,' snapped back Rueda.

'And stop pretending we're friends by calling me by my first name, Rodriguez. We're colleagues. Full stop. I'm not going to be buying you a beer or in your case a cocktail with a paper umbrella, anytime soon.'

'Wo, there! I'll just go quiet while you reel in your testosterone, Señor Rueda,' replied Rodriguez with a grin on his face.

Gomez cut across them. 'OK, girls, not now please. Rueda, look into who the major supporters are of this new party, PRUNE. And interview this banker and civil rights worker again, catch the banker when he brings in his laptop—no, second thoughts, get onto him now, tell him to bring it in now and then speak to him. See if either of them have had any other run-ins with Casa Social, then get Carrasco to visit the PRUNE party H.Q. See if there's been any other incident recently, ones they've not reported. And we need to see why some feel they can't report things. That's not what we're about. If any desk jockey has been rude or dismissive of any reported incident then I want to know. We're all fucking Spanish here. I will not tolerate any racism in my area.

And step-up vigilance on their building and the Mosque. Just in case. Rodriguez, see if you can wheedle anything more out of the Guardia Civil re this undercover agent, see if she or they can give us any more detail of any members of Casa who seem to be of the more violent type and if they know which groups they've been trading ideas with. And let me know asap if you trace where the e-mail came from and if it was sent to anyone else.'

'I'm on it, boss,' Rodriguez replied and swivelled his chair back to his desk.

'Something feels odd. It just doesn't seem like Casa Social's M.O. They've just been content with scaring the shit out of people up to now and being generally vile. This is not going to end well. I feel bad times might be about to descend on us. OK. Thank you both and, do me a favour, let's just keep this all in house at the moment. I don't want the press getting hold of it and stoking the fires. Social, and Martinez in particular, are too clever to go after directly—they're pretty good at labelling the police as always favouring Muslims etc over anyone else, so we don't want to give them any fuel either.

Get the full forensic report on Reda Al-Jayaani to my desk, José, as soon as possible, by the end of the day if you can. I agree this boy's death now looks more and more like murder but we need hard evidence for whenever we do go after Casa Social. In the meantime, let's make sure we watch any known members in Granada as close as skin.'

He rose from the table and left the room.

Only a few steps down the corridor and the door he'd just closed opened again. Matias Rodriguez called after him.

'Boss, I've literally just received an e mail with the last sighting of Martinez. She was in Madrid yesterday.'

'Doing what?' Gomez called back.

'Well, sounds odd but she was seen at a lecture on Moorish Art at the Caixa Forum. The local police had had her followed as a matter of course.'

'A lecture on Moorish Art? Really? Anything else?'

'Yep, she was seen speaking briefly to the main speaker at the end of the lecture.'

'Who the hell was the speaker?' Gomez was now back at the door's threshold.

Rodriguez looked down at his iPad.

'She was called, er yes, Lucy E. Hawksmoor. An expert apparently on all things to do with the Moors. It was about Boabdil in art apparently and…'

'Yes, thanks Rodriguez, enough. Well, well, Lucy E. Hawksmoor.'

'You know her?' Rueda called over Rodriguez's shoulder.

'Oh, yes. She's quite a lady. The question is, what did that daughter of a whore, Martinez, want with her? Rueda, get someone on to locating Miss Hawksmoor. See if she'll let us in on their chat. I somehow can't think Martinez was inviting her out for a drink and tapas. Actually, second thoughts, leave it with me. I'll speak to her.'

Rodriguez winked at him.

'Oh, grow up, Rodriguez. Anyway, she prefers women I believe.'

'One of your lot, Rodriguez!' Rueda shouted from inside the room.

'Oh, you have such a way with words, José! You know you really only have eyes for me!'

'Shut the fuck up, Rodriguez and I told you, don't call me fucking José!'

'I promise I will never call you 'fucking José'.'

Gomez smiled to himself and headed for the exit just as a plastic water bottle thrown by Rueda hit the door above the Rodriguez's head.

Chapter 10

Cordoba

Lucy let herself in to her flat. The air was still warm and outside autumnal colours were only just beginning to appear. She dumped her bags on the floor and called out she was home, but her greeting was not returned. 'And the silence rolled like thunder,' she muttered to the empty room.

Her cat, Jasper, gave out a half-hearted yawn come meow as his way of acknowledging her arrival but he was not sufficiently enamoured to stir from his place under the table where the shade was as cool as it could get in her flat. He just got up, stretched, turned round, judged she was not getting any food out to offer, lay back down and went promptly back to sleep.

'Hmmm. Nice welcome, gato! Gracias!'

No sign of her father, unless he was on the terrace. She shuffled off her Converses and revelled in the cool feel of the tiles beneath her feet. She opened the door that led off the kitchen up to the roof terrace.

'Dad!'

No reply from above either.

That's odd, she thought. Her father had known what time she was arriving and here she was in Cordoba at the flat only an hour later than promised, 4 p.m. He'd usually have met her at the station but as she was going to be a little late she'd texted him to just meet her at the flat and, more importantly, to make sure there was cold beer.

She opened the fridge to check, well, at least he'd managed that. She took a bottle of Estrella, her favourite beer, flipped off the top with the nonchalance of an expert and took a good swig. She picked up the post from the table and wandered up to the terrace. She had to pinch herself every time she looked out across the skyline of Cordoba from up here. She had a close up view of the arched roof and majestic tower of the church of Santa Marina, built in the second half of the 13th century where once a 7th-century Visigothic church and a mosque had stood. Sadly, no trace of either now remained. But it was still a beautiful building and it calmed her just to gaze at it.

The hotchpotch of surrounding roofs formed an undulating multicoloured quilt that seemed to go on endlessly, interspersed with all manner of oddly shaped TV ariels and satellite dishes. Lucy sat down, put her beer on the tiled tabletop in front of her and looked at her mail. Mostly advertising bumph.

There was a post card from Helena, an old friend from uni who was now a farmer in Suffolk. She'd obviously taken Lucy's advice and finally taken time out for a holiday. But Lucy wasn't sure that a week in Cromer was what she'd had in mind. Ah, well, only so much one can do for people, she mused.

The last piece of post was a plain white envelope, addressed to her in rather haphazard handwriting, but no stamp. Most of her post of any significance was always sent to her office in Granada. So, she couldn't believe it was work related. She opened it and looked inside. Just an umber coloured square business card. She lifted it out and recognised it immediately; it was for Casa Mazal, a Sephardic restaurant where she and her father were supposed to be eating this evening. On the back someone had written,

'9 p.m. Table for 3. Do not be late. Advice offered.'

OK, weird, very weird. Who else other than her father knew she'd be back in Cordoba today? And why for 3? Just then she heard the door open and footsteps coming quickly upstairs.

'Dad! Jesus! You frightened the crap out of me!'

'Hey, hello to you too!'

Her father was quite fit for a man in his late 60s. His hair was thin on top and still fair in places but whips of silver streaked his temples. It was shorter and spikier than the last time Lucy had seen him a week ago. He was dressed in all black, a t shirt, jeans and a pair of old Sketchers on his feet. He was quite tanned and his face, although lined, was of a man maybe ten years younger. Lucy got up and gave him a big hug.

'Sorry. I'm glad to see you, Dad, just had a shitty night last night with little sleep thanks to nightmares about that photo of the poor guy in Granada. And today's been rather strange too to say the least.'

'Let me get us more beers and we can talk all about it. Up here or downstairs?'

'Downstairs.'

'So, where've you been? I thought you'd be at the station to meet me.'

'I got caught up at the barbers and meant to meet you back here but then I got a return call from Alvaro Castilla. I'd had to leave him a message and you'll never believe it but by sheer fluke he's in Cordoba, which is fantastic timing for you. Then we talked too long and I lost track of time. I got back here only to realise I'd left my glasses at the barbers. I should've texted you or left a note, I'm sorry darling, but normally you don't like fuss. I guess this thing, this e-mail, has really got to you.'

He cracked open two beers and gave one to Lucy, then opened a tin of olives stuffed with anchovies and poured them into a bowl.

'Yeah, I guess. I was stood up this morning as well so when you weren't there, no message etcetera, I was feeling a little less than ten per cent on the 'poor me' scale. This second beer is helping though.'

'Stood up? You mean, Gloria hasn't come with you?'

'Nope. And, what is *very* odd, she didn't even call to explain. When it got past the time we were supposed to meet I tried calling her, but it just kept going straight to voicemail. Then suddenly I get a text saying, 'Thanks for yesterday. Hope we'll meet again soon.' No mention of Cordoba. Nothing.

I texted again. No reply. Nada. Zilch. I waited a while just in case, which is why I ended up catching a later train.' Lucy stared at her beer. 'She was so keen to come too.'

'Bizarre.'

'Is the right word for it.' They smiled at each other. Lucy felt a bit calmer in her father's presence.

'Do you think she's alright?' he asked.

'Why wouldn't she be? I mean, God, I hope so. She did think we were being spied on in one of the bars but I can't believe anything bad could've happened to her. Surely? I mean, why would it?'

'No, I'm sure not, but not to contact you, especially after her seeking you out for whatever reason. And, as you said, she was so keen to come. Didn't you say her father lived here?'

'Yes, she said he did.' Lucy paused and checked her phone again. 'You're worrying me now.'

Another silence whilst she sipped her beer.

'You OK, love?'

'Yes, I'm fine, I guess but I was trying to be cool and sensible, not thinking the worse but maybe something has happened to her. But surely no one would harm her?'

'I'm sure not. I think maybe you're jumping to conclusions based on very little.'

'Jumping to conclusions is high on my agenda at the moment after that horrific photo and threat.'

'Fair point. I'm sure she's fine and that there's a very good reason why she didn't show up. How about we try and find out where her father lives?'

'Yes, OK. Though no idea how we go about that.'

'Let me have a think. In the meantime, you can tell me about this paper she gave you. Unless you want to wait till later at the restaurant.'

Lucy suddenly remembered the letter.

'Have you booked a table at Casa Mazal, Dad?'

'Yes, for 9 p.m. That's what you said wasn't it?'

Lucy nodded. 'For how many?'

'I thought Gloria was coming so I booked a table for three.'

'Alright. This is my day getting seriously full on weird.' She took out the business card and put it on the table in front of her father.

'So? Their business card.' He picked it up and flipped it over.

Lucy watched him. 'That was delivered here, it was in an unstamped letter in the pile you left for me.'

Her Dad was thinking.

'It's peculiar, that's for sure. I didn't notice it when I picked your post up this morning. Well, I say morning. It didn't come as per usual till almost midday. It must've been in with the flyers and other stuff. I normally throw most of it away to be honest. Bit spooky that it's the same time as I booked and for the same number of people.'

Lucy took the card and looked at the handwriting closely. 'So, who's it from and why do they want to meet me without letting me know who they are? It's creepy, Dad. And why do I need advice and on what?'

'It's got to be related somehow to this thing with Gloria, what she told you. Come on, tell me and let's see if we can work out what's going on.'

'Are we still going to go to the restaurant?'

'Yes, I think we should. We'll be safe enough meeting whoever the mystery man or woman is in a restaurant. And together we can find out what this little charade is all about.'

He stood and headed for the fridge. 'Let me get us more beer and then we can sit on the sofa and you can fill me in on what Gloria had to say.'

Lucy crossed the room, sat down and wrapped herself in an orange and amber Moroccan throw. Her father's pragmatism always helped her refocus. She took the beer he offered and began to tell him all about what Gloria had told her and about the curious sheet of red paper.

Chapter 11

'An ocean of sadness raged inside us,
Our hearts, desperate, burn with eternal flame.
The city was so beautiful with its garden and rivers,
The nights were imbued with the sweet fragrance of narcissus.'

Ibn Amira 13th c

Aixa contemplated her son as he stared out across the darkening mountain scape. Her love for him was unconditional and immense but she had never been good at showing her emotions.

Many simply believed Aixa had no heart. She had lost much over the years, had witnessed horror and cruelty on an immense scale and had had to endure the ignominy of a husband belittling her and cheating on her after her first husband had died suddenly. She had then been married off unceremoniously to Abu l-Hasan Ali but it was a move only enacted for political reasons—there had never been a shred of affection between them. Yet no one had expected that her new spouse would run off with a slave girl and a Christian at that and marry her. Aixa, in fear for her life had gone into exile. She duly got her revenge a few years later when she sided, to the amazement of many of her advisors, with her ex-husband's enemies, the Abencerrages and had him deposed in favour of her son, the man who now stood before her.

She poured out her love silently across the space between them but she was unsure whether he loved her back or whether she had frightened him too much over the years with her imperious ways and, she had to admit, her tendency to criticise him so much. But she had always meant all her words to be for the best. She knew how on occasions his love for his fellow human beings, whoever they were, as well as his artistic slant, from time to time inclined him towards leniency or peace when what was needed was a demonstration of authority or strength. He was always reading, always writing verse, studying the Qur'an, was often to be found on one of the shadowy patios of the palace deep in conversation with that strange woman La Mora of Ubeda whose opinion he had always valued so much.

Aixa had always known that she had to be the strong one and, at times, the ruthless and bloody one. He would not be standing here had she not carefully negotiated his release from captivity when he had been held by the Catholic monarchs nine years earlier. She was a stateswoman and a powerhouse of the Nasrid dynasty, a survivor with few challengers, but she had had to use all her wiles over the years to overcome obstacles and defeat enemies.

Battles are not always won with swords. Being meek and polite was not what helped you survive in this world. Being open, wearing your heart on your sleeve was seen as a weakness by other men.

But, for the first time in her life she was now experiencing a feeling of real hopelessness, a feeling that all was truly lost, yet there was still perhaps one last deed she could do for her son. For, she reminded herself, she was Aixa—Aixa al-Horra—the honoured one, so called by many as she was one of the living descendants of the Prophet Muhammed. This always steeled her. Always gave her the strength to press on regardless of danger and an unfailing belief in herself. To many she came across as iron hard and icily arrogant but she knew that Allah was always with her, advising, cajoling, pushing, protecting.

Aixa knew she was approaching her end days in this world. She had already lost so much but, now she repeatedly told herself, was not the time to think of her needs. When had it ever been? She had to stay strong for her son and help in any way she could. And after he had spoken to her the previous evening, hinted at his plans for his future and the body of his beloved wife, Moraima, she had gone away to think.

Now she had to convince her son that her plan *would* work, for it was without doubt a truly audacious one and, because of the involvement of one person in particular, a person her son detested almost as much as he hated Isabella and Ferdinand, she knew Boabdil would need some persuading.

Boabdil sighed. Without turning around he spoke.

'So, mother, what can I do for you?'

'I believe I have a better plan than yours, my son.'

Boabdil lowered his head and smiled to himself. 'Well, it would be unusual for you to ever agree with anything I suggest. But please, speak. I do not wish to offend.' He sighed. 'Of course, I will listen.'

'Are we alone?'

'I am always alone these days, mother. I have never felt so alone. No one will overhear us out here. Our only company are the vultures watching from that distant outcrop. Quite poignant really.'

She moved a little closer, her long flowing robe flaring slightly in the warm breeze that came off the Vega.

'Are you sleeping at all, my son?'

'I close my eyes. I sleep in fits and starts. Sometimes I think I am asleep but I have strange visions on some nights which make me feel as if I am awake, they seem so real. I pray hard for the angel of the night to stop me thinking, to pour her blackness in to my eyes. But deep sleep will not come.'

'What do you see?'

'You may well think I am going mad, losing my grip on the real world. But…'

Aixa had not expected her son to actually tell her. He had rarely in the past opened up to her like this.

'I see a woman looking for me.'

'Moraima?'

'I wish to Allah it was. No. As hard as I try to bring her face in front of me, the more she seems to slip further away. But, somehow, I know not why, I believe this woman may have been sent to me by Moraima. I cannot explain, it is just a sense, a feeling quite ethereal, that she is a messenger. She comes into the room where I am sleeping, though it is not my room, nor even my palace. It has a low ceiling and carved words on the wall which I cannot decipher in the gloom.

The woman is dressed in strange vestments. Pale coloured hair. Long. Not of our people. But I feel, I know, she is there not to do me harm, but in some way to help. And, as hard as I try she will not turn to face me. I know she wants to find me but she cannot see me. And I try to call out to her but my words have no sound. There. Now you will think I have gone mad, mother. '

'You are perhaps grieving so much you are becoming ill.'

'Ill? Ha!' Boabdil turned to face his mother. 'I am certainly sick. Sick of this world. Sick of feeling so helpless.' He took a few steps towards his mother and placed his hands gently on her shoulders.'

'You are right, no doubt. You usually are. And this time I really, truly, hope you are, mother. Perhaps all this is as result of an affliction. Perhaps I will wake up one day and realise I just had a sickness of the mind. That none of this ever happened. That you and Moraima and my children will be standing by my bedside in the Alhambra when I awake from this nightmare.'

Aixa peered deep into his dark hazel eyes, as if searching for something.

'Son, you need to be stronger than ever. Do not dare give in now. Do not ever give in.' His mother's words were spoken gently for once. She took his hands in hers and led him to a couch.

'You must go over the sea, Abu.'

'I no longer wish to, mother.'

'I know. Not you. But you must go.'

'Now you talk in riddles.'

'Your place is here. I agree. I fear your plans are mortally dangerous but.'

'My lady, these forsaken mountains hold nothing for me. I would rather be a pauper in Granada than a King of nothing up here.'

'I know. Granada calls you and whatever your plan is, however it works out, I believe in you.'

Boabdil looked up and directly into Aixa's piercing hazel eyes.

'Now, I never thought I would hear those words from you, mother.'

Aixa, ignoring the sound of mild reproach in her son's words, stood and walked a few steps towards the balcony and then turned to her son.

'And if your plan stands any chance of succeeding you must be seen to leave these shores.'

She paused and then spoke firmly, without hesitation or doubt.

'I will go. I was always going to go with you and I will take someone with me, someone who the people of Fez and beyond will believe is you.'

'What? I am not quite understanding your words. Why?'

'Listen! Isabella has spies everywhere. If you leave Andarax and do not appear at the coast then they, the Christians, will know something is wrong. Isabella will know the minute you step foot outside these walls. And she will be expecting her spies to tell her that you have left and landed on a distant shore of Africa. If she believes you are out of Al-Andalus then she will sleep easier.'

'Let me get this clear in my head. You intend to leave and take someone who is masquerading as me to the Northern shores of Africa?'

She lowered her gaze and smiled. Boabdil had not seen such a smile on those lips for a long, long time.

'I was hoping you were about to say it is a wonderful plan?'

Boabdil nodded but was noncommittal.

'And who do you plan to take who looks like me?'

'We need to discuss that later. But I need to discuss your plans first, where you intend to go from here and when. '

'As you already know, my wife's mortal remains are on their way to rest in the grounds of the Alhambra. Not in the family plot, that would be impossible, obviously. More I cannot tell you. It is not that I do not trust you, mother, simply that the fewer people who know the fewer people can be held to account for my actions should anyone ever be questioned. Then, as for me, I will follow but what route I shall take or when I will go, well, of that I am as yet unsure.'

'Well, for what it may be worth, I believe you are right in your desire to return to the Alhambra itself. However, you go or wherever you stay, I know it is the correct decision, though I fear your chances of arriving unnoticed are not good. Nor do I understand what it is you think you might do once you are there. But with my plan no one will be looking out for you because everyone will think you have gone over the seas.'

Boabdil stared at his mother blankly.

She continued now with urgency in her voice.

'Do you not see? I repeat, no one will be looking for you once they think you are beyond these shores. Where better to hide than in plain sight, my child?'

Boabdil sat regarding his mother; rarely had she been so accepting of his ideas. Her easy acceptance of his plan to smuggle his wife's body back to the Alhambra grounds and of his own desire to head back there. And she too had clearly come up with a plan to in some way help him. A distraction on a grand scale. Yet, how could anyone pass as himself? Who even looked remotely like him?

'So, who is going to play my part?'

'I will tell you inside. Come. I need water.'

She rose and as she moved her silken robes flowed in such a way as to make it look as if she were floating, not walking. Boabdil sat for a moment longer, mesmerised, as if seeing her for the first time in a long while. Then he rose and followed her into the inner chamber where a large marble table dominated the room. On it were at least thirty candles burning brightly, sending spirit-like shadows dancing up the walls and across the ceiling. Branches of jasmine stood in highly decorated vases adding their heady scent to that of the perfumed candles.

He sat on a long couch covered in silks and cushions of velvet. Leaning forward Boabdil put his head in his hands and gently rubbed his temples. He briefly cursed himself for his lack of faith in his mother. As usual she had thought everything through and had come up with a brave and daring plan.

Without moving, he spoke gently. 'I am wrong not to trust you with my plan, to not tell you where I am going. Where I will hide. Indeed, where I will, one day Allah willing, lay down to rest. Alongside my wife.'

'It is not necessary to tell me. I understand. But somehow I think I actually know where you will go.'

Now he looked up and across at her, slightly stunned.

'You do? How?'

'Because I believe it is somewhere we have spoken of many times in other contexts. Somewhere right under Isabella and Ferdinand's noses, but a place of which neither is aware, even though it is within the very walls of the red palace.'

Boabdil suddenly realised his mother had indeed guessed correctly. 'By Allah. Mother!'

'You do not have to confirm it, that way I can never say you told me, if as you think I might possibly one day be held to account and asked. But I am thinking of Bib-al-Gudur.'

Boabdil sat back, speechless.

He laughed. 'Well, how about that! You knew all along. Was it that obvious?'

'No, my son, it would only be obvious to you and I, for who else knows that you asked Ferdinand to block the entrance up as one last favour, out of respect to the last sultan of Granada to leave through its arch.'

'You are right. No one else knew. And they indeed kept their word and that way out and into the tower is now blocked for eternity.'

Aixa again smiled. It was becoming a new habit of hers, Boabdil noticed and he watched as her face seemed to change shape, taking on a new, almost younger aspect as she let the smile spread wider.

'And fortunately for you, my son, they do not know its other name.'

'Long may that be so, mother. Long may that be so.'

'So, you will be forever close to your wife and children. I know that much at least, that you need to be near her.'

Boabdil sighed.

'If Al-Mulih succeeds in his quest. I expect word any day now from La Mora de Ubeda who set everything in motion. I have the utmost faith in them both, but I will feel a lot better when I know for certain that the first part of the plan has worked, even if it is the easiest part. Then I can follow in disguise as a lesser mortal.'

'I am sure you can blend in like a crow in the night. Few will remember you now I suspect. So many are leaving or have left the city who once knew us.'

'So, mother. Tell me of your plan. Who is to play my part in your venture?'

Aixa proceeded to explain her plan in detail and then, gently as possible, told him who would play his part. At first he was furious. He paced up and down the room, cursing, astonished beyond belief at who his mother had proposed, indeed who, it would appear, she had already asked.

Aixa let him blow his own fire out and after five minutes, he did indeed stop and stand stock still by the far wall. Then he turned to her. His face had changed from one of venom to one of angelic clarity. Then he laughed loud and long.

'My mother! When will you ever cease to surprise and amaze me? God in heaven! You are brilliant! I see it all. This solves so much! He will be once and for all out of Al Andalus and he will get what he has always desired; people to cheer him, welcome him, a place in the history books. And at the same time, for the first time ever, he will be helping us! Mother, you are indeed truly the wisest of the wise. I just do not know how you persuaded him?'

'That is not for now, my son. But let us say the thought of going to a safe haven where he will be welcomed as the exiled King of Al-Andalus, lodged in a palace no doubt with servants once again, was a vastly more appealing end to his days than wasting away his pitiful life hiding in the bleak caves of high Teruel.'

Later, as Boabdil lay in bed, all that he and his mother had spoken about whirled lightly like butterflies in his head. Perhaps after all, he thought, my plans are not folly. Perhaps he and Moraima would one day be able to lie side by side as they had always wished. His heart was now beating quicker. Bib-al-Gudur—the Gate of the Wells. For a strange moment he thought again of the woman of his dreams who was searching for him. He stared toward the window into the deep night.

'Do not stop looking, whoever you are. And Moraima, I know you are listening. We are going home.'

Once again, he felt alive. Aixa was without doubt a force, still very much, to be reckoned with.

Now, he had to ensure the Nasrids struggle to remain in Granada was not at an end.

It was in his hands.

Chapter 12

Cordoba

The light was just beginning to fade as Lucy and her father strolled through the quiet, narrow scented lanes towards the restaurant. Flowers were still in abundance at every turn, seemingly on every wall. Begonias, bougainvillea and gazanias created a rainbow of hues against the whitewashed backdrop of each building. Nowhere ever looks quite as beautiful as the narrow streets of Cordoba, Lucy mused as she for once turned her mind away from recent events. They took a turning past the Museo Taurino, the giant statue of the bull in the courtyard looking disturbingly life-like in the shadowy gloom of the courtyard it dominated.

As they emerged onto Calle Tomás Conde, Lucy noticed the scent of a different flower in the air, one she didn't recognise. Its perfume was intoxicating. She looked up to see several walls covered in a swathe of greenery with here and there little white and yellow blooms hanging like rows of fairy bells.

'What a gorgeous smell.'

Her father looked up. 'Isn't it? Just wonderful. I asked one of the locals what it was as I'm utterly hopeless with flower names but I was at least close with my guess. It's a winter clematis, though apparently they're not supposed to bloom 'til December. Blame it on global warming, I guess.'

'Let's not start that again,' Lucy smiled. 'I'll just accept them for just being here thanks and be glad they're out at this particular moment. I don't know how I've missed them in the past.'

As they approached the turn that would take them into the short alley leading to the restaurant, Lucy stopped and turned to her father.

'Don't look now, but there's a guy behind us, about three shops down, who I'm pretty sure has been following us since we left the house.'

'Really? I didn't see anyone.' He started to turn round. As he did so, the man Lucy was referring to briefly glanced at them then stepped into a shop.

'I said don't look round, Dad. Hopeless!'

'Sorry, love. I didn't really see his face, did you?'

'Not clearly. I'm maybe just imagining things. He actually didn't look too dodgy.'

'If he is following us he's not very good at it.'

'What time is it?'

'Just coming up to 9 p.m. Shall we go?'

'Yes, come on. I'm starving but my stomach is also doing nervous cartwheels.'

'You need a drink.'

'No shit, Dad! Let's go and see who our mystery date is.'

Further back, along the street, a man stepped out of a shop doorway back onto the pavement. This had to be the girl he was looking for. She certainly fitted the description. The chances of seeing her at the station earlier that day were slim but he'd struck gold. He'd wanted to approach her, had been told to do so, but he had to be sure for himself, had to be certain she was not involved with the others. There was so much at stake; one careless error of judgment and all would be lost.

Sometimes it was too much for him, this burden. He had often awoken in the dead of night wondering whether it was all worth it, if it actually meant anything. The thoughts were fleeting but he could not imagine what he would do if this turned out to all be a terrible waste of time.

'Allah forgive me,' he whispered to himself. But recent events had shaken him and now, real or not, clearly someone else wanted to share in the knowledge too and he knew whoever they were, they were extremely dangerous.

Just then his mobile rang. He looked up hoping those he was pursuing had not heard it, he cursed himself for having not switched it to silent mode.

Some spy I'd make, he thought. The voice on the other end sounded weak and tired. 'Have you seen her? Spoken to her?'

'No, I have not had a chance but I am following her.'

'You must see her now. Speak to her.'

'I am about to. Stay calm. I have to do it in my own time. I have arranged to meet up. Any minute.'

'OK. Tell her I really wanted to get in touch but I lost her number.'

'I will. Of course. Hassan will pick you up at the hospital. Tomorrow morning. He will drive you straight here.'

'Thank you, Papa.'

'Rest up until then. Good night my sapphire.'

He turned his phone off and decided to walk once round the block to clear his head then he would approach Lucy E. Hawksmoor. When he met her for himself, then he could rest easy and believe that they really had done the right thing.

***

'Good evening, Señora Hawksmoor! How are you?'

The waiter was tall, elegantly dressed and wearing a smile so bright, Lucy's father thought they could possibly turn the lights off and leave him simply to illuminate the place.

'I am well, Tariq and glad to be back here.'

'It is always a pleasure to have such a renowned personage as you in our restaurant. Do you have a table booked, not that it matters?'

'Well, actually, my dad here did, in our name but, well, I think someone else also booked a table for us, for three for 9 p.m.'

'OK, in what name?'

'Ah, that's where it gets hazy. I don't know, sounds bizarre I know but...'

A voice spoke from behind them.

'It is in the name of Sarmiyento, Faris Sarmiyento Yasin.'

Lucy turned quickly to look at who the voice belonged to. It was a face she recognised.

'Were you just following us?' Lucy's father asked in a low but stern voice. The waiter looked as if he was about to say something.

Lucy cut in. 'It's okay. Dad, I think I know this guy. Let's get to the table and we can sort this out quietly. OK, Tariq, lead the way.'

They sat down in a quiet corner, few tables this evening were occupied. The mellow ochre walls instantly relaxed all guests, though just at this moment Lucy wanted answers, then she could sit back and possibly, just possibly, relax.

'I recognised the name, you must be Gloria's father.'

'Yes and I apologise for the subterfuge, Miss Hawksmoor. The invitation was, as you English say, a bit 'cloak and dagger' but it gave me a chance to watch from afar. See who came and went, if anyone followed you when you left your apartment. I am not usually so circumspect but I am now far more nervous and wary than I have been in many a long year.'

Lucy smiled warily, the thought of being followed was not pleasant whatever the motive.

'OK, go on.'

'Thank you. I know of you, of course. And I know you know of me but after what happened to Gloria just after she left you, I had to be sure that you were who you said you were and that you had no connections to people who wish our people harm.'

'Gloria? She didn't show up this morning, is she OK?'

'You didn't know?'

'All I know is, I got a brief text saying she wouldn't make it. Nothing more since.'

'She didn't show up because, Miss Hawksmoor, she was in hospital.'

'Christ! In hospital. How come?'

'Yes, in hospital,' repeated Sarmiyento, emphasising the last word as if it was purgatory he was talking about. He breathed deeply and visibly seemed to calm down and just stared into the middle distance as if gathering his thoughts.

Lucy wanted to ask him to hurry up with the story but she bit her lip. He was clearly a man not to be rushed.

'She was, she believes, a victim of a theft in the Metro. It seems that two people pretending to help her after a fall in the train carriage took items from her bag, including her phone, without her knowing. The text you received was obviously not from her. Interesting that they bothered to send it. Clearly they seemed to know your plans.'

'Shit. That's not good.'

A woman dressed rather lavishly on another table looked over at her disapprovingly. Lucy mouthed the word 'Sorry.' Then she silently reprimanded herself for apologising.

Her father poured them all a glass of wine but Sarmiyento just drank water.

'So, please, tell me, why is she in hospital? Was she attacked?'

Gloria's father did not appear to hear her question but simply carried on with his story.

'What is worse still, she had obviously been followed for some time. Whoever it was seems to have known where she had been and where she would be going next. On the concourse of the Metro, Gloria was offered what she thought to be a free bottle of water from a vendor giving samples away. The police checked, no one had a license that day to do so. On CCTV the person clearly can be seen to wait for Gloria, give her the water, then pack up and leave. He had only been there a short while before she arrived and gave away no other bottles. But the water he gave my daughter was spiked with Rohypnol.'

'Rohypnol, fuck!' She could not believe what she was hearing. If there were any more disapproving stares at her language she was now beyond caring.

'According to reports, she passed out at the ticket barrier. Fortunately, an off-duty policeman was behind her and raised the alarm before any other harm could come to her.'

'Christ, that sounds awful. Poor girl.' James Hawksmoor looked very worried and glanced at Lucy. 'This is all turning rather nasty.'

'Yes, Mr Hawksmoor. Nasty is a good word.'

Lucy felt a bit sick. 'How is she now?'

'I am told she can leave hospital in the morning, my cousin is picking her up and driving her straight over to my house. This cannot be a coincidence, that the day she gets to meet you, takes you into our deepest confidence, this happens.'

'You're not blaming Lucy surely?'

'No, Dad, of course, he isn't.'

She looked at Gloria's father.

'Are you?'

'No, of course not, but…'

'But, what?' Lucy was feeling uncomfortable.

'Have you been careless? Were you careless? Where you spoke? Who could have overheard you? I have not had a chance to ask Gloria and the hospital said her memory of the day's events were unclear, though she remembers a lot about you it seems.'

Lucy couldn't figure out if he was angry with her or not.

'We were as secretive as you can be on the streets of Madrid. I wasn't aware at the time of the magnitude of what she was telling me though I'm sure coming up to speed on the dangers of it now. I was confronted at my talk by a rather hideous creature called Ximena Martinez. She told me in a rather threatening manner to steer clear of in any way highlighting good things about the Moors and specifically Boabdil, the subject of my lecture, in a good light.'

95

Sarmiyento had been staring at his hands but looked up at the mention of the last king of the Moors. Or maybe it was the name Martinez that stirred him. Whatever, Lucy could see he was deeply troubled.

'Martinez?' The look he gave Lucy made her feel that had they been in any other establishment and not one so posh he would have spat on the floor after speaking her name out loud.

'She is dangerous. I had not realised you met her. That though explains a lot. You must have been seen. And followed. I just hope to god you were not overheard.'

'We couldn't have been. Seriously, we couldn't.'

'In which case, they wanted to send out a message.'

James leant forward in his chair. 'But why Gloria? Why not attack Lucy, she's the one doing the digging so to speak and voicing support for Muslims in Granada.'

'Because attacking Gloria was a message to Lucy. To stay away from Muslims or they will harm them. And no one knows Gloria; attacking Lucy directly would bring the police down heavily on her party, Casa Social. She is too well known.'

'That's so horrible because of me she was attacked. I'm so sorry, Señor Saramiyento.'

'Don't be, please. Gloria would not blame you. And call me Faris. Look, one thing it has proved is how vital it is that they do not discover what Gloria told you.'

James ordered another bottle of wine and another large jug of iced water.

Then he asked Faris if he had heard about the boy who was found hanged in Granada. He had and was clearly upset about it. Lucy then told Faris all about the picture of this boy she'd received the day before.

He looked increasingly nervous during her account and turned his hands over and placed them, palms down on the tablecloth. Once she had finished he looked at her with eyes full of fear.

'These people are dangerous. They have done many unpleasant and harmful things, but no one has been killed by them before. This changes everything, puts us all in danger, especially you Miss Hawksmoor.'

She looked round at the other occupied tables in their corner of the restaurant. No one unsavoury met her eyes. Even the older lady who had glared at her language earlier was now completely ensconced in a conversation, clearly of a romantic nature, with the somewhat younger man sitting opposite her. Lucy took a long sip of her glass of Ribera.

She looked at her father, then at Faris.

'You need to call me Lucy and I can assure you no one is going to scare me off,' and, as if to show her lack of concern for her own safety, she let a light smile cross her lips.

She knew in her heart she was up for this fight and, though unsure of the consequences, she knew her research was somehow all linked in to this turn of events and that made it even more worthwhile pursuing her goal.

Faris stared at her, waiting for her to say something. Her father was a clearly enveloped in his own thoughts and sat stony faced.

After a moment's silence, Lucy spoke. 'I need to get moving with this paper and what it contains. Dad, did you get a reply from Alvaro Castilla about meeting up?'

'Ah, yes, sorry, meant to tell you, he can meet you at your place Saturday morning for an hour but no more if that's OK. On his way to the university. He's doing bits and pieces there this weekend as it's quiet, so he'll pop in on his way.'

'Brilliant, thanks, Dad.'

She then explained to Faris exactly who Alvaro was, as he was looking worried at the thought of involving anyone else.

'Don't worry. He's an expert on ancient Arabic texts and particularly in Aljamiado, which is what most of the text appears to be written in. And luckily for me, a good friend of my father's.'

'That's fine, Lucy, I trust your judgement on the course of action to take but let us speak no more of it here in public. We can meet tomorrow at my house when Gloria is back. I will text you. Now, as I invited you both here, let me buy us supper.'

'Don't be silly, Faris. There's no need.'

'I insist, Señor Hawksmoor, sorry, Lucy. Now, I will order my usual, Cous-cous con pollo harissa.'

'Good choice,' Lucy replied. 'Though I'm not too hungry now, really.'

Faris looked up at her with a very serious expression as if she had just uttered something treasonous.

'My dear, you must eat. You are going to need all your strength for the task ahead.'

Lucy did not want to offend, so gave in.

'Well, maybe you're right. I'll go for a small bowl of hummus and some of their flat bread. I'm glad you trust me, Faris. Thank you.'

'There is a lot resting on your shoulders young lady. I trust you to find the meaning to this piece of paper and prove that the faith of all those who have guarded it for so long was worthwhile. Gloria trusts you too. That means a lot. She is a good judge of character.'

The waiter arrived to take their order then Lucy excused herself and went to the loo.

Once there she closed the door behind her and looked at herself in the mirror. She had a very strange feeling, one so strong she almost felt dizzy. It was something she had never experienced before but deep in the well of her heart she knew that this was a task that had been waiting for her; almost as if someone somewhere had known that one day she would come along.

She considered for a second that she might be over playing it, she felt so lightheaded, yet she sensed that her search for the final resting place of the last king of the Moors was now a step closer. She could not have explained logically to anyone why this was; no doubt her colleagues would think she had gone mad getting so excited over something seemingly without much provenance. But she knew, just knew, that the piece of paper Gloria had given her was the key and that without realising it, it was something she had been looking for without knowing.

She suddenly shivered as if a ghost had walked over her grave.

She glimpsed over her shoulder then back at the mirror. Suddenly, she saw, as if through a haze of mist, the image of a man with his back to her leaning on a balustrade overlooking a mountain range.

She gasped. The bathroom door rattled. She momentarily turned her back on the mirror and when she whipped back round again, the image was gone.

Lucy threw water over her face and looked back at herself.

'Jesus, Mary, Michael and Joseph! Come on. Get a fucking grip girl.'

She wiped her face on a paper towel, took a deep breath and walked toward the door but then stopped. She turned again and looked back at the mirror. She had a feeling she knew who it was.

'I'm coming,' she whispered. She then felt foolish as she opened the door but somewhere in her head a distant voice sighed.

Chapter 13

The next morning, Lucy woke early, put the coffee pot on the stove and sat on her roof top terrace with a blanket wrapped round her. The air was cool and moist and she felt a new freshness in the air. Gloria was arriving at around midday, so in the meantime Lucy was taking stock of what had transpired over the last few days and planning her next moves. She was looking forward to meeting Alvaro Castilla at the weekend, though her father would not be accompanying them as he had to return to the U.K. He'd received an email inviting him to help with the setting up of a new museum in Cornwall on the Arthurian legends, an offer he couldn't refuse. But it meant he had to catch a flight back today in order to be in on the initial discussions.

There was that and the fact, he had joked, that her mother had said she would change the locks if he didn't come home soon. She could be wonderfully melodramatic at times; loved having him home but once he was back, after a few weeks she wanted him out from under her feet again. He had considered not going at all as he was worried about Lucy but she said she would kick him out if he didn't go and that he had nothing to worry about–she could look after herself.

Lucy went back over her meeting with Gloria in Madrid and then thought about whether she should be asking her to help her at all after the attack. She liked to have someone to bounce her own theories off and someone to challenge her thoughts and Gloria would be perfect for that she felt. Not that she always listened to others but it allowed her to run an argument or theory through its course. She reckoned that in Gloria's case she might be more open to providing challenging points of view, especially given her background.

Lucy switched her phone on and checked her e-mail cautiously; no unpleasant ones as far as she could make out, thank God. An update from her brother on his travel plans. After the usual gory tales of his love life and assorted gossip about their mutual friends and enemies, he ended by stating that he was definitely coming out to visit her in the not-too-distant future but, as ever, vague on dates. He was so exasperating at times. She replied briefly, once again, to warn him to check ahead and message her on WhatsApp when he was coming out as she couldn't be sure where she might be over the next few weeks and she didn't want him to book a flight to the wrong city.

She knew she didn't see him often enough these days, what with her work in Spain and his work jetting him off to various points on the globe from time to time, but if she could grab a day or two, even a week with him, then she'd love it. Not that this was great timing but she was too soft to put him off.

There was mail from the team in Fez saying Mohammad had come through as she had suggested he would and now they expected the DNA results on the body in the tomb back in the next 48 hours or so. The email ended by saying, 'If it is who we think it is, we bet you're beside yourself with regret that you ain't here to be part of it!'

Well, actually I'm not, she thought, because I'm certain that you'll find that whoever it is, it 'ain't' Boabdil. If he was anywhere in North Africa the Tlemcen site still seemed the favourite. The problem for the authorities of course was that it was a gamble testing the remains because if it wasn't Boabdil in Fez then it would cease to be a place of interest for a lot of visitors / tourists / historians and a loss of face for Fez folk in general and the city hierarchy in particular. Though Tlemcen didn't appear to have a body, it did have the tantalising tomb inscription. But somehow Lucy sensed these were all historical red herrings, designed to put people off looking in the right place. But why?

Then she nearly leapt out of her skin as her phone vibrated and rang in her hand at the same time.

She looked at the screen, a Madrid number.

Lucy answered cautiously.

'Hola?'

'Buenos dias. Am I speaking to Señora Hawksmoor?

'Depends who's asking.'

'Ah, yes. My name is Inspector Gomez, from the National Police force in Granada. We met once, a couple of years ago in the University.' Lucy's mind raced over reasons why he was phoning now. Gloria?

'Er, yes, I remember. The conference on diversity and tolerance. I remember your talk.'

'Ah, that's good. I trust it was not memorable for its dullness!'

'Not at all, it was interesting.' Dam, she thought, not a very convincing seal of approbation.

He continued, seemingly unfazed by her less than enthusiastic tone.

'I have followed your work since with interest by the way.'

A pause, Lucy was not sure what to say to that. She was not great on small talk on the phone and desperately wanted him to get to the point.

'I just wanted to ask a few questions about your lecture in the Caixa Forum last week, señora.'

'Oh, really? Why?' Her mind whizzed round the possibilities.

Gomez continued as if Lucy had not spoken. She bit her lip and chided herself for being so snappy.

'We believe you were approached at your talk by a woman, one by the name of Ximena Martinez. Is that so?'

Lucy suddenly realised what this was probably all about and relaxed slightly.

'Oh yes, her. Thanks for reminding me. Yes, she did have a few choice words of advice for me. Not sure she was too keen on my talk, nor me come to think of it. Not a fan.'

'Can I ask, did she threaten you at all?'

'Hmm, not sure if you would describe it quite as such but…'

'How would you describe it?' Lucy noted a tiny hint of impatience in his voice.

'Well, she clearly didn't like my research. The lecture was on Boabdil, the last king of the Moors in Granada and I'm researching into the location of his last resting place, as you no doubt know if, as you say, you are a detective and following my work.' Why on earth, she wondered, would he, a police inspector, be following her work on a long dead Moor?

'Yes, as you say, I do know. Please, continue?'

Jasper, her cat, suddenly jumped on her lap, demanding attention. Lucy stroked his head and felt a notch calmer.

'Ah OK, well, she said something along the lines of did I realise that not everyone liked my subject matter; clearly she meant Muslims.'

'And, if I may ask again, did she threaten you?'

'As I say, not as such, Inspector, though it felt threatening. She said words to the effect that she hoped my research didn't cause trouble for me. And that she hoped we did not have to meet again, something like that, and I can confirm with certainty that I have no wish at all to ever meet her at any point in the future. She spoke in a way that gave the distinct impression she hoped I would drop dead, if you know what I mean.'

The line went quiet.

Lucy wondered if they had been cut off. No, she could hear him breathing.

'Look, why exactly are you asking about this? I know who this woman is, Inspector. I know about Casa Social. Am I in danger or something?'

'No, we hope not.' That didn't especially allay Lucy's fears.

'Hope not? Is that supposed to reassure me?'

The Inspector realised he had to tread a little warily. He knew how feisty Miss Hawksmoor could be by reputation.

'We have no reason to believe at this stage that it was anything other than their usual tactics, to harass or intimidate. Casa Social rarely takes any action against people. It tends to be against buildings. Throwing fireworks, demonstrations, that sort of thing.'

'Well, let's hope this is not the start of her being 'unusual',' she replied, feeling now a little more concerned than she had been at the start of the call.

She was not sure he had understood what she'd just said. Still. Then she wondered if she should say anything about the e-mail.

'So, if that is the case, why are you phoning me? If she isn't dangerous?'

Again, he appeared to ignore her question.

'There have been some incidents in the last few days that we would not normally associate with Casa or Ximena Martinez in particular, but we have intelligence to suggest that they may be somehow involved, either directly or indirectly.'

'Incidents? What sort of incidents are we talking about here, Inspector? You are definitely beginning to worry me now.'

'I do not mean to. Look, there have been threats against some prominent pro Muslim figures. Some figures in politics, the justice system for example. And...'

'And what?' The image of the hanged student flashed once again before her eyes.

'There has been a murder, well, at this stage suspected murder, that could be a hate crime and not, as it was thought at first, a suicide.'

Lucy gasped. 'Oh shit!'

'I'm sorry? Senora Hawksmoor? Are you alright?'

'Yes, well, no, actually. I'm not 100% alright at all. Something happened when I was back in Madrid. I don't feel comfortable talking about it on the phone, though; I'd prefer to talk to you in person if that's possible. But it's connected to what you just mentioned.'

'OK, I understand.' Though he wished she could tell him over the phone. Still, what must be must be. 'Where are you at the moment? Granada?'

'No. I'm at my place in Cordoba. I've got some people I need to meet with regarding my current research but I'll be heading back to Granada later this month, if not before.'

Gomez thought for a moment. 'Look, I have to come to Cordoba anyway this week on a personal matter. I'll be in touch. Maybe we can talk further over a coffee. But, please, if you get worried about anything at all, ring me on this number. I have lots of contacts in Cordoba who can help you if necessary.'

He sounded genuinely caring. 'Great. Thank you.' Again, though, this was all sounding more and more serious.

Deep inside, she didn't feel that great at all. Moments after she had ended the call she wondered if she should have just told Gomez right away about the email but then again she didn't want to talk it through until she was sure of what was happening around her. Who she might be getting involved. Something wasn't right; that much was clear. Gloria's attack, the e-mail, the murder, Martinez confronting her.

What the hell? What has all this to do with my research into Boabdil? She was now wondering if this was more than a hate crime against someone pro Muslim. She had never experienced anything directly like this before and it bothered her more than she cared to admit but it also made her want to do something extra, something that would hit back at these people and put them in their place. The piece of red paper was the key.

There was a knock at the door. Lucy looked at the time on her iPhone.

'Shit! The taxi! Gloria! I'm late!' She wanted to get to the station and surprise her. She jumped up, jettisoning the poor cat onto the sofa in ungainly fashion. She grabbed her purse and keys and threw open the door. 'Sorry I'm running late but, Gloria!'

Lucy flung her arms around her. Gloria was laughing and gave Lucy the tightest of hugs back.

She was so glad to see her. She forgot her worries in a moment.

There were not going to be too many more like this.

Chapter 14

Lavapies Madrid

The room was poorly lit; the only bulb, bare and dangling from the ceiling by a noose-like cord, was doing its grim best to hang on to both light and life, but it was only really succeeding in adding a sickly hew to an already desperately grim space. The only possible inlet for natural illumination was a small skylight in one corner but it was covered thickly with moss and bird crap so was frankly of little value as a conduit for the sun's rays.

A long rectangular metal table, the kind you see in hospital wards or army bases, stood in the centre of the room, dented and scarred. There was little other furniture apart from six chairs, three either side of the table. Most of the occupants of the chairs stared at each other; no one seemingly willing to break eye contact.

On one side sat a young woman, who picked at her nails as if bored of the whole thing already and who seemingly had no desire to make eye contact with those seated opposite. She was flanked by two men in jeans and black tee shirts who sat, arms folded, as impassive as two living Buddhas. Slowly, she looked up and stared as she continued to pick each nail individually at the two bulky man mountains who sat across from her and then her gaze wandered up further to the only figure standing.

He avoided her stare and began to pace slowly up and down the small room as he broke the silence.

His Spanish was good, but it came with a hard-edged Germanic lilt.

'I have a feeling, señora, that you feel we are taking up your valuable time and that you would rather be somewhere else, doing such vitally important things as maybe leafleting or spraying graffiti.'

Ximena Martinez popped a piece of gum into her mouth, blew a bubble and let it pop.

'If I did not know better, Ximena, looking at you here now before me, I would think you were just a spoilt brat of a teenager playing dangerous political games and sticking your nose into things way above your head. But yet, everyone I talk to in our group recognises you as a smart and wily strategist. They say you have much potential and that you are moving in the right direction. Hard to believe looking at you at this moment but there we are.'

Ximena crossed her legs. 'Am I supposed to be flattered?'

'I only deal in facts, Ximena. I rarely hand out compliments and I do not play games. For the moment I show respect to you for what you've achieved so far. You have done well. Casa Social is an established group and even carries an air of respectability, at least amongst the poor and needy.'

He stopped by the only door and leant against the wall, his right Doctor Marten boot making a loud clunk as he crossed one leg over the other. He folded his arms and let out a sigh.

'I sense the word 'but' about to come from your lips, señor.' Ximena looked down again at her nails, disdain written large across her face.

'Maybe I really am boring you?' He came closer and stood behind his two associates, leaning over towards the table as he placed one hand on each of their chair backs. At the movement, Ximena looked up quickly and stared into his face. He was alarmingly tall and his shaved head and heavily pockmarked visage was not a pleasant sight. Ximena knew that he was really, deep down, just an old-school skinhead. Violence was ingrained in his DNA.

'I just want you to get to the point,' she said, as if she had been there for hours rather than minutes.

'Tell me, Ximena, tell me exactly what you think the 'point' is? The 'point' of your group? The 'point' indeed of you yourself?'

Before she could speak he held up his hand. Most of his fingers she noticed were adorned with heavy silver rings, some with skulls others with snakeheads, no doubt designed to cause maximum damage if he punched someone.

'No. Do not bother,' he retorted. 'You'll only waste more of my fucking time. The 'point' is, that you need to step up your game. Your demonstrations, occasional fireworks and clever posters are not getting our cause where we want to be fast enough. The government do not take you seriously enough. So, you need to step up attacks on all Muslim scum and their sympathisers.

We are not bank rolling you, just so you can call people nasty names and play politics. The far right is on the march across Europe, my dear Ximena and we want to be sure that Casa Social will play its part in Spain, helping to rid the land of these bastards who pray to Allah, rape our women and steal our jobs and houses. To that end we, in the shape of my two associates here, will remain in Madrid to aid your cause and direct operations, of course, alongside your good self.'

Ximena was trying hard to remain calm. She was not used to being told what to do.

'I take it, therefore, that the hanged Muslim student in Granada was your handy work?'

'Indeed. We felt you needed a helping hand. No need for any thanks.' His sarcasm was as subtle as the swastika tattoo on his throat.

'Please, see it as a starting point for you. Hopefully, if the police put two and two together they may start taking your group more seriously, as will others. We also let some of your enemies know we mean business by sending them a free poster of the hanged boy by email.'

She eyed him as steely as she felt possible. 'This also might mean the fucking police will just come down harder on us now.'

'They cannot trace anything back to you, yet.' The final word added as a rather too obvious veiled threat. Subtlety, Ximena knew, was not his strong point.

He smiled, if you could call the slight movement of his slash of a mouth towards his gnarled ears a smile.

'My dear, the time now has come for you and your group to be less political and more an agent of fear. Be more in the shadows, less in the limelight, strike more often and harder. So we scare the shit out of these motherfuckers so much they will scuttle off back to Africa, Arabia or whichever hole they crawled out of.'

'I want that as much as you do, Jurgen.' He flinched slightly at her use of his first name. His two associates leaned forward towards her as if ready to pounce. Clearly use of his given name was not welcome.

She continued unflustered, folding her arms across her scarlet v neck tee shirt emblazoned with the name of a band, *The Killers*, in white.

'So why the hurry now? If you want me to let these two baboons work for us, then you need to tell me what this is all about because clearly there is something I'm missing here. We can do violence if we have to, please do not worry on that account. But if we are going to endanger all the good work we have done infiltrating the poorer barrios of Madrid and helping to turn people against the Muslims, then we need to be in on the why. Because once the violence starts in earnest, once the proverbial shit hits the political fan, there'll be no going back and it will be us in the firing line, not you.'

'For one so bright, you say some stupid things sometimes. Is it not obvious? We want to be more forceful, more clear in our desires. We want to kick these people out, not just scare them. And,' he paused. 'And we also want to strike at those who support them, those who want to help them, those who believe the myths about history.

1492 was a great year for Spain, a great year for Europe, when the Moorish hordes were finally kicked out, along with the Jews. We now want all traces of them erased too. Their mosques, their statues, their graves, not just the people themselves. We want them to have no history here or anywhere in Europe.'

Ximena stared at him. 'I get all that. But you seriously want us to harm non-Muslims? Really? That is highly dangerous and could lead us to lose any support we have.'

'It is a matter of how you do it. How you scare them. Threaten their families, friends, loved ones etc.'

'Who have you already threatened, anyone?'

'It has already begun, yes. There is an English woman who needs distracting. She has allowed herself to become too interested in Muslim affairs and history.'

'The Hawksmoor girl?'

'Yes. We had to let her know we are on to her so we gave a friend of hers a 'gentle' scare shall we say. She is looking into the whereabouts of some long dead Moorish king's burial place and being cute and trying to rubbish the real history of Spain—the history of the mighty reconquistadors, Isabella and Ferdinand. The Spain that needs returning to the good old days of Franco.'

'Christ, all of a sudden you're a fucking historian.' The air between them froze again but Ximena rolled on unabashed. 'I know all about Hawksmoor, don't worry. I thought you'd asked *us* to follow her and fuck around with her?'

'Yes, we got your call and acted on your Intel appropriately. Thank you.'

'Would have been nice to keep me in the loop of what you'd done. Anyway, I'm not sure I understand why a search for a corpse from over 600 years ago is any big shit.'

'It's a 'big shit' as you so charmingly put it, because we don't want anyone digging up these bastards or their history. Let's surmise, for example, what would happen if she found his tomb? Let's throw in that she finds it in Spain because from what we have heard there is a legend that he may have never left this land.'

'That's crap. Everyone Spaniard knows our history that Boabdil went into exile in North Africa.'

'What if he didn't? What if he *is* discovered here in Spain? Suddenly we are back into the territory of Spain as the natural Islamic homeland and Muslims and fucking jihadis flocking here in their thousands, claiming it as their land.'

'Jesus, Mary and Joseph! I can't believe we're arguing about fucking history now.'

'This is your weakness, woman. You do not see the bigger picture. History matters. The winners write it.'

He paused and dropped his voice so it could only just be heard over the noise of traffic outside.

'If working with us is a problem, just say and we can look at ending our association. And I mean ending.'

'If that's a threat, Jurgen my angel, then you misjudge me.'

Again, he bristled at the use of his first name but he felt in complete control of his emotions, for once.

'Let's hope so, my dear. Let's hope you grow some balls and start showing how tough you and your poster pasting people are.'

She'd now had enough. Ximena rose from her chair and it tipped backwards, clanging angrily onto the tiled floor.

'Fuck you. Fuck your help. We've got the message loud and clear but we don't need the fucking sermons, Adolf. We're leaving.'

She and her companions moved towards the door, watched all the way by Jurgen and his men. At the door, she stopped and turned around. She breathed in deeply, calming herself down yet still red in the face with anger. No one, she thought, speaks to me like this.

'We are stronger than you bastards think. I've not spent the last ten years of my life making Casa Social a force to be reckoned with, just so you lot think you can just fucking waltz in and take over.'

Jurgen had the sense to just watch and wait as she defused.

'Send us what intelligence you have by the usual route and *we* will take care of the enemies of our fucking land ourselves this time, with no need for your help. Understand?'

'As you wish, Ximena. But don't let us down. We will be watching. Before you go, one thing I do want is for you to watch this Hawksmoor woman closely and let nothing, I emphasise, nothing, stand in your way of preventing her from finding anything, nichts, nada. She must not find this tomb anywhere, especially here in your beautiful country. I will send you of course what we have on her and on the rumours we have picked up about her research.

Now, you clearly seem in a hurry. Do not let me keep you and your two gay boys here any longer.' Ximena's companions suddenly moved as if to jump at Jurgen, but, with surprising swiftness, she caught their arms and shouted 'No!'

They shrugged her off, one spat on the floor and then turned and stormed out, leaving Ximena to shake her head at Jurgen as if in pity.

Jurgen and his men started to laugh.

Once outside Ximena was faced with the realisation that now everything had to change, that things would get taken out of her hands if Casa Social did not take action, no longer in their own way, but in a way that showed they meant business like more than ever before. It was not her path of choice but she knew deep in her soul that she had to take it and it would be a path lined with blood.

Back in the room Jurgen was now sitting tapping his rings on the metal table's surface.

'Keep track of her, both of you. Everywhere she goes, everyone she talks to. I want to know all her plans as soon as they are made, before if possible. Get to someone inside her group. I need to know in particular what she is doing about the Hawksmoor woman. We cannot afford any weak link in our plans. And let our dear Ximena Martinez know we are watching her. If she does not act soon, then we will. Miss Martinez is not indispensable. '

Chapter 15

Cordoba

It was another glorious late autumn day, one that most Northern Europeans would have been glad to accept in mid-summer and Plaza de la Corredera was filling up slowly. Like the Plaza Mayor in Madrid, it was a focal point for tourists as well as locals mooching about during lunch breaks from work or old men chewing over the politics of the day, as well as a place for Spanish 'ladies who lunch' to show off their latest outfit or hair do.

But to Lucy it would always be a place that conjured up images of death, she found it hard to forget that not only were violent and bloody bullfights held here in the past, but it was also the site of trials held by the Spanish Inquisition. She always felt she could sense the ghosts of those innocent men and women who had lost their lives in violent and gory ways at the hands of cruel human beings who purported to be doing it all in the name of God. Well, if that was so, it was certainly not a god she wanted anything to do with.

Sometimes she envied the tourists who could sweep through such a place without allowing any of the past to touch them, who could remain content in their ignorance and see the square as just another photo opportunity or atmospheric watering hole. Maybe, Lucy thought, it's just me, maybe it's just my problem.

Her brother often teased her by saying he wished she would live for the day and not the yesterday; it was one thing to study history, but it was another thing entirely to get so emotionally involved in it. It was over! All that mattered, he would say, is the here and now. If only she could follow that advice, but she was of the firm persuasion that if the human race did not learn from their past, then their future would be not much to look forward to.

And in Spain, as in so many other places, the crimes of the past are inextricably linked to the present. She had several good friends who were currently working with a commission to uncover mass graves from the Civil War of 36-39. But, for as many people who wanted to know where their loved ones who had disappeared were buried, many just wanted the whole episode to be forgotten, consigned to the past, entombed with the long dead, hidden away and never spoken about. Her friends had encountered hope and hostility in almost equal measures.

Now here she was encountering hostility because she was searching for the last resting place of a man who died over 500 years ago. And she feared that this was far more serious than people just wanting to forget an episode in history; this was about religion and racism.

It began with two royal cousins, Isabella and Ferdinand, who caused so much pain and suffering in the past and now people on the far right of politics wanted to once again stir up hatred and enmity against Muslims. Some people, Lucy reckoned, simply had an evil DNA chip somewhere, no doubt inherited, that would simply not let people live together in harmony. She knew all too well how bigots used history to their own ends to distort the present and blame minorities for their own failings and problems. She looked over at Gloria who was busy watching a mime artist dressed as Oliver Hardy and reflected on her words.

Over several coffees and various pastries, Gloria had explained to Lucy in as much detail as she could, what had taken place on the Metro after they had parted in Madrid. Gloria was convinced that in some way the attack was linked to the secret she carried, as was her father and she was sure that one of the men she had seen on the train had also been in one of the bars that they had visited together in Madrid.

Lucy had told her in return about the call from the police officer in Granada. At this time, she decided to say nothing to her about the e-mail she'd received and the boy who was hanged. It didn't seem right and she thought it would only worry Gloria more. No doubt Gloria's father would tell her before she got round to it anyway.

Lucy ordered two small beers and spoke quietly as tables nearby began filling up.

'It's all looking too dangerous, Gloria. But I'm not going to stop searching for Boabdil's resting place. I honestly, seriously, would fully understand if you don't want to help me anymore.'

'Of course, I do,' she replied. 'It's going to take a lot more to scare me off, Lucy. Nothing would please me more than working alongside you and finding out exactly what it is my family have been guarding for so long.'

111

Lucy sighed, pleased at her response but she kept her emotions in check. 'But we'll need to be extra careful from now on about where we go, who we talk to.'

Gloria nodded as she took a sip of the ice cold Mahou beer. 'What's next on the agenda then?'

'A meeting with Alvaro Castilla tomorrow. He's the guy my father knows, the expert on ancient Arabic script, remember. You said you knew him already.'

'Well, not quite know him, I know of him, all students of Arabic do. His work has always fascinated me.'

'Well, we'll show him the piece of paper, see what he makes of it. Hopefully, find out what it says, its significance, provenance and so on.'

Gloria stared into her glass. 'I hope the provenance is not in doubt.'

'No, you know what I mean, I mean just establishing it is written by who we hope it is—we couldn't go further without getting it authenticated, it's not that I don't believe you. It's just the way it is.'

'Yes, I know.' A couple of sparrows landed on a nearby empty chair and Lucy threw them some breadcrumbs. Lucy started singing,

'Feed the birds, tuppence a bag

Tuppence, tuppence, tuppence a bag.'

Gloria laughed. 'Where's that from?'

'Ah, it's a song from Mary Poppins. My mum used to sing it to me and Lance whenever she fed the birds in our garden when we were little.'

'Mary Poppins? Never heard of it.'

'Ooh! Then you, señorita, are in for a real treat,' laughed Lucy. 'Maybe we'll watch it online together sometime.'

Gloria looked down at her beer glass again, not quite sure what to say. Lucy suddenly felt awkward, but Gloria changed the subject.

'It's going to be weird finding out what it actually says. The paper. Scary in some ways. Have you any idea what you think it might say?'

A beggar suddenly appeared beside Lucy's chair offering her a packet of tissues in return for a few coins.

'No gracias, pero esto es para usted,' and she handed him a 2-euro coin. His ancient eyes that had clearly seen too many bad days lit up and he thanked her with a broad smile and a soft touch on her shoulder. He then crossed himself and bestowed an imaginary blessing on her. He smiled wistfully and moved on but they both noticed that he had no such luck at other tables nearby.

'There for the grace of God,' said Lucy.

'You're too nice, that's your problem,' joked Gloria.

'Maybe it's me salving my conscience. I just can't abide seeing people reduced to this. I'm not sure they're all genuine, but I tend towards the side of optimism. Anyway, where were we?'.

'You were about to give me your thoughts on our paper's contents.'

'Our paper, I like that! Well, I've looked at it a lot. Whatever it says I get the feeling deep down that it is to do with his last days. The fact that it is almost in a code of sorts obviously means that he did not want it to get into the wrong hands. And I have a suspicion that it may also include a key of some sort. But to what I can only speculate. I know what I want it to be.'

She drained her glass in one.

'Hey, whatever. We should know tomorrow all being well. Let's go get some lunch, girl. I know the perfect place, blissfully free from tourists.'

Ten minutes later they were sitting in the quiet secluded courtyard of El Rincon de Carmen just off Calle Romero, and Maria, the owner, was in her element. Her favourite customer had returned. Lucy gave her a hug, though as she introduced Gloria she noticed that Maria was a little less enthusiastic, not that Gloria noticed.

Lucy knew very well what Maria's feeling for her were and although the feeling was not mutual, Lucy still liked her a great deal as a good friend and her occasional overt overtures were worth putting up with for the amazing food she served.

She and Gloria shared a goat's cheese salad and a heavenly plate of lightly fried aubergine slices drizzled with honey followed by a plate each of oven baked sea bass with vegetables.

All was going so well and the afternoon was slipping into a tranquil haze when the sharp trill of Lucy's mobile brought her back to reality. She looked at the screen. A new message. She clicked it open.

She wished she hadn't.

'I need to make a call,' she said quickly, giving no eye contact.

Before Gloria could ask if all was OK, Lucy had got up and wandered out of the courtyard where they were sitting and into the street, mobile pressed to her ear.

No one at the other tables seemed to pay attention and Gloria sat back. Maria came through with the bill.

'Has Lucy left?'

'No, she's making a call.'

Maria stared out into the street. She could see Lucy on the phone on the far pavement, seemingly listening more than speaking, just nodding every now and then.

'Have you known Lucy long, Maria?'

Maria turned and looked down at Gloria. She seemed to take a while to gather her thoughts as if troubled by something.

'Er, yes, a few years now. This has been her favourite restaurant, well one of them, for some time. She's a good customer, recommends us to all her friends and colleagues. She's always friendly, interested in others, a good listener.' Maria suddenly sat down in Lucy's chair.

'How do you know her, if it's not rude to ask?'

Gloria was slightly thrown. 'No, no it's not rude. It's just a work thing. We have the same field of interest in terms of history and archaeology. I attended a lecture of hers and introduced myself afterwards hoping I could offer my services, you know, maybe as a researcher or something. We got chatting and here we are. I'm not sure where it's heading but I hope I'll be here for a while.'

Maria stared at her. 'Where what's heading?'

'Sorry?' Gloria was a little confused.

'Do you mean the work you're doing?'

'Yes, of course, what else?'

Maria looked back out again at the street. Lucy had obviously wandered a bit further along and was now out of sight. 'You don't seem her type?'

'Type? Oh god, I don't fancy her and I don't think she fancies me. It's just a work thing, I assure you. We're both a little more mature than that I hope, letting our feelings come into our work.'

Gloria was hoping she sounded convincing before adding, 'And I'm sorry but, no offence, it's actually none of your business.'

Maria leaned forward and whispered quietly. 'If it concerns my friend Lucy, it is my business. I'm sure I've seen you before in Cordoba.'

'I guess that may well be possible. My father lives here.'

'Are you really who you say you are?'

'Sorry? Who the hell do you think I am?' Gloria could feel herself getting increasingly angry with this woman who seemed a little deranged and clearly possessive towards Lucy.

'I wonder. I wonder. I hope you're not after anything else.'

Now Gloria suddenly fell a little guilty, as if Maria could read her mind and actually did know what she was doing. But that was crazy.

Before she could reply, Lucy was standing over them. She looked at the bill and quickly popped two 20 euro notes on the table.

'I have to fly I'm afraid. Urgent business, I need to sort out. See you, Maria, thanks as always.' Then she was gone.

Gloria felt embarrassed at Lucy ignoring her, knowing full well that Maria was lapping all this up.

Maria said nothing, got up, took the money, then nodded and smiled at Gloria, but it was a smile as sharp as a dagger. All Gloria wanted to do now was leave as quickly as possible.

She accidentally banged into a nearby table as she headed off, sending a glass flying to the floor. She didn't pause to apologise. Her mind was now firmly elsewhere and she needed to try to work out what had bothered Lucy so much.

Problem was, she was sure she already knew.

Chapter 16

Cordoba

Gloria had had to pinch herself several times. She couldn't quite believe that she was sitting opposite Alvaro Castilla from the School of Arabic studies at Spain's Higher Scientific Research Council. Along with his team he had decoded and identified almost half of the 10,000 inscriptions carved all over the interior walls of the Alhambra. They were sitting on the terrace at the top of Lucy's apartment drinking sweetened mint tea in the late morning sun. Despite the time of year, the celestial orb was still giving off enough heat to allow for daytime chats and drinks outdoors for the good people of Cordoba

Up until now their conversation had consisted mostly of idle pleasantries. Lucy had said little since he arrived. She was still bothered by the text message she had received the day before but had no desire to discuss it, at least not yet. Gloria had been worried about Lucy as she had sat alone in the restaurant and also, frankly, a bit pissed off as she thought they had agreed to share everything in order to stay safe. Somehow, she knew Lucy was keeping something to herself. Something she feared that had to do with her. Not good.

They both simultaneously left their own worlds behind and focussed on the present.

Gloria spoke first. 'So, Señor Castilla, please tell me a little more about your work. I wish I had been there at the time.'

He smiled and breathed in heavily.

'Oh, I'm not sure you would have done. The work could get extremely dull at times and very tiring. Mind you, many a scholar has for many centuries spent half their life ruining their eyesight scrutinising the messages at the Alhambra. They very much laid the foundations of the work we have done. They certainly suffered a lot more.'

'You're too modest, señor.'

'Call me Alvaro, please. We are among friends.' Alvaro Castilla was a tall man, but seated he seemed to somehow fold up like a concertina as if trying to hide his height. With his slicked back greying wavy dark hair and bushy moustache, he reminded Gloria of pictures she had seen of Gabriel Garcia Marquez, the Colombian author. He spoke gently and yet with a calm, firm assurance. She thought of just how much she would have loved to have sat in on one of his lectures.

'So, what do most of the inscriptions say?'

Lucy butted in all of a sudden. 'I can't believe you haven't got a copy of Alvaro's DVD. It has it all on there.'

Gloria suddenly felt embarrassed. It probably was something she should have done but never got round too. She had read much about his work and had been fascinated by it but had not gone into it in as much detail as she should have done due to, well other circumstances. Now she wished she had.

She looked at Lucy. She felt cross that she had snapped at her, but Lucy was gazing into the middle distance, seemingly unaware of any hurt caused. Alvaro clearly was oblivious to it as well or had politely chosen to ignore it. Maybe she was making too much of it.

Alvaro continued unperturbed.

'What is peculiar is that there are not as many words as we thought. Inscriptions of poetry and verses from the Qur'an represent only a small percentage of the texts that adorn the walls. It's funny but even having published much of my research, many people still believe that they are smothered in writings of this kind.

Anyway, the motto of the Nasrid dynasty—'There is no victor but Allah'—is repeated hundreds of times on walls, arches and columns. There are lots of isolated words like 'happiness' and 'blessing' which were seen as divine expressions protecting the people within, especially the Sultan. Aphorisms abound such as 'Rejoice in good fortune, because Allah helps you' and 'Be sparse in words and you will go in peace.'

'A few of my colleagues could do with that last one emblazoned on their study walls,' chipped in Lucy.

Alvaro smiled. 'Indeed, words of the wise from the past can teach us a lot. We could do with a few more wise owls who listen more and speak less in our politics.'

Gloria nodded. She felt she had to prove to Lucy that she did remember some things from her reading of Alvaro's work.

'I believe you translated verses by some of the famous Islamic poets such as Ibn al Khatib and Ibn Zamrak.' She noticed out of the corner of her eye Lucy watching her closely.

'Yes, indeed. They mostly appear in places that they actually describe such as the Hall of the Two Sisters, which represents a garden.'

'Why was it so hard to decipher?' Lucy was beginning to look more interested and less sullen though clearly not firing on all four friendly cylinders just yet.

'Ah, well, the form of script used is angular kufic, whose uprights spout into decorative foliage or intertwine and also the wonderfully named curlicue cursive and, at times, it is a marvellous mixture of both. It looks in places just like fabulous design rather than words and as there is no form of punctuation it is not easy to tell where one idea stops and another phrase starts. Makes translation challenging shall we say!'

Lucy nodded. 'Wasn't Kufic used for quotations from the Qur'an?'

'Indeed, it was, my dear Lucy. They tend to be high up on the walls, while the poetry is lower down, further away from heaven, man knowing his place!'

His smile was a warm glow of satisfaction, a man clearly at one with himself and his work. And happy to talk about it, even if it was probably for the umpteenth time.

'So, young Gloria.' He turned his scrutinous gaze on her as he spoke like the sagely professor he was. 'With the modern technology at our disposal, including a 3D laser scanner, we can transcribe the verses much more easily and at the touch of a mouse, everyone, from scholar to the idly curious can see exactly where they are located in the palace, how often they are repeated on the walls and of course, learn the meaning of these ancient words. The DVD we have produced, as Lucy mentions, has everything contained therein, I shall send you a copy, as a gift.'

Gloria felt herself going red, a little embarrassed and a little annoyed with herself too.

'So,' Alvaro continued, 'let's get down to why I am here shall we, so I do not waste anymore of your precious time than necessary.'

Lucy liked the switch of emphasis.

'I think it's your time we don't want to waste, Alvaro. Thank you so much for agreeing to come in the first place. I know how busy you are.'

'As are you too, my dear lady. I know of your work and it is clearly time consuming! Come to the point. How can I be of assistance?'

Gloria looked round as if expecting someone to be spying on them. But there were no visible living creatures in sight other than a parakeet in a cage on a balcony opposite.

She told her story to Alvaro who listened with great concentration. When she had finished he unclasped his hands from beneath his chin and breathed in deeply.

'And I assume you have the paper with you now?'

Lucy produced the paper from a folder on her lap. 'We have this copy. Gloria has the original safely hidden.'

Alvaro took it gently as if taking the real thing itself.

'I may have to eventually see the actual paper but for now, let us see what we can make of this. Hmm, we will need to go inside. It is too bright up here and I need to look at it closely under a lamp if you have one.'

Two minutes later they were seated around Lucy's kitchen table.

Alvaro spent almost ten minutes staring at the paper through a small powerful pocket magnifying glass under the light of Lucy's angle poise lamp taken from her bedroom. Alvaro occasionally made odd, low noises that sounded to Lucy like puzzlement and sometimes like 'a ha!'

Lucy desperately fancied a beer but dared not move for fear of spoiling his concentration.

Almost on cue, he looked up, as if reading her mind and just said, 'Don't suppose you have a beer do you?'

Lucy almost jolted where she sat. Bloody hell, she thought. He reads minds as well. 'Yes, of course.'

She came back with 3 beers. Gloria declined hers.

'I'll get myself some water in a minute. Thanks anyway.'

Lucy nodded and sat back down behind Alvaro in hushed expectation.

After another few minutes and several swigs of the ice-cold lager, he sat back, put the paper down and folded up his magnifying glass with more than a little sense of theatre. He clearly loved being centre stage.

'Well, you really have something of major importance here, Lucy Hawksmoor.'

'Important as in?'

'Important as in, it's a big deal, as in, I'm almost lost for words. Almost! As in you may have Boabdil's final plans for himself and his wife post Alhambra. Possibly written in his own hand. Not that plans necessarily come true, of course. However, it could prove a huge advantage to your search for his final resting place, because…' Alvaro paused.

Gloria couldn't wait. 'Because what?'

'Well, because, if I am reading this correctly, it contains cryptic clues as to his intentions for his future and in particular where he and Moraima are to be laid to rest.'

Lucy stared at him. 'Are you certain?'

'Well, I am never 100% certain of anything in this field and less in life until I have authenticated it as far as is humanly and scientifically possible. I will need to spend more time transcribing it in detail, some of the words don't seem to make sense but that may be me. Oh and I will need to see the original.'

Gloria looked nervous. 'Why?'

'Well, my dear, I need to see the actual inks used, as I have a suspicion that there may be more than one person's handwriting here. I am almost certain that the drawing of the hand at the foot of the paper is by a different writer to the text. It's a real puzzle for sure but…' He paused and looked at them both, his hands open wide in a pleading gesture.

'Well, we will see. And, if allowed, I need to date the actual paper. That will help certify it and ensure no one goes on a bogus treasure hunt.'

Lucy got up from her seat and started walked to the fridge for another beer. 'So, how can you tell for sure who actually wrote this? I mean prove that it is Boabdil's handwriting?'

Alvaro nodded to her. 'Well, we have copies of his handwriting at the centre. From his diaries.'

Gloria looked perplexed. She was still puzzled by something Alvaro had said earlier.

'You referred just now to the picture as a hand. But surely, is it not more than that? Isn't it the hand of Fatima?'

'Well, yes and no. It is in the style for sure, but there is one striking difference.'

Lucy and Gloria said almost in harmony, 'What?'

'This hand has 7 fingers.'

Chapter 17

Lucy was walking to the shops, striding out as always, head down, ponytail swinging in the light breeze. Alvaro had headed off with Lucy's photocopy of the red paper and they had agreed to meet tomorrow afternoon at a lab in the University of Cordoba which was put at his disposal whenever he was in town. Sunday was a good day as it would be quiet and fewer people would be around to ask questions. Gloria had agreed to bring the original too, though she seemed nervous at the prospect of it leaving her father's house and its place of safe keeping. Alvaro thanked her for agreeing to do so and promised he should then be able to give a more accurate translation in full and hopefully certify its provenance.

Lucy had left Gloria sitting back up on the terrace. She had really wanted her to go back home to her father's but she hadn't taken the hint when Lucy had said she was going out to the shops to buy food for later and had also declined the offer of her company.

She stopped and bought a mango and some oranges from a street vendor. Then she went on to the small convenience store near the river.

Gloria, Gloria, Gloria, what the fuck are you up to, she thought as she mooched between the aisles. She knew she really needed to confront her with the contents of the message she had received from one of her researchers. It was nagging away at her but she was not sure what it all meant or, if she were honest with herself, whether she even wanted to say anything at all to her.

But she had to. She held a chilled water bottle to her face and sighed. Putting aside her feelings for Gloria, Lucy knew she had to be hardnosed about this. The implications for this whole matter could be serious if Gloria's role in all of it was bogus. But how could it be? The girl had been poisoned for god's sake! Lucy reprimanded her softer self and bit her lip.

She bought a bottle of Albariño, a baguette and a small local curado cheese. Nothing more. Cheese, fruit and wine would be enough as she realised she was now not as hungry as she had thought.

On the way back, she sat on a bench and mulled over Alvaro's words. Something seemed odd about the whole thing, somehow contrived. Could it really be this easy? Think, Lucy. After all these years of research, a complete stranger just happens to turn up out of the Madrid thin air with a mysterious piece of paper which just happens to be a shout out from Boabdil himself from across the centuries telling her exactly where his tomb lies.

She felt frustrated that Alvaro had not been able to just translate it all there and then but she realised that she would do exactly the same in his shoes. He was a perfectionist and no doubt needed peace and quiet as well as time in order to get it right rather than having to chance getting it wrong whilst she and Gloria stood over him hanging on every word.

Dating the paper was a must, whatever it said. Gloria had seemed nervous when he mentioned this. But Lucy knew it was vital for credibility's sake and she certainly did not want to waste her time, or anyone else's, on a wild goose chase. She didn't want to get her hopes up just yet and she told herself to stay calm, keep an open mind, stay focussed. Hopefully, the way forward would be much clearer after tomorrow. In the meantime, she had to speak to Gloria and find out what was going on there. She was still angry with her for seemingly lying but Lucy wanted to give her a decent chance to explain why.

Then her phone rang.

'Hello?'

'Señora Hawksmoor. It's Gomez again from the National Police. I am in Cordoba already. I wondered if we could meet to continue our conversation. If you can spare me half an hour.'

'Yes, fine. Erm, how about tomorrow morning?'

'Perfect. Shall I come to you?'

'No, let's meet somewhere less central. Let me think. How about La Bicicleta, a nice quiet cafe on Calle Cardenal Gonzalez. It's in La Ribera near the river.'

'OK. I'll find it. Time?'

'It opens at 10 so I'll see you then. I'm afraid I have to be at the University late morning so I hope an hour will be OK?'

'I am sure it will. Until then.'

He cut the call. Lucy wondered if it was all worth it, going through what happened all over again but she had a feeling she needed to keep the police informed. She still didn't know what she was up against. How the threats fitted in to her search for Boabdil. How closely she was being watched.

Right, time to face Gloria.

She headed back to her apartment.

But when she got there, Gloria had gone. Ah well, maybe she did get the hint. Their heart-to-heart chat would have to wait till later.

Then Lucy's phone pinged with a new WhatsApp message as she was putting the wine in the fridge. She took it out of her jean's back pocket and opened the message.

The text was from Gloria and it was brief.

'My father's been attacked.'

*****

An hour later, Lucy was sitting next to Gloria in a rather too bright waiting room in the Hospital Universitario Reina Sofía. Gloria's eyes seemed to have sunk deeper into their sockets and she was wringing her hands as if trying to squeeze out her pain. She had told Lucy what happened in a torrent of words and it was hard to take it all in.

She had received a call from a neighbour not long after Lucy had gone out. The details were sparse but the neighbour had awoken to the noise of breaking glass just as dawn broke. She and her husband had found the door of her father's apartment open and when they entered they found him crying and trying to pull himself up from the floor. He had knocked a bottle and several glasses onto the floor in the effort. The husband had looked out of the window to see two men driving off at speed on a motorbike.

Her father was covered in blood and the room looked as if a whirlwind had swept through it. When Gloria got to the hospital, her father was in surgery.

A young rather tired looking policewoman told her that when they spoke to him he said he had no idea who the intruders could be, just that he had awoken to find two hooded men in his bedroom who began asking him lots of questions, particularly what he had of value in the house and did he have a safe. He told them (she apparently checked her notes at this point as if in a court room being cross examined, which had somehow irritated Gloria, she did not need every piece of minutiae at this point just the gist) that he was hiding nothing, that he had no safe but they then hit him several times, dragged him from his bed and told him to show them where he hid his valuables.

Nothing seems to have been taken as far as the police could see and her father had said they were uninterested in the money he offered them—it wasn't much but all he had in the house—a couple of hundred euros. The policewoman added that her father had seemed traumatised, not surprisingly, by the attack, but remarkably stoical and had said nothing more until the ambulance arrived.

Lucy listened carefully then put her arm round Gloria and gave her a hug. 'Why did no one call you earlier?'

'New phone remember, new number too.' She stared at the floor. 'My neighbours found my father's phone on the ground floor outside, it looked as if it had been thrown out of the window but was still working despite the cracked screen. Fortunately, my new number was on there, I had added it for him. Good job my father never locks his phone, despite me always pleading with him to do so.'

Lucy's mind raced ahead.

'But did they find the pouch?'

'No. It's still where it's always been. I went to check before I took a taxi to the hospital. I thought there would be police there on guard or something but they were already packing up when I arrived. They'd waited for me, asked me a few cursory questions and then left, except for the young policewoman whose job had been to fill me in with those bare facts. Once she'd gone I took a quick look and it was where it's always been.' Lucy was keen to ask where but thought it might sound odd.

'Thank Christ for that. Did the police say nothing more?'

'They just said, they'd be back in touch in the next 24 hours. Sadly, a part of me wonders if my father were not a Muslim whether they would show more interest. They almost seemed a little suspicious. As if my father was hiding something, drugs or whatever. They even asked if he owed anybody anything, for fuck's sake.'

Lucy sighed. 'Do you think it has anything to do with what we're on to?'

'It must. Why else would someone break in and threaten him?'

'But no one else knows or has known for hundreds of years, about it. How would they find out now? And why the hell would they care?'

Gloria now had her head in her hands as she spoke.

124

'It's all my fault. I've gone over everything that has happened, trying to think of how anyone could know and then it hit me.'

She looked up with teary eyes surrounded my smudged mascara.

'My phone. When I was attacked in Madrid, they took my phone. It had your number on there and my home address.'

'That's not going to be of much use to anyone.'

'Ah but…'

'Ah but, what?'

Gloria looked down at the floor and closed her eyes.

Lucy pressed on. 'Ah but what Gloria, for god's sake! Tell me.'

Gloria took in a large breath, holding further tears at bay, just.

'I, I'd taken a photo of the paper before I gave it to you. I'd intended at first just to show you that. And, well, I forgot to erase it. If whoever had my phone has got into it they must have seen it.'

'Oh shit, Gloria. Shit, shit, shit, shit! Not clever!' Lucy walked up and down hands on her head.

She stood in thought for a moment and then walked over and took both of Gloria's hands in hers, scolding herself for her outburst which she knew was not really very helpful in the circumstances.

'OK, let's look on the bright side. If they have seen it, well it doesn't mean that they understood what it was. That's a big leap from seeing a photo of a piece of writing to attacking someone because of it.'

'Unless,'

'Unless what?'

'Unless they already know.'

'They can't. Can they?'

'There must be other people I guess who can read aljamiado. I just think someone is watching us, someone who wonders why I approached you, someone who has put two and two together, not got 4 maybe but close enough. Think. You get approached by the leader of a far-right anti- Muslim group. We get followed. I get attacked and drugged. You get sent a picture of a dead Muslim student. Now my father, a man who is Mr Invisible most of his life gets attacked in his own home by people 'looking for something.'

Think of the consequences if Boabdil's body was to be discovered still on mainland Spain. The far right already fears the growth of Muslims and the number of new mosques being built. They are doing everything they can to dissuade other Muslims from coming here and to a degree they're being successful but through tolerance and community work our people are being accepted back more and more. Slow progress but it is happening. They despise the new initiatives of Muslim and non-Muslims working in harmony to recreate what Spain lost when it kicked out the Moors all those years ago.'

Lucy stood up and leant on the wall opposite with her feet crossed, hands in pockets. No one else was about. The corridor seemed unnaturally quiet.

'You should be a lecturer you know.' She almost smiled. 'But seriously, well, I know. You're dead right. I guess they fear the tomb if it was to be found here in Spain, could become a rallying point for the radical Muslims who have openly said they want to regain Andalucia for Islam.'

'Exactly,'

'It just seems so crazy though. Using history like this. Threatening people. Killing people. But sadly, I guess that's what the world is coming to—old wounds being unpicked by the far right. New barricades going up, real and metaphorical. I think, Gloria, you, we, need to get this pouch and its contents relocated at some point. They may come back.'

Before Gloria could reply a trolley emerged from around the corner carrying medicines and rattled its way between them, pushed by a lady who looked like she'd been pushing rattling trolleys for way too long.

A door opened and a young doctor appeared and approached where now they both stood.

'Your father, señora, is in a stable condition. He has a ruptured spleen, two broken ribs and a lot of bruising. We are also monitoring him for delayed concussion but he's a strong ox and I believe he will make a full recovery. We may need to remove the spleen, but we will wait until tomorrow to see how it is. He will be in for a few days at least. But it could have been a lot worse.'

Gloria let out a sigh of relief and thanked the doctor. She liked the comparison to an ox. That was him all over. Slow and steady, strong of will.

'When can I see him?'

'Not for an hour or so, I'm afraid. He's on strong medication and would not be very responsive. Once the consultant has assessed him on his next round I am sure you will be able to look in on him. If you want to go for a walk or whatever, I can get the lady on reception to text you if you like?'

Gloria declined the offer. 'It's fine. I'll just come back in an hour. Thank you.'

They walked in the late afternoon sun towards the nearby botanical gardens.

Gloria was the first to break the silence that seemed to have enveloped them both.

'Thank you for coming to the hospital. I appreciate it.' Lucy just nodded. 'Are you going to tell me why you left so suddenly yesterday, why you were not really wanting to talk to me this morning when we were with Alvaro?'

Lucy looked straight ahead. 'Probably not the best time to discuss it. Let's wait till you're in a better place, headspace wise.'

Gloria didn't look impressed.

'I'm fine thanks. I'm a big girl. You don't need to go easy on me. I may look soft but I'm tougher than you think. My father and I have had to put up with a lot over the years, especially since my mother left us.'

'God, I'm sorry, I didn't know she'd left you. I somehow got to thinking, well, with you not mentioning her, that she'd died. Not sure why.'

'Hmm, may have been better all-round if she had, god forgive me for saying so. She was not a nice woman. She bullied my father a lot. She aspired to a 'better life' whatever the hell that meant. I always seemed to be a disappointment to her, possibly because I spent so much time with my father reading or being read to, discussing life, religion, politics.

And then, when I was 21, he let me in on the secret, about the bag and its contents. He never breathed a word to my mother though. Funny how two people can just fall apart like that. He never explained why it had all gone wrong, didn't even say anything really bad against her, despite her verbal attacks on him. And when she left he seemed to grow younger.

But later I found out from an aunt that she was obsessed with sex, couldn't get enough apparently and my father turned his back on her when he found out she was seeing other men. He was deeply ashamed, almost as if it was his fault apparently. But no, she was just a rather unpleasant and spiteful person. So, there you have it, but I've not suffered as a result. I don't hate her. I have no feelings at all for her now. I just don't ever really think about her. I don't know where she is and I don't want to know.'

'That's tough on you.'

Lucy stopped at a kiosk and bought them a bottle of water each and a newspaper.

Gloria looked closely at the bottle and grinned.

'You sure this water isn't spiked?'

'Oh shit!' said Lucy. 'That's not funny!' But she smiled nonetheless.

They sat on a bench and watched some mothers in the distance push their children on the playground swings. Lucy never got especially broody watching such scenes but maybe one day she'd like to have a kid of her own. Not yet though.

One child blew giant bubbles from a machine of some sort and then lay himself down and watched as they drifted off skywards. What a nice life thought Lucy. How I'd love to do that again. A picture filled her head, of lying flat on the lawn back at home when she was 8 or so, cloud busting with her dad and her brother.

Gloria's voice snapped her back to the here and now.

'Come on then. Why were you angry with me?'

Lucy took a deep breath.

'Well, look, I'm a naturally inquisitive person and I, well, you may be cross but I ran some background checks on you. Well, my secretary did, back in Granada. Whoever I work with, I always want to know who they are, that they're kosher etc, I guess. I've been messed around quite a bit in the past by people not being quite as open as they should about their motives or background. It's a habit, I didn't expect to find out anything. I like you for God's sake, so I was a bit upset to say the least when I got a text suggesting you hadn't quite been truthful with me.'

The sky clouded over and both Lucy and Gloria involuntarily shivered.

Gloria looked at Lucy. Oddly she didn't look angry, more resigned.

'I thought as much. Is it about uni?'

'Yes. But, I'd like to hear it from you though. Why you told me you worked at Salamanca University. There is no record of a Gloria Sarmiyento Ruiz in the Arabic Studies Department. In fact, there is not a jot on you at all out there, except that you do work for an online magazine, Muslim Spain Info Monthly, if I recall. I've even read a few of your articles, they're good. You're certainly clued up on politics and history. So why lie?'

'I would've thought it was obvious. I just didn't think you'd take me seriously if I just turned up with no credentials. I guess I wanted you to see me as a fellow academic. Otherwise, you may not have wanted to give me the time. I'm sorry. It was stupid of me.'

'I'd like to think I would have done,' Lucy replied, 'though you appearing just after Ximena Martinez's unpleasantries was fortunate timing; it got me out of a nasty spot and cheered me up. I think you could have said you were from anywhere frankly and I'd have gone with you just to get away. It was just unnecessary is what I'm trying to say. I get the jitters when I find out someone's not telling me the truth.'

'I guess that's fair. I'm sorry, Lucy, I really am.'

'OK. Anything else I should know about you? Skeletons, cupboards, false identities?'

'You're mocking me now I know and I deserve it, but I did apply to uni in Salamanca, I did, but I failed to get the grades I needed. I got really down, low style depression, suffered from anxiety attacks, stopped eating. Usual stuff I guess amongst teenagers, unsure of themselves or their place in the world, well that's what I read. Anyway, my father was really worried about me, so I decided to give up on university, travelled a little then went back home and studied in my own time. That's when I started writing too. I sent stuff off to various blogs and this website liked my work and asked me to contribute regularly. And that's when I got involved with the Partido de Nacimiento y Unión de España.'

'OK, I've heard of them. The Party for Revival and Union in Spain, right?'

'That's it. PRUNE for short.'

Lucy smiled. 'Not the best acronym for a serious political party.'

'Why?' Gloria asked. 'Oh, of course, ah, the fruit! Yes, in your country it would be very odd, I guess, to have a party called PRUNE.'

'Yes, they'd have to all be vegetarians or something,' Lucy joked and for the first time in a while felt almost quite good. 'So, what's the Spanish for prune?'

'La ciruela pasa.'

'Ah yes, la ciruela pasa, a much better name for a fruity laxative.'

Gloria smiled but then she leaned forward and spoke quietly. 'But don't tell my father. He has no idea. He'd be furious if he knew. He abhors politics and trusts no politicians.'

'Wise man.'

'He'd also think I was jeopardising our secret too. Though I'm not sure why.'

A small dog yapped up to them and Gloria ruffled his coat. The owner called out and the dog turned and ran off, not before giving Gloria's hand a good lick.

'OK, next question. How are you involved with this party?'

At this, Gloria seemed to go quiet. The silence was long enough for Lucy to wonder whether the dog owner was watching them. Paranoia setting in she said to herself,

'I've helped them with a few things.'

'Such as?'

Two cyclists went past, a boy and girl precariously holding hands as they rode in parallel.

A siren blared in the distance and as it melded into the general hubbub of the city sounds, Gloria turned to Lucy.

'I've not been totally honest with you. It's not, well, it's all as I have already explained but, well, I told someone in the organisation that I knew you were investigating the whereabouts of Boabdil's last resting place.'

'Which is true. No big secret. So?'

'So, I kind of suggested, put forward the idea, that you were of the belief that he was buried somewhere in Granada.'

'Which at that time I was not. And despite your paper, I still have no idea where he is. Not yet. So why did you tell whoever it was that I thought that?'

'Because we needed a rallying call. We need to have an aim that is tangible, that will strengthen the Muslims position in Spain. This would prove that Boabdil was not defeated totally, that he fooled Isabella and Ferdinand and remained here in Spain somehow. Then our people would have the courage to ask for more freedom in our worship. We could get more mosques built.'

'Wo, Jesus, slow down. I'm confused here. So, you are a practising Muslim, fine, but you are also clearly way more politicised than you'd let on, Gloria.'

'It's what we need to get a voice as a people. No one listens to us. If we can say we have found Boabdil's tomb in Granada, then Granada will once again become our spiritual home. History will have to be rewritten.'

Lucy stood up and tossed her empty water bottle into a nearby empty bin with a well-aimed lob.

'You are jumping way ahead, Gloria. Way ahead. What if we don't find him in Spain? Wait, what if we do. I don't want all this to become a circus.'

She undid then retied her ponytail. 'Right, I need to go and have a long think.'

'What about?' Gloria looked worried.

'About everything really; you, who you are, what you're up to and all this political stuff that we're now wrapped up in. Oh and the fact that you're making history up now. As of this very moment we have no proof where Boabdil is buried. None. Zilch. Nada.'

'But what about the paper, the code?'

'Oh yes, the red paper. Yes, it might change everything, I admit.' She stared at Gloria. 'If it's real. And I hope for your sake that, well, that it's not just a ruse to get me involved in all this. Use my name whatever.'

'No! It is real. My father knows it's real. You must believe me on this.'

'God, Gloria, I want to. But something doesn't feel right. Your father seems to be genuine. But until we know what that piece of paper says I have no idea where we're heading. So, I would appreciate it if you said no more to anyone about anything, OK?'

'Of course,' She bit her lip. She looked as if she might cry. 'So, you think my father is genuine but not me?'

'It's not whether you're genuine or not, it's what you're involved in. Was the attack on the Metro random? Or do these people know about who you really are?'

Gloria looked away. 'I'm not answering that.'

'OK. Fine. I'm off. When I find out what Alvaro has to say and, all being well, that the paper's genuine, I might, I stress *might*, get back to you.'

'Might? Hold on, you mean I can't come with you?

'I would rather you didn't until I get my head round this, whether it's all a wild goose chase, a political football, or a potential time bomb. People have got hurt, your father, you and someone has already been killed, Gloria. His death and the subsequent e-mail picture of him very dead was clearly a real direct threat to me because of my work. That's not a good thought, but worse, I don't like the idea of people being killed because of what I'm doing. I need space to think.'

'Hold on. Dead guy? What dead guy?'

Fuck! It suddenly dawned on Lucy that Gloria didn't know about the dead student.

'I didn't tell you. I was going to but after you got out of hospital it didn't seem a good time. Sorry. And your father clearly didn't mention it either? I guess I thought he might.'

Gloria just stared at her. 'He knew too? Joder!'

Lucy hadn't seen Gloria angry before. Her face grew dark.

'I was going to tell you at some point.'

'Someone gets murdered, you get a threatening e-mail and you don't think that was something I ought to know? Really?'

Lucy for once was lost for a reply.

'So, who was it? The guy who died?'

'A young Muslim student. Hanged himself, though the police don't think it was suicide. And I got sent an image of him. A threat really. Blaming me. Bizarre, horrible and seriously unsettling.'

'Lucy, please, please, sit back down, tell me again everything that happened.'

'No, not now. I need to go.'

Lucy felt she wanted to desperately be somewhere else as quickly as possible. 'I hope your father gets better soon. Send him my love. I'll be in touch.'

'Please get in touch soon. My intentions on all fronts are genuine and real, I promise.'

Lucy paused momentarily wondering what that meant exactly.

'Well, if I do, then I hope you'll be more honest and open with me. Let's just see what happens in the next few days.'

Gloria nodded and a tear rolled down her cheek. 'Then she remembered. 'Lucy,' she called. 'You need the real thing for Alvaro to see.'

Bugger, thought, Lucy, how the hell did I forget that? She took a few steps back towards Gloria.

'Of course. Look, I'll text you and give you a time to meet me somewhere near the University. OK?'

'Yes, OK.'

Lucy turned and walked away. Gloria watched her go with a bad feeling in her stomach. She needed to keep close to Lucy. She couldn't afford to be cut out of the search now. She sat back on the bench and wiped her eyes. Martinez and Casa Social were no doubt onto them, all because of that stupid photo. Why did she take it? But the bad feeling she had was compounded by Lucy's news of the student's death.

She had an awful feeling swirling around in her stomach She took out her phone and googled the news.

And then there it was, a picture of him. 'Oh fuck, no!' she whispered. 'Please, no.'

A photo of Reda al-Jayyani and his mother Yamina. Gloria knew him.

Knew him well.

She made a call.

A quiet male voice answered.

Gloria was beyond angry but tried to remain as calm as she could.

'Why did no one let me know what happened to Reda?'

The man ignored her. 'We wondered when you would get in touch.'

'I'll ask again,'

He cut her off. 'We tried. But you were not answering your phone. Then, next thing we know we discover you've been attacked and the police are involved. So, we hung back. We reckoned you would eventually see it on social media anyhow and get in touch.' He paused. 'Which you have. Maybe you can understand now why we want you to work with us, not against us. We all only want what is best for our brothers and sisters in this land. Come back to Granada. Sit with us. Share with us.'

'I can't, my father...'

'Will be fine,' he said gently. 'I will have someone watch over him and ensure he is safe from any further violence. My promise to you.'

'How the hell do you know about my father?'

'We have friends everywhere, Gloria. You should not be surprised by that. I heard of what took place, though I do not as yet understand why. Maybe you can enlighten me when we meet. Tomorrow?'

'Fuck you,' she said and cut the call.

But she knew she would have to meet him. She would have to return to Granada. Have to try to sort out the mess she had made.

But it was going to be difficult. Now she knew she was being watched by both sides.

Not good. Not good at all.

Chapter 18

The next day, Lucy reluctantly kept her appointment with Inspector Gomez. She had awoken that morning too early, feeling pretty shitty about Gloria but the rational side of her took over and gave her a metaphorical boot up the backside. This was work, not a game and any feelings she may have had for the girl had begun to evaporate and generally put into cold storage. Her researcher, Alma, had not only told Lucy about a no-show in the university records for Gloria, she had also found some dubious tweets Gloria had put out a few years back, ones that were clearly politically motivated and not about keeping the peace.

She needed to find out more about the party's members, as she had always been led to believe that they were a peaceful organisation. Maybe there were some rogue players hidden away in there. She prayed to God Gloria was not one of them. But it was not looking promising.

Over a café con leché and a side order of toast, tomatoes and olive oil, Lucy regained her sense of equilibrium in the universe and she gave the Inspector a blow-by-blow account of all that had transpired since she was initially harassed by Ximena Martinez. Gomez listened intently and took copious notes.

Lucy couldn't help but notice his perfectly manicured fingernails as he scratched away with his pen; she was actually quite jealous and was tempted to ask him where he got them done but reckoned he might be embarrassed. It was certainly something she was always impressed by; how Spanish men seemed to take their appearance a lot more seriously than many English guys she knew. Gomez leant back in his chair. He looked concerned, as well as tired and Lucy wondered when he had last had a good night's sleep.

'Señora,'

'Call me Lucy, please.'

'OK, Lucy, I have to tell you that I am very concerned about these incidents. I can tell you they are not isolated, other figures in other walks of life have also been targeted. It would appear that what you all have in common is your interest in Muslim society in Spain, either promoting its values, supporting them financially or, as in your case, showing interest in their history.'

'Jesus, really? Other people? Shit. Look, it's kind of hard for me to believe that my research into the last resting place of the King of Granada who died over 500 years ago is sufficient reason to be so aggressive and threatening. It's crazy really when you think about it. But I'm sure sensing the gravitas of the situation I'm in on an almost daily basis, Inspector. I just have to accept the reality, I guess, that I'm causing waves.'

'Crazy it certainly is. And real it certainly is, but unfortunately these people are extremely racist and if it were up to them they would imitate Isabella and Ferdinand and expel every last Muslim, gypsy, Jew and several other peoples whom they regard as not Spanish from these shores as soon as possible. My fear is that they have only just begun.

Our office has had intelligence over the last 24 hours to also suggest that Casa Social has been approached by other extreme right-wing organisations from within Europe, organisations who are more intent on using serious violence rather than politics or simply scare tactics.'

'Christ, really?' She ordered more coffee for them both. 'So, what do you want me to do about it? I mean, is there anything I should be doing differently? Or not doing? I'm certainly not going to stop my research.'

'I just want you to be careful, extra careful, extra vigilant. Be wary of any strangers who might approach you either at home or in the street. One of their ways of working is to befriend you or get you into a conversation. Maybe lure you into meeting in a remote place.

I have no doubt, I am afraid, that they want to stop what you are doing. They will not want you to find this man's burial site in Spain. They will want to quash any chance that it will draw attention to Muslim history. Ridiculous as that sounds. These are not normal people we're dealing with. They are out and out racists of the worst kind. And they want to scare away anyone who has any dealings with our Muslim nationals.'

Gomez took a sip of his second coffee and loosened his tie.

'Sadly, they see Muslim society as a blight. Any signs, symbols of their culture they will want to attack, destroy, vandalise. This is happening all over Europe, as I am sure you know.'

Lucy sighed. 'Yes, it's happening back in the U.K. big time. The whole Brexit farce opened up a Pandora 's Box giving credence and airtime to racists, bigots and homophobes, not just amongst the people but within the media too. The lid will not be put back anytime soon, I fear.

Over the last few years I've read things in the papers that they could not have printed a few years back for fear of a backlash. Not now. Hunting season for anyone who does not fit into the all-white, Anglo-Saxon born and bred, St George flag tattooed, Christian, heterosexual mould has well and truly been reopened.' Lucy smiled. 'Ah well, off my soap box now. You get my drift anyway.'

'I do, I understand and as I said those sentiments of isolationism and nationalism are rife throughout Europe now and these dangerous people come in all hues and guises. We believe a lot of these thugs are just the foot soldiers for groups higher up in society who want to return to the old days of empire and keep... erm... what's that expression you have in England? Ah, yes, I remember, yes, that's it, Johnny Foreigner at bay.'

Lucy laughed. 'I've not heard that expression for a while. That's one from my dad's era. You clearly know your idiomatic English, Inspector.' Gomez felt himself going a little red.

'I study a lot of history in my spare time, what little I get. Especially about the days of empires. We don't seem to learn from our mistakes, do we?'

'We definitely do not. And you think the rot goes higher then?'

'Oh yes, we have some serious right-wing parties here in Spain, who have gained seat after seat in the Congress of Deputies. Worrying times. And remember, after Franco died, many of his ministers just hid themselves away in other parties and roles.'

He finished his coffee.

'So, you do not think you will return to England anytime soon?'

'For good? No, definitely not. I've got family there and visit now and then but Spain is my home. The place is in my blood. It's got its faults like anywhere but to me the people are more caring here, more friendly and of course, there's the sun, oh and the food, and yes, the wine. And my work at the moment is here and will be for the foreseeable future. I'll go back to lecturing at Granada Uni once this work is put to bed. If it ever is.'

Gomez realised he was staring at her. He coughed. 'So, how is the research going?'

'It's stalled a little lately, for obvious reasons, but we have some good leads and hopefully I'll get back to the grindstone soon and we'll make progress.'

'This Gloria who was attacked, she is helping you then still?'

'Hmmm, on hold. The jury is out on that one.'

The Inspector looked a little blankly at her.

She tried to vaguely clarify. 'I mean I need to just double check her credentials so to speak.'

'Why?'

'I want to keep politics out of my work as much as possible, especially given all this recent shit. I need to keep it out. I need to appear non-judgemental, but I think Gloria may have ulterior motives for wanting to help.'

'But, she was, as you explained, attacked, no?'

'Exactly. She was, but why, was it because of my work or because of hers?'

'I can look into that if it helps.'

Lucy thought for a moment. She didn't like the idea of checking up on Gloria through the police but on the other hand she didn't think it could do any harm. Lucy gave Gomez Gloria's full name and he added it to his notes.

'I will be discreet, I assure you, Lucy. But at the moment it is probably just as well that you trust no one until they have been checked out. I am sure I will find nothing to concern you.'

'OK, fine.'

She looked at her iPhone to check the time.

'Lordy, sorry Inspector, I need to make a move. Things to do, people to meet.'

She flicked back her ponytail over her shoulder and noticed the Inspector's watching her a little too intently.

He blushed and looked away.

Lucy stood and smiled at him. He tightened the knot on his tie and mopped his brow.

'It's warm in here.'

'It is, Inspector. Are you alright?'

'Yes, I'm fine. Just a bit tired.'

It had been a while since she had really noticed a man paying attention to her and it was quite funny in a way. She had no sexual feelings towards men but it made her realise that at least this policeman was human.

The Inspector rose too, handed a few euros to a passing waitress and walked to the door with Lucy.

'I will be in touch, Lucy. Please, as I said before…'

'I know! Look after myself. I will, I promise.' She smiled at him. She knew he meant well.

'And if I find anything I will let you know, or if I get any Intel that might affect you or your work, you will be the first to know.'

'I appreciate that, Inspector. Thanks.' She felt he was spinning it out now.

'You have my number. Call anytime if anything worries you. I will let the Cordoba police know of the situation; ensure they are on the lookout for anyone who might cause problems. And when you return to Granada, let me know and we will help in any way we can.'

Lucy felt he was now definitely going above and beyond his remit, but that was fine.

'Terrific, Inspector. Thank you. Now if you can…'

'Yes, sorry.' He moved to one side and opened the door for Lucy.

She headed off to the university, reassured to some extent that at least the police were onto things. But at the moment she wanted no one else to find out what she was up to, nor would she let the Inspector know when she returned to Granada. The fewer people who knew from now on, the better. Even the police.

Chapter 19

That evening when she got back to her apartment, Lucy sat on her sofa, snuggled into her wrap and closed her eyes. She needed time to think about all that had happened since she met the Inspector. It was hard to take in everything Alvaro Castilla had said and it made her feel a little dizzy with excitement but also filled her with a fair slab of trepidation.

Gloria had not met her as planned but instead sent her a text saying that she'd left a package for her at El Rincon with their mutual friend, Maria (*mutual friend? What the hell was that all about?*) She had gone to the restaurant where a rather amused Maria said that Gloria had popped in and left a package, something about a 'leaving present'. Lucy had a quick glass of vermouth and a few olives before managing to make an excuse and leave.

Maria had seemed clearly delighted that Gloria had apparently left town. She touched briefly on the conversation the two of them had had, whilst Lucy had been on the phone that lunchtime. Said she thought Gloria was pleasant enough but a little too young. Lucy had asked for whom? Maria ignored her and added that she was a little too inquisitive for her liking. Lucy ignored the bait. Maybe another time. She had needed to get to the lab and put the package in the safe hands of Alvaro Castilla asap.

In the lift at the university she had opened the top of the well sellotaped box to find a brief note.

'Lucy, good luck with this. I know it is in safe hands. I hope you let me know what you find. I have to go to Granada. The boy who died, I knew him. I can't get my head round what's happening. There are things I need to do. I'm not sure when, or if, we will see each other again but I hope with all my heart that we do. Forgive me.

Hasta pronto mi querida, Gloria. Beso x'

Lucy had felt momentarily very guilty. Gloria knew him, the guy in the photo. Fuck. She wondered how she knew him. She worried too what it was that Gloria needed to do. And what was this thing about forgiveness? What had she done apart from tell a lie about university? She shuddered to think. But all that could wait. Her 'to do' and 'get back to' lists were growing.

And then Lucy peered into the box again and there, snuggling amongst swathes of tissue paper, was the actual pouch, containing the actual original piece of red paper. A shiver had run through her whole body like an electric eel. She closed her eyes and prayed.

***

Moments later she had been stood in a small lab with just Alvaro and the pouch. The paper had been carefully removed from the lining and the expert set to work.

He had taken his time, during which Lucy had run coffee errand upon coffee errand for him, Alvaro had admitted to Lucy's amusement that he had only drunk mint tea at her place to be polite, he loathed the stuff. Coffee, thick Arabic style coffee was his poison. Lucy loved coffee, too, but this stuff? One had been more than enough, she was so buzzing with caffeine she'd felt like she was about to take off and fly around the room several times.

After an hour or so, he had drawn up a chair and sat for the first time, inviting Lucy to do the same. When he spoke, he had sounded more serious than she had expected, his usual jovial nature parked up for the moment.

'You have something here of tremendous value and also problematic. Because what it reveals is potentially game changing for the history of Spain.'

Lucy had decided not to speak. He was in the zone.

'Can you lock the door, please, Lucy. I do not want any interruptions.' She had done as he said and that simple act had brought the fear back into play.

'I am in no doubt that this was written by the hand of Abu Abdallah Muhammad, Boabdil as he is commonly referred to. I could get other experts to look at it for confirmation but I think that would not be wise just yet. I have compared it to copies of known extant letters he wrote to Isabella prior to the surrender of Granada. He was unusual, in that, as you know, he often put pen to paper himself, rather than dictating it to a secretary, trust was at a premium in those last dark days of Nasrid rule.'

Lucy knew all this but did not want to interrupt his flow.

'He is clearly giving instructions to, I believe, La Mora of Ubeda, a constant sounding post in his retinue whilst in power. He addresses her as 'Mi profesora', my teacher, though in aljamiado it looks quite different. He is asking her to prepare a place or places for two eagles, who need rest and shelter. An allusion no doubt to himself and his wife.'

'Are you positive?' Lucy had asked.

'Well, who else? But what clinches, it is the drawing of the hand—my guess is this was done possibly by La Mora herself. It is packed full of imagery alluding to royalty and secrets.'

'All in that tiny drawing?'

'Indeed. It is a work of art, one possibly lost now. A Hamzah hand, the hand of Fatima, daughter of Muhammad himself. Everyone knows that, but this hand is different, significantly so.'

'I remember, you said it had 7 fingers.'

'Indeed! Not easy to spot with such intricate tracery. Her hand must have been steady as a rock. But it is the 7th finger that is the most interesting—it bears a picture of a small owl and the aljamiado word for malik or king.'

'Why the owl? Hold on, it's not what I think it is, is it? Something to do with death?'

'Indeed, I think it is, the owl is an Arabic symbol of death. The three things together must mean something, seventh finger, owl, king.'

'Oh Jesus. Are you thinking what I'm thinking?'

'Most likely.'

'Boabdil is buried in the Tower of the Seven Floors.'

'Well, if he is, it certainly and unequivocally, in your parlance, 'buggers up' a lot of history, Lucy.'

They had laughed but Lucy's mind had started to race.

'This would mean he managed to smuggle himself and his wife back into the Alhambra—right under the noses of Los Reyes Católicos.'

'It would indeed but what also is curious is whether he went before or after his wife Moraima passed away. There's no indication here.'

'And why would he go? What would be the point? I don't get it. That surely is a sticking point.'

'He'd left a lot of his ancestors buried in the family cemetery in Mondújar in the Valle de Lecrín remember. Maybe he wanted he and his wife to be buried there too?'

'No, she must have been dead by then surely. She died not long after they got to the Alpujarras remember. He would no way have had time to make such intricate and dangerous arrangements. And he was still only in his 30s, Alvaro. He wasn't ready for the grim reaper at the end of 1492.'

'Broken heart?'

'Hmm. He certainly idolised her by all accounts. And the other thing is, there are records of his departure, writings by Isabella's royal secretary, Hernando de Zafra, who spent a long time negotiating his exile. Boabdil even wrote a long letter in the form of a poem to the King of Fez, asking to allow him to go and live there. Zafra mentions it in his writings and passed the news on to his masters.'

'A beautiful piece of writing. It was entitled, correct me if I'm wrong, *Garden which Pleasingly Perfumes the Spirit.*'

'Spot on and yes it is indeed a wonderfully executed plea for him to be allowed to settle there.'

'Some say it was dictated to a poet called Abdullah Muhammad, the court poet, but I just get the feeling it was his own words.'

'Me too. It was so well structured and sounded so genuine, so from the heart, unless,'

'Unless what, Lucy?'

'Unless that was a ruse? Part of a plan to throw the Christians and Zafra in particular, off the scent.'

'But there is confirmation that he *did* sail, Zafra rejoiced in the fact when he wrote to Isabella.'

'Well. Somebody sailed. Somebody arrived. Did the King of Fez know what Boabdil looked like? No Sky news in those days, no Instagram or Facebook for those guys.'

'Praise be to Allah!'

'Yes and Boabdil probably guessed as much too. That no one would know the difference between him and a credible lookalike.'

'So, what are you thinking. How do we move forward with this?'

'Simple. We go to Granada and search the Tower of the Seven Floors.'

'Define your version of 'simple'.'

'Oh, come on, Alvaro. I'm talking theory here, not practice, I know it will be tricky to do all this without raising suspicion.'

'That's an understatement.'

But Lucy was on a role and details were not getting any spotlight.

'Anyway. Look, all that aside, my hunch is that Boabdil must be in that tower and possibly on the seventh floor given your reading of the hand.'

'Yes, but only two floors have ever been discovered.'

'All the more reason to look again then, Alvaro. This has to be what the paper is telling us. The paper has been kept all this time, passed down from century to century because Boabdil was waiting for the right moment to be found.'

A silence had wafted into the room as if a host of spectral listeners were hanging on every word.

'Alvaro, I think this is the right moment, don't you? Archaeologically? Politically? Are you up for it?'

'Up for it?' His grin was almost as broad as his shoulders. 'Miss Hawksmoor, I would not miss this adventure for the world, but why me?'

'Because your knowledge of ancient Arabic and aljamiado, along with your in-depth knowledge of the Alhambra will come in very handy. And, you are the only person who knows about this that I actually trust. All we have to do now is figure how we get in without alerting the whole world what we are up to. If or when we find anything, then we can figure what to do.'

'Getting into the red palace without any fuss. Right.' He frowned then he smiled. 'Now with that, I think I may well be able to help.'

'You can?'

'I think so. Getting in should be the easier part. Getting access beyond will be the challenge. But leave it with me, one step at a time.'

****

She watched her cat on the windowsill crouched on its haunches as it watched a bird on a roof opposite. She could not help thinking about the inherent danger of what they were about to attempt. They needed to find Boabdil before anyone caught the slightest sniff of their plan. If the likes of Casa Social or any other far right nut jobs found out, then the whole thing could be sabotaged. She was also worried about Gloria and her friends finding out too; if any of them were extremists and she feared that Gloria was naive enough not to realise the difference, then they too could use any resulting find for their own ends. Lucy felt a bit like that bird perched on the roof, unaware of the hunter that was watching her every move.

She rose from the sofa.

'Come on, Jasper. Let's get you fed before you act on those evil thoughts of yours.'

She rattled his biscuits and with a last withering look at the winged food opposite he jumped down, stretched and accepted the offering of biscuits in his bowl.

'What a life you lead, eh. I wish I was a cat right now.'

She opened her iPhone as she poured herself a cold glass of crisp Rueda.

She texted her dad, hoped his new venture was going well. Then she messaged her mum to ask how things were with her. Nothing from Lance as per usual but she sent him a message nonetheless saying she was leaving Cordoba shortly and if he was coming over, reminding him to give her advance notice.

Not that the coming days, or possibly more likely, months would be a good time for him to visit, but with Lance she always felt as if she needed to just let him know that she was there for him if he needed to escape from his job for a while. He probably wouldn't come anyway but she knew he liked to think he could. And deep down she missed him, though she wouldn't tell him that. They both knew how close they were without spelling it out.

She needed to start planning for Granada asap and tying up a few loose ends here before she left.

Alvaro Castilla was going to spend the next few days putting his plan into action and making the necessary contacts at the Alhambra. Christ, Lucy thought, we need to get moving with this. But she also knew her normal way of working was slow and steady. If she slipped into headless chicken mode then it could all go pear shaped.

She poured another glass of wine and cut herself a slice of tortilla. She heard laughter outside her window and remembered it was Friday night; people were beginning to head out for pre drinks before they went off to a party or a concert or a meal or, perhaps, as was more often the case, just hitting bar after bar, tapas after tapas.

Then in quick succession, her phone rang and the door buzzer went. She jumped.

'Fuck! Calm down, girl!' She looked at her phone; it was Lance. He'd obviously got her text. Not like him to ring though. She answered as the door buzzer sounded again.

'Hi, how are you?'

'I'm fine, Scally. How are you? You sound a bit tense.'

'Someone won't stop pressing my fucking door buzzer and it's freaking me out. There's been some weird shit happening and I'm starting to feel I'm being watched.'

'Yeah, Dad told me about all the stuff with the e-mail. Nasty. That's why I'm ringing. Better go see who's at the door first though. I'll hang on, make sure you're OK.'

'Hey, I'm not that scared, thank you. Well, a bit. Hang on.' She opened her flat door and shouted down the stairs to the main courtyard door, 'I'm coming!'

And then she headed down the double flight of stairs. It was times like this that she was glad there was no entry phone fitted in her flat, just the buzzer. She was not sure now why she was so worried. She felt a little daft but prudence cost nothing she reminded herself.

'I'm just going to check through the peep hole, Lance. It's obviously some idiot trying to scare me or else they're drunk.'

'I'm not drunk, I can assure you.'

'No, I know I, hold on! No way. It's not you, is it?'

She peered through the peep hole.

Standing there, rucksack over one shoulder, huge grin on his face, waving at her, was her brother, Lance.

'You daft bugger!'

Chapter 20

The next morning, Lucy was in the middle of packing for her trip back to Granada. In the background one of her favourite playlists, Arab Café, kept her company on Spotify. Jasper had taken himself up to the terrace and was busy doing little except his usual bit of bird-watching, eyeing the pigeons and doves as they came and went, always frustratingly just out of his reach.

Lance had gone out for a stroll and some cigarette papers. Despite her best efforts her kid brother had not kicked the habit. Still, it did seem to keep him calm and she had got to the point where she felt she had to stop nagging; he listened to her more than to their parents, but he was old enough now to make his own choices. He was happy in his job and was doing very well for himself financially. She wished that he would get a girlfriend and settle down but that was clearly not going to happen anytime soon. They'd always been close and Lance was one of the few people in the world who really understood her.

She was glad he was here but she wondered what would happen when they got to Granada. He had said he would come for a few days then get a train up to Madrid before he had to fly back to London. But Lucy knew she had to get down to work as soon as she arrived at the Alhambra. Maybe she would have to explain what was happening in more detail so he would understand; she knew he'd already guessed that something was up and he'd said as much late last night when they were talking about recent events and her fears that she was being followed. She didn't want to tell him too much though, didn't want him to get involved because she worried he might get hurt defending her against some of the seriously unpleasant people she was currently having to deal with.

As always, being the brother he was, he wanted to protect her and keep her company for a while at least. He had stood up for her on many occasions in the past, especially when boys came on to her uninvited in pubs and clubs when they were younger. Some guys back then took it personally when she had told them she fancied girls, not boys, as if somehow their manhood was being challenged.

One guy had followed her out into the street from a club in Reading when she was out celebrating a birthday in her late teens with Lance and some friends. He'd started to abuse her, then tried to grab her before Lance came out and pinned him up against a wall. Her brother had said that night that he would always be there for her when she needed him. And he had. He'd even vetted some of her girlfriends in the early days, making sure they were not just messing her around. Lucy smiled at the memories.

But the people who wished her harm this time were not just a few drunken boys from a club; they were violent thugs who seemingly had killed someone in order to frighten her.

Lucy went to make a pot of coffee. She still couldn't get her head around all that had happened since meeting Gloria. She was excited about getting the chance to find out Boabdil's last resting place but couldn't still quite take in why anyone would go to such extreme lengths to stop her. She paused as she put the coffee pot on the gas stove.

Gloria had seemed convinced that the finding of Boabdil would be a boon for Spanish Muslims, but clearly there were those who did not want him found. It seemed crazy to Lucy that such things mattered so much in the 21st century but equally she knew how mad the far right were, way beyond crazy sadly. Lucy just knew too that Gloria was not telling her the whole truth, that there was more to this.

'What are you up to, Gloria?'

Then her mobile sprang into life, interrupting the music. A Cordoba number. She flipped from Bluetooth speaker to her mobile's speaker.

'Hi.'

'Miss Hawksmoor, Lucy, sorry, it is the father of Gloria, Faris Sarmiyento.'

'Oh, hi, Faris, how are you?'

'I am still in hospital but I can sit up now. Still quite a bit of discomfort but the painkillers are doing their best work.'

'I'm glad, that was a horrible thing that happened.'

Lucy popped him on speaker phone and turned the gas on under her coffee pot.

'But that is not why I am phoning you. My injuries are unimportant. It is Gloria who is worrying me. Have you heard from her?'

'Not since she left for Granada yesterday. You did know she was going I hope or I have just seriously put my foot in it.'

'Yes, I did. Don't worry but she said she would call me last night and let me know she had arrived safely. But she didn't. And she told me that she knew about what happened to her friend, the young man who was hanged. That worried me even more. I should have told her, she was angry with me.'

'Why didn't you?'

'Sorry?'

'Why didn't you tell her about the murder?'

'The boy, Reda, he was a troublemaker, well I believed so. Gloria always denied it, but I'd heard from his family how he had changed in recent months after meeting some new members of PRUNE—he had apparently become radicalised—no father sadly to guide him, a mother who suffers ill-health since her husband died. But again, Gloria argued, that had nothing to do with it, he was just more passionate than the others who she often considered too weak to stand up for Muslim rights. You can't tell young people anything these days. I knew if I told her she would want to run back to Granada and do something silly.'

Lucy suddenly realised she didn't know where Gloria actually lived, originally she'd assumed it was Salamanca until the lie was exposed, but now it was clear Granada was her hometown. She didn't really know Gloria well at all.

'Were they a couple?'

'Oh, no. Reda is in fact loosely related to us. But they worked together quite closely and she considered him a good friend. Maybe on Reda's part, maybe he felt something for Gloria. How do I know? I sometimes wonder if I know Gloria at all since she moved to Granada.'

'That's where she lives then? Granada.'

'Yes, for the last year or so. She rents a room from a cousin of mine. But he says he has not heard from her.'

'Does she work there?'

'Work? Hmm, she does some waitressing at a bar and some freelance journalism though I don't get to hear much about either. But she does come and visit me quite often, so I don't complain.'

She thought again about the note, 'Things I have to do.' It was not sounding good.

'So, what do you think Gloria is going to do in Granada?'

'I'm not sure, but I fear since the attack in Madrid she is in real danger and now with this, she may not act rationally. I know she told me she'll be fine, said I had nothing to worry about. But I am very worried and I don't know what to do.' Lucy heard suppressed anguish in his voice, as if he was holding back tears, just.

Lucy poured herself a strong cup of coffee and added a tiny splash of milk.

'Faris? Are you still there?'

When he finally spoke, his voice sounded distinctly more grave.

'There are more things you need to know about Gloria, Lucy. She has, I fear, like Reda, got involved with the wrong people. This PRUNE group, you know of them?'

'Yes, I do now. Gloria mentioned them and I've done a bit of reading up on them. They seem relatively harmless. Aren't they?'

'Yes, but they acquired a new member a year ago who friends of mine tell me is not what he seems.'

'Meaning?'

'Look, I tried to warn Gloria but she wouldn't listen to me, said I was being paranoid. But good friends, one indeed a cousin of mine (Lucy marvelled at just how many cousins Faris seemed to have) contacted me a while ago to say they think that PRUNE has been infiltrated by extremists. This new man, in particular.'

'Does he have a name?'

'Yes, Abdul Qadir Jilani. I think he is a Moroccan Muslim. My cousin hears from his sources that he may have been fighting in Afghanistan at some point. But Gloria apparently seems to think he is a decent person. My cousin and his friends, they too tried to speak to Gloria to warn her but they told me that she wouldn't listen.'

'Faris, why would these extremists infiltrate such a group?'

'He thinks that they want to radicalise the group, turn it from its peaceful ways to more proactive violence. Under the guise of PRUNE they can stand for office in local elections. If this man gets in, he will be dangerous. And he is dangerous, anyway.'

'Yes, I can see that.'

'But whatever Gloria told you, she did not tell you about any of this, about this man, about me warning her?'

'No, she didn't, but we kind of, well kind of fell out a bit over it, I'm afraid. Because I don't in my line of work get involved with politics if I can help it and Gloria certainly came across as being politicised and that's not helpful when clear thinking or judgment is required, deciding how to proceed in any research. The reason for me looking for Boabdil cannot be made a political one.'

'I fear it may be too late to stop that. Unless you stop looking for him, of course.'

'No, I'm not stopping. I want to find him. I want to give him his proper place in history and solve the puzzle of what happened to him. It's what I do. I just don't like the idea of people turning him into a political pawn to serve their own ends. But, as you say, I guess it might be too late for that.'

She paused to think. Downstairs she heard Lance's voice singing a Kanye West song as he ascended the stairs. It struck her as bizarrely incongruous.

'Look, Faris, I'm heading off to Granada later today for work.' Lucy decided not to tell him what she was actually going to be doing. 'I'll phone her when I arrive. If I get in touch with her, I'll ask her to call you asap. Text me her address and I'll try there if I hear nothing. If no luck, I'll ask around at PRUNE headquarters, see if anyone has seen her.'

'If you go looking for her at PRUNE be wary, Lucy. This man, Jilani, he is dangerous.'

In the background Lucy could hear voices. Doctors?

'Are you OK, Faris?'

'There's a doctor waving at me, telling me to hurry up. I think I'm due for some medicine or tablets or something. But did you hear what I said? Be careful. And please try to find Gloria. She is in way over her head I fear. I am not sure she is as good a judge of who to trust as I thought, apart from you; that goes without saying.'

'That's kind. And of course, I'll do my best. Try not to worry. Get lots of rest. You need to get your strength back.' Lucy was unsure how reassuring she really sounded.

'And you also must do what is best with the knowledge that you now have from what Gloria passed on to you. I trust you to do the right thing. You are now the one to act on this. After all these hundreds of years it is down to you to discover what the meaning behind all this is. I hope all those who have guarded this—yes, I'm coming!—sorry, Lucy, damned doctor.'

'I know what you're going to say. I will do everything I can to make what they've done worthwhile.'

Lance was now in the room and signalling to her and mouthing, 'Beer?'

She shook her head, pointed at her coffee and mouthed back, 'I'm nearly finished.'

'I have to go, Lucy. May Allah watch over you.'

'Thank you. Take care, Faris. I'll be in touch as soon as I have any news.'

She ran off. Lance was already halfway down a bottle of Estrella Galicia.

'All OK?'

'Not sure, really,' She then spent a few minutes explaining who Faris was.

Lance nodded. 'Are you going to tell me what all this is really about, Scally? I mean, I sort of get why these nutters are unhappy about you being interested in this last Moor guy but at the end of the day, that was a fucking long time ago.'

'You have such a wonderful way with the English language, Lance. You should have been a journalist. Look, we need to get the AVE to Granada at midday so how about I tell you what I know on the journey?'

'Who looks after Jasper?'

'He looks after himself mostly, but a lady across the way leaves food out for her cat and she doesn't seem to mind him sharing.'

'Who? The other cat or the woman?'

'Ha! Both!'

Lucy went to the bathroom and leaned against the sink. She was angry with Gloria and at the same time afraid for her. A storm was looming that could cause lasting damage but she also knew that there was now no avoiding it. The present and the past were about to clash head on. Worries and doubts came flooding back, but Gloria and Boabdil now seemed inextricably linked–both needed finding.

That was all she had to focus on. She knew if she thought too much about the politics and the dangers she would not be able to think straight. This was new territory for her. Two groups of extremists seemingly hell bent on making Boabdil a modern focus of their hatred for each other and it was in Lucy's hands which way the pendulum swung.

Chapter 21

Granada

The Banuelo Abajo Té is a small teteria nestled in a two-storey house high up in the Albayzin close to where it merges into Sacromonte, with a flower and plant decked terrace overlooking the mighty Alhambra. Unlike the Arabic tea rooms on the Calle Calderería Nueva, this one is rarely frequented by tourists and is not easy to find unless you know it's there. Its clientele are the locals of the area who appreciate the owner's discretion and the dimly lit back rooms which smell of sandalwood and jasmine intermingled with occasional musky whiffs of marijuana. It is a heady cocktail. Any tourists who do wander in are ushered out to the terrace to drink pots of mint tea and be instantly captivated by the view, thus leaving the locals in peace.

In one of the more remote back rooms, behind a studded doorway hidden by a lace curtain, a man sat waiting at a low table on an old leather stool, his legs crossed beneath him. He was dressed in a long white flowing robe called a thobe; he had his prayer beads in his right hand and every now and then he flicked them into his left, murmuring something then placed them back on his lap.

There was an air of calmness and tranquillity around him which did not seem to filter out to the two men in his presence. They guarded the doorway, alert and tense, their eyes seemingly never to blink. Suddenly, there are words spoken in the room beyond near the entrance to the tearoom and one of the guards gives an almost imperceivable nod to the seated man. He beckons in return with a little movement of his head, the curtain is held back and a young woman enters. Nothing is said at first. They both just stare at each other like two gladiators assessing the situation.

She feels his stare is too intense for her to resist any longer and breaks the silence.

'You wanted to see me. Apparently.'

A smile crossed his lips. 'Please, sit down, Gloria. This has been a shock for you, for all of us.'

'Really? For you? You're the one who always wanted to step up our game against the far right and now you have the perfect reason to do so.' She sits down heavily

'That does not mean I am not saddened by what happened to Reda. I have been praying for his soul constantly. And of course, we want to find the people who did this to him. It is obvious to all, including the police I am told, that this was no suicide as you know. He was a good friend of yours. It must have been hard learning of his death.'

'I didn't learn of it as I would have wished.'

'We tried to contact you.'

'Yeah, right,' She put her head in her hands and tears came to her eyes. 'What's happened to us? He was a good guy. He didn't deserve this.'

'Of course not. But our enemies are everywhere, Gloria. We are all shocked at this escalation. We will not, cannot, just ignore it. Reda's death has changed things.'

'It has certainly done that. It's scared the shit out of me and now I'm worried about how you're going to react. We're supposed to be a peaceful party, remember. You feeding guys like Reda all this radical stuff is dangerous for all of us. You tried it with me but I didn't take you as serious as I should have done. I know how you pushed him, pushed both of us, but he listened. Sadly. And now I'm worried what you're going to do. What you suggested before. If you overreact and strike back, strike back like that, how will that solve anything?'

'Hmm. I am not sure I understand what you mean, Gloria. Who is talking about striking back? And how does Reda getting murdered have anything to do with me? I am merely keen on furthering the cause of PRUNE. That is all I am here for. I have been asked to help and I am doing my best to ensure we have a louder voice in local government here in Granada and eventually in Andalucia as a whole. Is that not what you too wish for?'

'You know I do, Jilani. But not using the ways you're thinking about. Our group must be better than the far right, not use the same tactics of fear and bullying.'

'I hope you have not spoken to any of our brothers in the party about this, or about Reda? I would hate to have to talk to your father about you.'

'I don't need to talk to anyone. I think many suspects already what you are. Many of them are just frightened of you. But they want a peaceful revolution, Jilani. And leave my father out of this. You promised you would never say anything.'

Jilani ignore her.

'You misunderstand my intentions, Gloria. Look, surely, you believe Reda needs justice?'

'Justice yes but not an eye for an eye.'

'I do not understand what you are talking about. Really, I do not. I simply want to fight fire with fire. Peaceful demonstrations, leafleting and sending petitions to the government is all well and good, but do you see the far right doing that? And sadly, the far right have infiltrated the thoughts and minds of those in power. We are struggling against all those who spread lies and venom against our people.

It is all around the world, this hatred, not just here in Spain, Gloria. So many politicians and commentators in the so-called civilised west, feed the hatred against Muslims worldwide. They do the job for the racists very well. Do you think when Trump says. 'I think Muslims hate us,' or one of his top advisors calls Islam the most radical religion in the world, that people are not being brainwashed against us? Muslims are demonised at every turn. Demonising Muslims is a vote winner in so many countries around the world, from Australia to Canada.

Not long ago, a Fox News host in the United States of America. berated a Muslim congresswoman for wearing a Muslim headscarf–declaring that doing so meant she wouldn't be loyal to the US constitution. Such rhetoric from both the media and politicians allows those on the far right to feel vindicated in their actions when they bomb a mosque or shoot our people at prayer. And here, Gloria, here in Spain, just listen to those in the Voz party spreading lies and falsehoods about Muslims.

Last year, the leader of this vile party, released a video of himself alongside dozens of men on horseback riding across an open plain with the slogan, The Reconquista will begin in Andalusian lands.'

Jilani hardly pauses to catch his breath; Gloria just stands and stares as the lecture continues.

'And, earlier this month, he launched the Voz electoral campaign in the village of Covadonga, where it is claimed the first Christian victory against the then Muslim rulers took place.

Voz's anti-Muslim approach has helped win the party favour with Europe's largest far right political groups. They claim an affinity with France's ultra-conservative Marine Le Pen for what they laughingly call their mutual protection of 'Christian Europe'. Le Pen, along with Geert Wilders of the far right in the Netherlands, have even openly supported Voz through expressing hopes that the party will gain seats in the next European parliamentary elections. This growing coordination between Europe's far right parties only threatens to strengthen the institutional legs of a continent-wide Islamophobia.'

Jilani's voice was now more strident and beginning to rise above the whispered tone he had used so far.

'Can you not see? Not understand what is happening? Am I wrong?'

He leant forward and rapped the table. 'Tell me, am... I... wrong? Are we to just sit back and write letters, Gloria? Be polite while others plan to kick us out? No one, I repeat, no one will help us if we do not help ourselves. The government here are too weak, too fragmented, to take any decisive action. We need to know who is standing with us and who is against us.'

Gloria suddenly felt out of her depth. So much of what he said was true. You only needed to read the papers to see the shocking depths to which such parties as Voz would stoop to win votes, to scare people, to characterise Muslims as evil foreigners invading their lands, as being all jihadists on a mission to kill Christians. She could never understand how anyone with any intelligence could believe all these stupid lies. But there they were, sitting in parliament. A minority but a growing one.

'I know your words are true, Jilani. I guess I'm just scared that your methods to combat these people will turn more against us. Make us appear to be the very terrorists they want to believe we are.'

'The action I crave is simply to rally all Muslims in this land, indeed from this land down to and beyond North Africa, to come together to take our rightful place at the table. Does not the Qur'an tell all Muslims, *Drive them out from where they drove you out.* And to me, Gloria, this means that any land that belonged to the Muslims at any time belongs by right to the Muslims forever. That includes Spain.'

He held his hands up to prevent her interrupting.

'And, despite your fear of me, we can begin at least with a statement. One that you can help with. One that you promised to us, to bring to fruition with the help of this woman, Lucy Hawksmoor. I need to know what is happening. The rest of our party need to know. What have you discovered?'

Gloria eyed him with a look of quiet disgust, yet at the same time with a rather terrifying admiration, which scared her even more. She knew she was wavering between two worlds.

'What I have discovered, Jilani, is that we have to be careful not to bring the Muslim world into disrespect and feed what you call the demonisation of our people. We cannot use the same tactics the far right use, if we do, we are no better. I do not want to be a member of any party that includes terrorists.'

'Terrorists? Oh, Gloria. You look at the world through such simple eyes. I will ignore your disrespect; I am assuming it is me you are referring to as a terrorist. I will put it down to ignorance. You are not looking at things from the right perspective and we must work on that. In the meantime, just tell me, has the English girl discovered what the red paper says? Does it lead us to Boabdil or to anything he hid in the Alhambra?'

Gloria did not get a chance to reply. A commotion outside the door diverted her attention, raised voices and sounds of a brief argument.

'Do not say anything further, Señora Ruiz.'

The voice came from just beyond the curtain. Gloria stood and in walked a female, brushing past the guard who reluctantly held back the curtain for her. Evidently, she had convinced him in no uncertain terms that he should not stand in her way. The woman was dressed in tight black jeans, black polo shirt and a leather jacket. Her sleek ink black hair hung down her back in a tight ponytail. Above her left eye a sharp scar followed the line of her eyebrow, which, though it caught Gloria's attention, did not detract from the woman's beauty.

Jilani smiled, but it was bereft of any warmth.

'Ah, Señora Carrasco. To what do we have the pleasure of your company today?'

Gloria was sure she recognised her. 'Do I know you?'

'I know you, that is all that matters here. And more to the point I know this gentleman, if that is the correct term.' She returned Jilani's smile with an equal amount of coldness.

Jilani spoke to Gloria but without taking his eyes off Carrasco.

'This is our friendly neighbourhood policewoman, Gloria.'

'Police? You're kidding?'

'No, she is indeed a police officer and fortunately she sympathises with our cause. She gets us information, keeps us in the picture regarding anything that might threaten our people in Granada, comings and goings of the far right, Voz rallies, etcetera, etcetera. And she keeps a close eye out for the Muslim community in Granada. Don't you, my dear?'

'Fuck off, Jilani. I don't get anything for you. I do it for the good of PRUNE, for the Muslim community, all peaceful people, not animals like you. Gloria, we are going now. Come with me.' Jilani did not stir as Gloria moved to follow Carrasco out. A guard stood in their way. Carrasco tilted her head to one side and eyed him up and down.

'Seriously? You want to stop me leaving?' Jilani nodded and the guard stepped aside. 'We will be in touch Gloria to finish our conversation.'

'No, you won't,' Gloria heard Carrasco whisper as they exited the room.

'Once we leave the building, we walk quickly back down in the direction of the Mirador San Nicolas. OK?

'OK. But what's this all about?'

Carrasco didn't make any eye contact at all as they left the teteria and headed south.

'Just keep walking. We need to be as far from here as possible before the church clocks strike the hour. We have ten minutes.'

Once out of sight of the front door, they almost broke into a run. Having passed the church of the Parroquia del Salvador, Carrasco slowed down and Gloria was able to catch up and walk in step.

'Can you hear anything?'

Gloria listened but apart from the sound of a distant guitar player, a busker no doubt, she couldn't hear a thing.

'No, what am I listening for?'

Then suddenly, filtering through the late morning air came the faint sound of a siren.

'What's happening?'

'Let's go over to that café. It's quiet in there and I know the owner.'

Minutes later they were sat at a small table drinking espresso. Gloria felt the caffeine course through her veins and she visibly relaxed.

'OK, three questions; what's all this about, why the dramatic entrance and are you really a police officer?'

'I am.' She ignored the first two questions. She flashed her warrant card.

'And you spy for PRUNE?'

'That is a strong word. I look out for them. I have gypsy blood, but I also have Muslim blood on my mother's side of the family. The police force know of my ancestry and are happy to use me as a go-between for the Muslim community and, yes, I act as a community police officer for them.

I also think it has stopped me getting any promotion sadly. So, for a few years now I have liaised with PRUNE leaders to ensure safe demonstrations, keep an eye out for troublemakers who might agitate at meetings and so on. But to my great sadness, I could not prevent Reda getting murdered.'

'You knew him?'

'I was asked by a few of the elders in PRUNE to keep an eye out for some of their more enthusiastic members, Reda amongst them, those whom they felt might get into trouble, push their luck too far with the likes of Voz and Casa Social. But I did not see this coming.

What I do know is that we believe that Reda's death was the work of an extreme right-wing group led by a German thug by the name of Jurgen Schneider, though he probably has several aliases, who have entered the country, despite there being a warrant out for Schneider's arrest from both the German authorities and our own. Several people who have connections with the Muslim community were sent photos of his body.'

Gloria lowered her head. 'I know.'

'We've been trying to keep an eye on you and Miss Hawksmoor too. My boss has spoken to her and tried to work out why she should be targeted. I am not sure why she should be in danger, just for being a historian, but it seems she is. And you too, clearly. I heard what happened to you in Madrid.'

'You did? How?' Gloria's sense of relief was being swiftly tempered by the knowledge that the police had been watching her and Lucy.

'We have an undercover agent in Casa Social in the capital. We now believe the attack was the work of Casa, they're clearly stepping up their game. It's not their usual method. And, anyway, I'm rambling. One of the PRUNE workers, Ahmed Bakaar, whom you know, asked me to keep an eye out for you. He said you were on your way back from Cordoba and he feared you were being sucked in by Jilani.'

'I am not as weak as you might think.'

'Well, I guess, but he can be persuasive I believe. Anyway, I had him followed for a day or two. He's not as street wise as he thinks, but he is a dangerous man or one with the potential to be. Many PRUNE members are frightened of him but feared he had the backing of some powerful radicals in Morocco and Afghanistan who, it turned out, have been trying to bankroll PRUNE and use it as a legit front for a terror group. They didn't know what to do. So, I've gambled.'

'Gambled? How?'

'I told my boss about where he was going to be today. I've been following up leads for our department regarding Casa's influence in Granada since Reda's murder and I radioed in to say I had got a tip off from an unknown source about this guy who appears to be a possible terrorist threat. Turns out he's on a wanted list. Well, he was as of 6 p.m. last night when a friend of mine in the G.E.O.* put a warrant out for him. It's who you know in this job that gets the wheels turning. Not totally kosher but it's not easy to catch criminals without bending the rules sometimes. Anyway, I got to you just before I phoned it in.'

'But won't Jilani try and convince your boss that you work for him?'

'I doubt it. Because other PRUNE members know I don't, as they're grateful for me keeping an eye out for them. My boss knows how I work and wouldn't believe Jilani, and the G.E.O. won't give a fuck what he says frankly. They just want him in prison and then extradited most likely.'

Gloria suddenly felt the need to go to the toilet. Her stomach was in a whirl as well as her head. As she locked the door behind her she leant against the wall and wondered how much the police really knew. A wave of guilt ran through her once again when she thought of Reda, she knew he had a bit of a crush on her, she knew that much and they'd had some fun evenings together as well as attending marches and rallies on behalf of PRUNE. But she had felt he was too young and too hot headed for her and anyway he happily shared his affections around so at least she knew he wasn't totally fixated on her.

But clearly this Schneider guy must have been watching them for some time. Maybe still watching. And what worried her was that he might well be the one who had access to her mobile, in which case he could have been the one who saw the photos and therefore might have an inkling as to what Lucy might be up to. Shit. She needed to warn Lucy as soon as possible.

* G.E.O. - Grupo Especial de Operaciones. The Special Group for Operations is the tactical unit of the Spanish National Police. It is responsible for countering and responding to terrorism, as well as VIP protection duties.

She got back to the table ready to make an excuse to leave but Carrasco was already standing by the doorway.

'I have to go, Gloria. HQ's called me in. They're going to take Jilani into custody, so you can breathe easy.'

Gloria nodded. She suddenly realised what had been bothering her since Carrasco turned up.

'Before you go, I need to ask. How much did you hear of what Jilani was saying to me?'

'Well, I heard him threatening you, but I heard little else. I caught the name Boabdil, I've heard of him, who hasn't in Spain. Odd topic of conversation. Going to tell me anything I should've heard? Anything important?'

Gloria took her sunglasses out of her pocket and put them on. 'No, nothing that can't wait. I'll tell you sometime.'

Carrasco gave a knowing smile. Gloria knew she wasn't convinced. 'And maybe you can tell me too about the red paper and more about Lucy?' Gloria felt her hands sweating. She walked through the door and turned back to Carrasco. She was trying to think on her feet.

'I think Jilani had his wires crossed. I've no idea what he was on about, but I'll ask Lucy if she knows what it means when I speak to her. Let you know as soon as I know.'

Carrasco knew Gloria was not telling the truth, but she was in a hurry and her boss would be getting more and more irate.

'OK. But remember, I'm on your side. If you ever need help, just ring this number.' She handed Gloria a card.

Gloria pocketed it and spoke to Carrasco without looking up. 'Thanks for the coffee. I'll keep the card safe. But don't worry, I'm good to look after myself.'

She turned and hurried off.

Carrasco watched her go, then lit a cigarette and headed off towards the town centre, musing on what Boabdil's tomb had to do with any of this. She needed to tell Gomez. She'd heard more than she had let on to Gloria.

In the shadow of a shop doorway nearby, a man watched them both go their separate ways from behind a carousel of faded postcards. He raised the hood of his old waterproof over his head, stepped onto the pavement, spat on the ground and followed the direction taken by Gloria.

Chapter 22

Carrasco's walk back to the station was cut short by a phone call. It was her boss, Gomez. 'You might like to get yourself over to the teteria, now.'

'Why, what's up?'

'What's up is I have several members of the G.E.O. here who've just swept through this building. And, to cut a long story very short, the mother of a whore rat has vanished.'

'What the fuck? That's not possible. I heard you arriving only seconds after I'd left. Someone said you had him in custody.'

'After you had left? Shit, Carrasco, what the hell were you doing there? I thought you had just called it in?'

Silence.

'Oh Jesus, Joseph and Santa Maria, please don't tell me you were actually talking to him?'

'You're ignoring the question. Why did HQ say you had him in custody?'

'Old news. One of our lot caught this guy running away, took him down. But turns out he was just some guy who'd been doing a little dealing in there.'

Silence again. Carrasco was now worried about Gloria.

'So, Carrasco? Answer my question. Why were you there, for Christ's sake! That was dangerous.'

'I'm on my way. I'll explain.'

'Yes, you should and it better be a solid gold 24 carat, watertight, no shit explanation.'

He cut the call. Carrasco looked up at the sky.

'Fuck, fuck, mother of god fuck!'

A short while later she was back at the teteria. Two men were in handcuffs and were being pushed into a van. Gomez didn't look at her.

'Those are the two goons who were here with Jilani. No shots fired, thank Christ.'

He now turned his gaze on Carrasco. 'You can tell me later what the hell you were playing at being at the scene but first show me where you were.'

A small crowd had gathered but were kept at a distance behind a makeshift cordon manned by police. Carrasco noticed some hostile glares in their direction.

'This doesn't look good,' she murmured,

Gomez agreed. 'Hopefully once we put out in the press who we were after, the locals will be more understanding.'

'I doubt it, not if we don't have him in custody. It'll look like we're just out to bust members of the local Muslim party. And the far right will be full of 'told you so' shit. PRUNE are just a front for jihadist terrorists, they'll be saying.'

'Thanks for the heartening words.'

'And it's the election tomorrow,' added Carrasco. 'Maybe the timing was not great, but...'

Gomez disagreed. 'More like whatever we do we'd annoy one side or the other.'

Carrasco then took a moment to explain to Gomez about Gloria and why she had to intervene. She'd heard from a source, she didn't go further, that Jilani might push Gloria to do something stupid. She's been tailing Jilani until he finally ended up at the teteria.

She'd just called it in, when Gloria turned up. She had to get her out before the SWAT team from the G.E.O arrived. It had been a risk she admitted but she had also learnt something interesting. From the overheard conversation, it sounded like Jilani had involved Lucy Hawksmoor somehow, or at least Hawksmoor was involved in something that interested Jilani.

'Jesus.' Gomez paused for a moment. 'It has to be something to do with her research. What else could it be? The Casa woman, Ximena Martinez turned up at one of her talks a while ago. Then she got sent a threatening e-mail, most likely from Casa or an associated far right group. Now Jilani's sticking his nose in.'

They entered the building and Carrasco showed her boss to the room where she'd met Jilani.

'So, how the fuck did he get out when the whole place was surrounded by the G.E.O. team?'

He looked at the doorway and it was obvious to both that there was no way out other than that.

Carrasco looked around the room again. Something was not quite right. She stepped back to the doorway and studied the room again, trying to recall exactly where Gloria and Jilani were both sat. She knew where Gloria had been but the chair where Jilani had been sitting had moved, probably not surprisingly, but now she looked again, so had the low, wooden table. She bent down and looked beneath it.

She then rose, put her fingers to her lips, pointed to the table and then said, 'No, idea boss. A complete fucking mystery. Let's check outside again.'

As they left the room, she pulled Gomez to one side. 'There's a trapdoor in the floor beneath the table, I could just see the corner of it. The rug and table had not been put back properly in the rush to conceal it.'

Gomez nodded. 'That would explain the Houdini-like disappearance of our friend. I'm going to get the G.E.O. guys back in. You need to stay outside with me.'

'I need to see his face when we find him.'

'You'll see him when he's led out. That is, of course, if he is even down there. Depends where the trap door leads. He could be miles away. But if he is down there, he may be armed. So, stay out here.'

Carrasco moved to one side and tucked herself into a small alcove as Gomez spoke into his walkie talkie.

Minutes later, the SWAT team from G.E.O. were back in the room. As quietly as possible they first removed the table and then the carpet from the scene. The trapdoor appeared to have no lock, just a flat bolt, so, after positioning themselves ready for the swiftest entry, one of the team slid back the bolt carefully with one hand whilst pointing his 9mm SIG SAUER pistol at the door with the other. He flipped it open. The image was chillingly bizarre.

Jilani was lying in a coffin-like space, his hands clasped together. The soldier thought he was raising his hands in surrender but instead he realised too late that he had pulled a pin from a grenade. In an instant, there was an explosion of gunfire mingling seamlessly with the ear shattering sound of the grenade detonating and something else. Glass blew out of the window and screams ripped the air outside and in.

Gomez ran in ignoring warnings from another G.E.O. officer. A claustrophobic scene of bloody carnage met his gaze. A trooper was lying with half his face missing, despite having worn a protective helmet, none of which remained. Jilani's body lay torn apart in the floor space; one of his hands missing and his chest cavity bloodily exposed. It was clearly not just a grenade that had exploded. Gomez realised Jilani had somehow attached a small explosive vest before hiding, unless, Gomez thought, he wore it as a matter of course. Or it was down there already. A vest had to be the reason given the injuries he had sustained and the god almighty bang that had filled the building.

The smell of cordite was everywhere. Fuck, why didn't I expect this? He stood with his hands on his head, his ears still ringing. It should have been a reasonably routine exercise as these things go, arresting a known terrorist, but Jilani was clearly someone who'd not wanted to be caught, had decided to go out on a high.

Gomez was pale. The other members of the G.E.O. were getting to their feet; only one other seemed to have been injured fortunately and he was being swiftly attended to. The guy who opened the trapdoor had taken the full blast and possibly inadvertently saved others' lives. Or so it seemed. Gomez looked around and there, behind a low leather chair, he saw a pair of black boots protruding. He moved the chair and, to his horror, he saw the still body of Office Carrasco.

'Oh no, oh fuck, no, please!'

She'd clearly disregarded his orders and must have crept in to see the arrest of Jilani. He bent to feel her pulse. It was light but it was there. Just. Her hair was matted with dark swathes of blood and diamond-like shards of glass sparkled incongruously amidst her locks, probably from the mirror which lay wrecked beside her. Blood was oozing from a gash to her throat. Gomez could not believe it. He was joined by a paramedic who appeared as if from nowhere and knelt beside him.

'Sir, please, you best go outside now. Leave this to me.'

'Is she going to be OK?'

'Just go outside, sir, please.'

Another officer took his arm and guided him away from the scene as he said several prayers for Carrasco.

He lowered his head as he left the building and, for the first time in many a long year, tears ran down his cheeks.

This was not how this day was supposed to turn out.

Chapter 23

Lucy had not been back in Granada long but already she had fielded two disturbing phone calls. The first was from the police; Inspector Gomez warning her that not only were the far right on her trail, but the guy who had blown himself up—the story had been all over the news—had also apparently expressed an unhealthy interest in her work and he was a known Islamic extremist who had hidden himself away within a moderate Muslim group much to their embarrassment. As he spoke, Lucy had begun to wonder about Gloria's role in all this when, to her complete amazement, he mentioned her by name. She refocused and asked him to repeat what he had said. He quickly related the story as far as he knew it, how Gloria had been speaking to Jilani just before the police arrived but all Gomez knew for certain was that Jilani had been trying to get information from her about Lucy's work. One officer had died in the explosion and another two badly injured.

'So, where the hell is Gloria, is she OK?'

He didn't know, she'd left before the police arrived, but she was now missing. The police were looking for her. Gomez asked Lucy what it was about her work that everyone was so interested in. She stalled him, said she would pop down to the station the next day and talk it through.

So, where the fuck was Gloria, thought Lucy. And what the hell is she doing talking to this Jilani guy? She was getting increasingly bad feelings about all this. And about Gloria. Try to be positive, Lucy. Don't be negative. But shit it was hard not to be.

She had not long been off the phone to the Inspector when her mobile had chirped again and this time, despite the screen reading *Caller ID Unknown*, she answered it. She wished she hadn't. A cold voice told her to stay away from Granada, to go home and to stop meddling in Spanish affairs. Except, his vocabulary was a little more visceral and ugly.

'Who the fuck are you?' she shouted.

'You are a Muslim loving fucking little bitch and if you don't get back to the fuck where you came from you'll find out who I am and I'll cut you into little pieces you…'

She cut him off before she heard anymore.

When she relayed this to Lance, he couldn't believe what she was telling him. She was clearly shaken and she'd gone pale. Lance gave her a huge hug and held her tight as he spoke.

'How the hell have they got your phone number?'

Lucy could only think of one thing. 'When Gloria was attacked in the Metro, her phone was stolen. It had my number on it which makes it obvious, I guess, that this bastard must be with either Casa or some far right crowd linked to them.'

Her room at the university was not huge; one living space that just managed to squeeze in a double bed and a sofa squashed into a room littered with books, swathes of A4 sheets covered in her not very attractive scrawl and lots of academic magazines.

No kitchen, though she had a small electric hotplate and a mini microwave and a tiny bathroom with a shower cubicle completed the flat. Two people in this glorified box were not good for her thought process, even if they were family. She already felt hemmed in. She slipped out of Lance's arms and gave him a peck on the cheek.

'Let's go out, Lance, I need a beer and fresh air fast.'

'Now you're talking, Scally. Come on, drinks are on me.' Lance grabbed his wallet and they headed out to find a bar.

***

Back at Police Headquarters, Gomez, after having talked to Lucy, went straight in to speak to his number two, Rueda. He had his head in his hands and just behind him, Rodriguez was at his computer but staring vacantly into space. Rueda looked up as Gomez entered.

'You don't look great, Josef. Are you sure you should be in?'

'I'm OK. It's going to take some time to get over this fiasco. It's not really sunk in. I didn't think things like that happened in Granada. Losing that officer was avoidable. It's such a fucking waste. And if Carrasco doesn't pull through it'll be two dead.'

Rodriguez turned round. 'I'll get coffee for us.'

No one replied but he went just the same. There was a tangible air of sadness mixed with nervous tension in the office since the incident. No one wanted to answer the phone if it rang for fear it was bad news about Carrasco.

Rueda stood up and loosened his tie, tucked his shirt in and turned to his boss. 'So? What now?'

His eyes looked puffy and red as if he had not slept for a while. He had been at Carrasco's bed side for several hours and clearly it had upset him. Gomez hadn't marked him down as having this softer side. He had never seen him like this before. He chose not to comment on it. Rueda would hate it.

'Well, we need to put a watch on Lucy Hawksmoor while she's in Granada. She's attracting the wrong sort of attention and I have a horrible feeling someone might do something to her to make a statement.'

'I'm on to it. Does she know she'll have a tail?'

'No, I think she'd refuse. And also I want to know what she's planning to do. She says she's popping into the office tomorrow to brief me, but I sense there's something she doesn't want me to know. We'll see.'

Rodriguez returned with the coffees. He put them on the table, with a plate of cold churros on the side.

'Boss, there's something you need to know. You may or may not remember but there is the Voz rally tomorrow in Plaza Virgen del Carmen and it's going to be taking up a lot of our manpower as it is but to make matters potentially worse, PRUNE is holding an open-air meeting in Placeta Comino less than half a kilometre away, at more or less the same time, 11 a.m.'

'Christ, who gave them permission?'

'Well, with the election next Sunday, Voz is one of several parties allowed to hold a stall to gather support, hand out leaflets etc and the PRUNE one was arranged a long time ago with the town hall. It's a kind of information, shake people's hands, marketing one too, but for local council elections next month, not the general election tomorrow. It was apparently organised before the current one was called.'

Another general election, Gomez thought. Another waste of everyone's time and taxpayer's money. Another hung parliament, another chance for trouble to flair in Catalonia, another chance for the far right to take more seats in the government. When would the politicians not see the writing on the wall and work together to keep these fanatics, the likes of Voz, out of the picture?

Probably never, sadly,

'Can't we get them to cancel or postpone? Or just make them?'

'Er, we could but that may not go down well with the Muslim fraternity,' chipped in Rueda.

Rodriguez sipped his coffee. 'And, this news is not going to do your worry lines any good at all I fear, boss, but.' He hesitated.

Gomez took a long gulp of coffee as if a torrent of caffeine might prepare him better for Rodriguez news.

'To add to the perfect shit storm, gents, there is Intel in this morning to suggest that some of Casa Social's merry men and a few of their new far right mates are heading this way to join the fun.'

'What? For fuck's sake! Agent provocateurs are all we need. Are they coming because of Voz or the PRUNE rally?' Gomez answered his own question. 'Probably both, but if there's trouble and I find out anyone in Voz is connected to them, or invited them, then I'll piss on their parade. Big time. Rueda, alert the Guardia Civil. We need as much deterrent on the street as possible. But get them to be low key. Side streets for the vans. Get the dogs in, mounted guys too. But hold them back unless they're needed. I don't want to spook the locals unnecessarily.'

He walked back to his office thinking he would have to delay Lucy Hawksmoor's visit to the station. Tomorrow was going to be a busy day, hopefully not another bad one. Yet he had a horrible feeling that trouble was almost a foregone conclusion if the Intel was right.

And it usually was.

He rang the mayor. He explained the situation and it was agreed to cancel all leave for the next 48 hours for the local police. A request would also be sent out to close the Alhambra and several other potential targets for the far-right mob heading their way. Also, a detail of plain clothes police would be posted tomorrow to watch over the Mosque. Maybe they were overreacting, but Gomez had to protect his city as best he could.

He then called Rueda in to his office and told him to put plain clothes officers at the train and bus station. They were going to play a watching brief rather than go in heavy handed and prevent anyone entering the city who they were concerned about. The mayor had voiced his concerns that with the elections coming up, any show of unprovoked police force, however warranted, may backfire on them. The last thing he wanted was for Voz to have a field day accusing the state of preventing free speech etc, etc. Gomez got the point. Rueda less so. He huffed but nodded his assent.

Then he rang Lucy Hawksmoor again.

***

Lucy and Lance were in a bar on the Camino del Sacramonte, a laid-back spot called Casa Juanillo. They had walked farther than Lance had wanted to but he had kept quiet, as Lucy was in a deep reverie and he knew her too well to interrupt her thought processes. Once sat down, he had wasted no time ordering a tapas of cod and red peppers plus some chipirones, his favourite and a plate of pimientos de padrón. A cerveza grande for himself and a glass of Toro for Lucy. When the food arrived, she picked at it, Lance pounced on it. She stared at him with amusement.

'Sorry, I'm ravenous.' Then he ordered more bread.

When her phone rang, this time she knew straight away it was Gomez as she had saved him to contacts—she had decided to answer no more withheld calls. His first question was abrupt.

'Where are you?'

'And hello to you too, Inspector.'

'Sorry, hi, Lucy. I'm just worried about you, just wanted to check all is OK.'

'All is OK, in so far as my brother and I are in a quiet bar and it appears we were not followed here, I took a few deviations to check.'

'Good. You are turning into quite the spy, Lucy.'

'No. I'm turning into someone who doesn't want to be attacked, Inspector.'

'Apologies, that was flippant of me.'

'So, any news, anything I need to know. I'm sure you have lots of other things you need to be worried about rather than just a professor of history trying to go about her business. I'm not used to getting checked up on by concerned policemen. It's a bit unnerving.'

'I'm sorry, but I wanted to tell you that tomorrow is not a good day to come to the station. There are political rallies in town ahead of Sunday's election and there is also the Muslim party, PRUNE, running an open-air talk, so all my men will be on the streets, me too.'

'Right, OK, thanks for letting me know.' Lucy's mind started turning and she was keen to end the call.

'One more thing. Might be good to take extra special care tomorrow. We have word that there are some rather unpleasant people heading our way. We will try and intercept them if they arrive at the train or bus station but that might not be easy. But suffice to say, they belong to Casa Social and potentially accompanied by some members of a neo–Nazi group. The guys we spoke about before.'

'Thanks for the heads up. I promise I'll stay clear of the centre tomorrow. May not even go out.'

'Have you been threatened again or has anyone contacted you in any way?'

'I received a pretty nasty phone call from some abusive bastard who doesn't want me in Granada but apart from him everyone has been as lovely as usual.'

'Hmm, now you are being flippant, Lucy.'

'I guess. I'm just seriously pissed off with the whole thing. I have no idea who to trust or not at the moment.'

'I get that, but just please take care. Ten mucho cuidado.'

'Si, gracias. I will.'

'And next time phone me straight away if anyone in anyway threatens you again.'

'I will.'

'Right,' Gomez paused. He wanted to push Lucy on why she was back in Granada and what she was up to. But he thought better of it. She wouldn't tell him anyway.

Lance looked up as she put her phone down.

'All OK?'

She smiled her most vague smile; one he knew well, the one she employed when she wasn't keen on saying too much.

'Yes, all is fine, apart from a possible clash of ideologies on the streets of Granada tomorrow, followed by general mayhem and minor carnage.'

'Right. I see. I think I do. And are you as you said there, going to stay in tomorrow?'

'Let's wait and see. I certainly won't be going looking for a fight in the centre. That's for sure.'

She ordered more drinks. The waiter returned her request with an almost imperceptible nod as he continued popping different plates of tapas on the counter. The aromas were now starting to make Lucy seriously hungry. Her appetite had taken a turn for the worse over the last few days but she was beginning to think she would need a lot of sustenance for what lay ahead over the next 24 hours or so.

'Lance, I need to speak to this guy called Alvaro Castilla, the one I told you about, who wants to help with some work I'm doing at the Alhambra.'

'Really? Wow. I thought it was all guns blazing on this Boabdil guy. Is the work connected?'

'Kind of.'

Lucy didn't want to embroil her brother too much in her world.

Lance got the hint. 'OK, so, shall I occupy myself for a while?' He held his hands up in a mock gesture of hurt.

'It's fine, don't worry. Chill. Actually, Scally, I could do with catching up on some sleep when we leave here.'

'Great. Here's the keys. I won't be long. We could get supper later. But I think I may well not be much company tomorrow, just to warn you.'

'No, I understand. It's been nice to catch up, even if briefly. I may head up to Madrid tomorrow. Andres Jarabo said he was in town if I had a chance to look him up.'

'Andres? The wine tour guy?'

'Yeah, he's been in touch about financial advice regarding expanding his business. He's also got into stocks and shares. Not much I can do to help but it'll be nice to go out with him. Have a beer or three. It's been a while since I saw him. Last time was when Dad was there.'

'I've never met him but from what I've heard he sounds good company. Better than me at the moment for sure.'

Lance finished his drink, gave Lucy a hug and left but not before giving her a short lecture on watching out for herself. Any problems she could message him and he'd come straight back out.

Lucy then paid and went outside to sit at a table with the remains of her wine. She messaged Alvaro who messaged her back straight away. Then he was on the phone.

She listened to him cough for a moment before he spoke.

'Hello, Lucy.' He sounded for a second as if he'd been choking.

'Are you OK, Alvaro?'

'Yes, just a few pipas choosing to go down the wrong way.'

'I don't know how you eat those things; they always get stuck in my teeth.'

'It's an art, you are born with it if you are Spanish.'

171

'Unless you choke on them, that's not very arty.'

'It's a hazard worth living for and they take my mind off smoking.'

'Ah, OK. Sounds fair enough. Right. What's with your plans? Any luck?'

'Big luck. Big luck. But let's not talk over the phone. Can we meet? How about Mirador San Nicolas in half an hour?'

'I'm on my way, Alvaro.'

Lucy finished her drink and ordered a third and final glass. Dutch courage, she thought to herself. She now knew for certain that, one way or another, tomorrow was going to be a momentous day in her search for Boabdil. Maybe even a make-or-break day. If Alvaro had opened the metaphorical doors he had spoken to her about, then some literal doors may well be opened too. What lay behind them, or how easy they were to open, she would soon find out.

It gave her a buzz but at the same time she had to be honest with herself and admit to feeling a little scared. She had no idea why. It wasn't the physical threats of the thugs and racists, more oddly a fear of letting Boabdil down, which sounded ridiculous, but to her Boabdil deserved to be found. Not to just be consigned to history as the weak Moor who cried as he left the Alhambra to the conquistadors. Who fled to North Africa and disappeared off the face of the Earth?

To find Boabdil, meant rediscovering the beauty and splendour of the 800 years of Moorish rule. Setting the history books straight, the ones written by the conquerors. For this was Spanish history. These Moors were Spaniards who tied their flag to the Iberian mast and had helped build Spain into the country that had been the envy of Europe for several centuries.

As she stepped outside the sun hid behind a dark bank of clouds and a chill seemed to reach for her bones. She felt a strange tug on her sleeve, as if someone was trying to pull her along. No one was there. She shivered and looked around. The street was empty. She walked until she could see the distant snow-capped Alpujarras. Her eyes then followed a line down towards the Red Palace. She sensed the answers all lay deep within the magnificently imposing array of buildings that contained so much beauty yet hid so much bloodshed and tragedy. Lucy bit her lip, told herself to focus, turned up the fleecy collar of her denim jacket and then headed off to meet Alvaro.

Chapter 24

Alvaro's plan was simple but audacious. He had contacted a good friend of his, Victor Morata, senior sculpture conservator at the Victoria and Albert Museum in London, who was currently engaged in a two-year project in the Alhambra, working on the plasterwork of the Nasrid dynasty; copying, restoring and identifying what was genuine and what was a later addition in each room of the entire palace. A mammoth job.

They were only working on small areas at a time so as not to disturb the daily tsunami of tourists too much. There was a team of 12 helpers working with Morata and they were dotted around the site, each with a specific task of their own, a small area to record, photograph and then, where necessary, restore. Alvaro had asked if he and Lucy could tag along and observe the work. Of course, they could come along. Morata was honoured to have such distinguished guests.

Lucy had been almost bursting to tell Alvaro of the plan to shut the Alhambra the next day due to the potential risk of trouble but Alvaro was already one step ahead. Morata had been alerted directly by the police and had been granted permission to continue his work behind locked doors. He had suggested to Alvaro that with the peace and quiet it would be a perfect time to visit. Alvaro knew it was their chance, possibly their only chance, to try and access the Tower of the Seven Floors and find a possible way down below the only two floors currently known. It would mean an early start if they were going to make the most of this golden opportunity.

He had mentioned that Lucy was working on a history of Boabdil and had asked if it was alright if Lucy was given access to the ancient burial site, close to the walls of one of the palaces, as it was where most of the Nasrid dynasty had at one time been laid to rest. This would be a rare chance to photograph its layout, etc, etc. Alvaro had spun a good tale and it sounded authentic.

Normally, it was off limits due to its fragile state; in some areas it was prone to subsidence. Morata had agreed that she would be most welcome. He would clear it with the authorities but if they knew she was with him, then there would be no problem, as long, obviously, as she took the necessary precautions and followed the necessary risk assessment procedures and a set route, etc.

Lucy listened attentively to Alvaro's plan. It seemed a good one but she wished that she had more time to prepare, to gather her thoughts and work out different scenarios. She had learned to be more meticulous over the course of the last few years, at times to the point of being highly irritating to some of her colleagues. But now she would have to revert to being the younger version of herself, thinking quickly on her feet, following gut feeling rather than a well thought through plan. She hoped that she could uncover somewhere some sign or symbol that could be linked to the writing on the red paper.

If she stopped to think too hard and long then she couldn't help but see it all as ridiculous that they could stand any chance of finding something that had remained undiscovered for many centuries now. Alvaro had been surprisingly positive when she had initially voiced her doubts.

No one had tried for a long time to search for these hidden floors. Most experts thought they no longer existed or maybe never even did. Or some believed they were destroyed possibly when Napoleon's retreating army blew up sections of the gate. But he thought maybe that was what led to the entrances being hidden in the first place, under rubble and, when the tower was restored in the 70s, maybe no one unearthed the floors because their entrances were just that, hidden. Lucy found it hard to believe they would have missed them if they were there but Alvaro reminded her that they had apparently not used any ground penetrating devices back then due to cost.

Alvaro had laughed gently and just said, 'Have faith, Lucy.'

Victor and his team started early most days, so she would have to be there around 7 in the morning. She now had just a short evening to prepare herself for the morrow's adventure. She felt very tired and wanted to go home to sleep but she had reading to do, sketches of the Alhambra to study to refresh her memory of its layout. She wouldn't be able to take much with her and, as Alvaro had said, nothing that would arouse suspicion or hinder her progress. Her worry was that she would not have the gear she needed and the whole thing could turn out to be huge waste of time. But at least if she got a lead then maybe they could go back officially at a later date.

When she got home, Lance had already packed his few things and left. A brief note explained he was catching a late train to Madrid and said he'd keep in touch.

Just as well, she thought. One less person to worry about. But she missed him already.

***

She knew she had to take a brief nap or her eyes would not make it through the evening. They were starting to feel full of that gritty tiredness that makes them ache from the inside out. Taking out her iPhone, she clicked on her Calm app, chose the sound of rain on leaves and set the timer duration for 20 minutes—that should do the trick. It was something she did every day as often as she could, her version of a siesta. She found it helped her to switch off, recharge her batteries and forget all her worries for a while. She rarely slipped into unconsciousness, just into a state of tranquillity, slightly south of the land of sleep. But this time she had only just lay down on her bed when she felt as if she was somewhere else.

On closing her eyes, Lucy saw all the paintings she had studied of Boabdil's departure from the Alhambra swim before her. She felt lightheaded, as though she was walking on air. She drifted into one of the pictures, floating effortlessly over 3D horses and white cloaked figures. Now she was walking down a snowy path lined with eucalyptus and jacaranda trees, the mountains of the Alpujarras in the grey blue swirling distance. The path narrowed as she continued her journey, her breath streaming out in plumes of frozen air ahead of her. Lucy could hear not only her own breath but her heart beating in rhythm with her footsteps.

Then she found herself in a clearing, but somehow it was high up and she could see on either side of her, the world slope away towards deep dark valleys. From nowhere, a snowy owl flew toward her and she ducked just in time; its wings brushing her hair. She turned around to see the bird alight on a tree branch. It turned its head 180 degrees and stared, but not at her. She sensed someone was now behind her. She slowly looked round and in a small space amongst the trees she saw a stone tomb covered in ivy.

For all the world it felt like a scene from a fairy story. A beautiful young woman in a long blue robe was lying on top of the lid. As Lucy approached, she

175

could see that her skin was alabaster white. There was no sign of life. Lucy stood transfixed as, without warning, the lid began to move, sliding towards her, just enough to leave a small gap. Lucy was about to look into the tomb when a pair of hands emerged, gripping the edge. Lucy wanted to run but her legs would not move. She was now like one of the eucalyptus trees, rooted to the spot and her arms had entwined with their lower branches.

A man's head slowly appeared and it was clear from the look on his face that he was using all his effort to pull himself up from a deep pit from beneath the tomb. Then he was out and his form seemed to shimmer and pulse, like a faulty hologram. He leant forward and kissed the forehead of the woman lying on the lid. His features were those of a young man but his face was contorted with so much grief and anguish, that it was as if he was ageing before her eyes.

Lucy could sense it was a face that had experienced much heartache and suffering. She realised he was going to look her way and she tried to melt into the trees either side of her. And then he was there, right in front of her. He tilted his head to one side, dark hazel eyes piercing hers as if he was trying to stare into her very soul. As if he was searching for something within her. He reached out a hand to touch her cheek and a cascade of snow suddenly blinded her. When it had stopped, she opened her eyes but no one was there. In the distance she saw the tomb slowly sinking into the ground, no body now atop it. Instead, there stood an owl and a bluebird, gazing at her. Then the tomb was gone and bells rang loudly in Lucy's head.

***

The next morning after a fitful sleep, Lucy stood, more alert than she had expected, outside a side entrance to the Alhambra—one reserved for staff only. It was 6:50 a.m. and she shivered a little in the crisp early morning air. She seemed to be shivering a lot recently—it was a sign of someone walking over her grave her mum always said—rather macabre but possibly appropriate today—though not *her* grave. The sky was blue and clear and no one was about other than a street sweeper who ambled sedately from litter piece to litter piece. She checked the time on her phone. 6:55 a.m. Alvaro should have been here by now. Victor Morata would not unlock the door until he arrived as he was awaiting Alvaro's call to let him know they were outside. Lucy began to worry whether she was in the right place.

Suddenly, a bright red Seat Ibiza came hurtling around the bend. Its brakes screeched unnaturally as it came to a halt by the kerbside opposite. She felt a shot of alarm kick her stomach. The passenger door swung open and Lucy was stunned to see none other than Gloria rushing across to her. Before she could say anything, Gloria had wrapped her arms around her in a tight embrace.

'Don't say anything. There's no time.'

A swarm of questions buzzed through Lucy's brain.

'What? Christ, are you OK? And how did you know I'd be here? And fuck, I've missed you and been worried sick.'

'I'm OK, Lucy. Please. But time is not on my side. Alvaro told me you'd be meeting him here this morning. I spoke to him late last night. I haven't phoned because so much is happening and things have been done and said that are not true and I have to put them right. And I knew you'd be busy with... this...' she gestured towards the Alhambra.

'And I'm being watched since the death of Jilani, by the police and the far right. Probably more than being watched but hey, lucky me. I think my phone's been hacked too, so I've got rid of it. Look, I have to go. There's going to be a demonstration against Voz and I need to be there. If anyone asks, please don't say you saw me.'

She took out two letters from her jacket pocket and pushed them into Lucy's hands.

'One is for my father; one is for you. Don't read yours till tonight. My prayers are with you, Lucy Hawksmoor that you find what you are looking for. Please, find it for you, find it for my people. Find it for Boabdil.'

Before Lucy could say anything, Gloria kissed her lightly on her lips then she was back across the road, in the car and away.

Lucy felt she could hardly breathe. She felt so stupid that she had said so little. Gloria's words had poured out like a rainstorm. She looked at the letters then put them both in her canvas messenger bag. What the hell was going on? She could still taste Gloria's vanilla lip balm. And her mind was a washing machine of worry. Why were the police following her? What had she done?

She was worried about Gloria going to the demo, especially after what Inspector Gomez had told her. Why the hell was she going? Why was she being watched by anyone? Lucy looked at the time. 7:07. And where the fuck was Alvaro! 7.07? Lucy looked back at where the car had vanished into the distance.

Then it struck her. Who goes to a demo at 7.07 in the morning? She needed to talk to Gomez as soon as possible.

***

The street sweeper pushed his cart a little further down the road, then sat on a bench, took out a cigarette and lit it. Then he flipped open a mobile and, eyes still on Lucy, made a call.

'She's still here. No sign of anyone else. Not sure what she's doing if I'm honest.

Oh and you were right, that girl, the other one. She just turned up out of the blue, ran over to the Hawksmoor woman, seemed to say a few things then got back in a car and sped off. I've texted you the make and licence plate.'

A pause whilst the voice on the other end spoke.

'Only thing looked odd is that she appeared to hand something to Hawksmoor, papers or something. She has them in her bag. I don't think she was waiting for her, she looked very surprised to see her.'

A pause.

'No, I couldn't see the colour of the paper. Yeah, I can get the bag. Anything else? OK, I'm parked nearby so I'll be with you as soon as I get it.'

He hung up.

Lucy was seriously worried now. Without Alvaro this was all a useless waste of time and time she sensed was not on her side today for some reason. She knew they'd need every minute in there that they could. As she turned back to the road to look for Alvaro's arrival, she noticed the street sweeper coming up her side of the street. He glanced at her and she smiled. He didn't smile back.

Lucy suddenly had a bad feeling. The street was empty apart from the two of them and if she stepped away it would look odd yet he seemed to be walking straight towards her. She glanced over her shoulder in case he was headed for a waste bin she hadn't noticed. She told herself she was being paranoid. But she wasn't.

In that moment, she felt an arm push her and hands grabbing at her bag as she fell. Then she heard a dull thud. The sweeper's eyes rolled in his head and he fell forward narrowly missing landing on top of her.

There stood Alvaro clutching a long heavy rubberised torch, now clearly broken. More importantly he was standing in front of an open door into the walls of the palace. He helped Lucy to her feet and, as the sweeper began to rise to his, he pushed her through the doorway and slammed the door behind them.

Chapter 25

Lucy found herself in a narrow corridor. The only light came from a narrow slit high up in the wall above the doorway. The sharp shaft of sun's rays hummed with dust particles that seemed to be gently basking in the glow. Alvaro was leaning against the opposite wall, hands on knees catching his breath.

'What the hell was that all about? Alvaro, are you OK?'

'I'm fine, just a bit old for fighting.'

'Well, that wasn't much of a fight. You were amazing. You stopped him with one blow. Thank you. But who the hell was he? And why didn't you meet me outside? I was worried.'

Alvaro straightened up. Lucy could plainly see that whacking the guy so hard had taken a lot out of him. She went over and gave him a hug.

'Too many questions, Alvaro, I'm sorry.'

'No, I'm sorry, Lucy. Leaving you out there put you in danger. But I was followed this morning and so I decided to enter through the conventional entrance. Victor Morata met me there and let me in. I think he realised something was wrong by my manner. I am not used to being tailed like that. It put the wind up me I have to tell you.'

'I bet it did. Who do you think it was?'

'No idea, but he didn't look friendly. It was odd.'

'Why?'

'Well, it almost felt like he wanted me to know that he was following me.'

Lucy realised that the plan had been to separate the two of them, leaving her alone and vulnerable.

'I'd had to explain to Victor why we were really here. Not to the letter though, just that you had a theory you wanted to explore before going public with it. I'm not much good at lying when eye to eye.'

'He knows about the paper?'

'Oh, no! Just that you have a hunch based on some research that there may be an undiscovered tomb here of one of the emirs.'

'And he was okay with that?'

'Surprisingly so. He even joked that if you needed any help with anything Nasrid he would be happy to help as long as he got first refusal.'

'I reckon he thinks I'm on a wild goose chase and maybe just doesn't care.'

'No, not true. He's even offered you help in the form of one of his workers, a young guy called Diego, who is short but built like a small Mosque.'

'Are you not coming with me?'

'No, I don't think so. I am happy to wait near the front hall, make sure we get no unwanted visitors. You can move quicker on your own. We only have an hour or so, not much more. I'm going to phone the police too. Report the attack on you. Maybe if we get a police car down here it may scare off any who intend to do us further harm. I am an inveterate coward, I fear.'

'If you phone, ask for Inspector Gomez. He seems to have an interest in my work and may take it more seriously than others. I hope they don't ask to speak to me.'

'I will tell them you've gone home by taxi but that I fear the attacker is still around.'

'OK, not sure whether they'll buy that but let's see. Mind you, with what's happening today demonstrations wise there may not be many police spare.'

'Spare?'

'Available.'

'Ah! Spare! I was thinking like a spare tyre. Sorry.'

Lucy couldn't help but smile at the guy. He'd make someone a great uncle.

'So, where to now?'

Alvaro pointed to his left. 'Follow me.'

They walked for a minute or two until they came to an archway that led out to a very small courtyard, no more than 10 meters square. A miniature fountain took up most of the space and the cold stone stare of a lion gargoyle met Lucy's gaze.

'Where are we, Alvaro? Just so I can get my bearings. I'm pretty sure I've never been here before.'

'We are just on the southern side of the palace and through that small doorway you will follow a path down to Bib-al-Gudur and your guide, Diego, will show you how to get from there to the graveyard that lies close to the Tower of the Seven Floors.'

At that moment, a stocky young guy in his early twenties appeared, dressed in paint covered denim shorts and a white t shirt so tight Lucy thought he might burst out of it any moment. He had a friendly face, handsome she guessed and a nice smile, which was just as well as, despite his size—he wasn't much taller than her—she wouldn't like to get on the wrong side of him. His muscles were beyond rippling, they were like steel ropes waiting to be unleashed. Lucy imagined that to many girls this would no doubt be very appealing.

'Diego, please, meet an esteemed colleague of mine, Lucy Hawksmoor. Be kind enough to guide her where she wants to go, but don't let her get lost!'

Diego grinned. He clearly was a man of few words. Just as well, thought Lucy.

'English, Diego? Or my broken Spanish?'

'English is okay, señora. Speak slowly and me, I am fine.' More grinning.

'Great, let's get going then. Thanks, Alvaro. Meet you at the front entrance as soon as I can.'

'Keep an eye on the time, Lucy.'

'Noted. Come on then, Macduff, lead on.'

Diego looked at her and, grinning again, opened the low doorway and they both stooped to pass through.

Alvaro said a prayer and headed back to the entrance to wait.

The graveyard was a series of rubble piles and pits, presumably once tombs. The sky above was patchy and the light changed from minute to minute as clouds drifted past the sun. Lucy made for the graves nearest the original entrance to the tower. Diego sat on a rock and just watched as she moved from spot to spot.

'You are looking for what, señora?'

'Not sure really. Any remaining markings that have not already been destroyed or removed I guess. In particular, an owl.'

'Owl?'

'Búho.'

'Ah, el búho. Entiendo!'

Lucy watched him for a moment as he seemed to practise saying the English version over and over. He looked like a Buddha who'd taken up weightlifting as he sat on the rocks. Then he looked up and called over to Lucy.

'I help?'

'OK. Si, gracias.'

Diego started towards the tower and began searching with Lucy. She was conscious of the time it was taking but didn't want to rush. Whilst Diego roamed around, head down, occasionally dropping into a pit out of sight, Lucy tried to look at the place from Boabdil's viewpoint. If he had come back, if, he would have needed to gain entry. The tower was the perfect spot as the Christians had adhered to his wishes and sealed up the gate and no one had used it for centuries after.

So, presumably, thought Lucy, it would not have been well defended. But there had been more tombs here then. And seven floors. Seven. She kept thinking back to the paper and the seven fingered Hand of Fatima. And the owl. The sign of kingship. Seven. Such a sacred number.

Lucy rested for a moment and took a water bottle form her shoulder bag.

Seven. She had read up the night before once again on the symbolism of this number. It had always held a fascination for her, how prime numbers in particular feature so heavily in different religious texts, architecture and even nature itself. She had read how in the Qur'an, seven is a literary device rather than sacred.

The reference to seven heavens and seven hells meant that there are innumerable layers. Seven is simply used to just suggest cosmic scale, which summed up her chances now of finding anything. They were on their own cosmic scale. But to the Arabs of the ancient world, pre-Islam it did have a more magical element to it. Magic. If only she could conjure up some magic now to point the way. But she couldn't see her getting anywhere in the time left. She picked up and counted out seven stones and began lobbing them gently toward the tower. Diego's head rose out of one of the pits.

'You, OK, señora?'

'Yes, sorry. I'm fine. Just frustrated.'

She was about to continue her search when Diego's voice rang out for the pit.

'Señora! Aqui! Aqui!'

She ran over, stumbling on the uneven surface. Diego's head was just below the pit and he was staring at what appeared to be a long stone lintel that edged the pit.

'Mira! Mira!'

Lucy jumped down and stared at where Diego's chubby index finger was pointing. There in the rock was an engraving.

183

Of an owl.

'Búho! Owl!'

Lucy could hardly believe her eyes. A carving of an owl, no more than 3 or 4 centimetres in height. Not the most ornate, in fact a rather crude representation, stylised, probably done in a hurry, but nevertheless, very clearly, an owl. She took a small brush from her bag and dusted away some umber sand to get a closer look. She stepped back and tried to take in its relevance. Why was it here? In this spot. So much had been disturbed over the centuries, was this the original place it was laid?

She looked up to the tower and then down towards its arched entrance. Something must have stood between here and the tower at one time, but what. This lintel, whatever it was seemed out of place somehow. Had it been put here, removed from somewhere else?

'Diego, how much do you know about Bib-al-Gudur?' She repeated it again, slowly.

'Si, yes, I have studied Alhambra for long time. I am studying antropología. How the people live here, what each part function as. So, I know this well.'

'An anthropologist. Wow.' Lucy had had him down for just a dog's body, how wrong she was.

'So,' she took out a small map of the southern section of the walls. 'Has the Tower always looked like this? Was there ever anything else here that is not here now. I know it's been rebuilt since 1812, but it was supposed to be an accurate rebuild of the original.'

'Pasos. They were here. Not here now. I think they were never replaced.'

'Pasos?'

'Si, pasos. It is another word for steps. Old use. Sorry, an old use. There was a lot of confusing in traducción, translation? Yes? Well.'

He was thinking hard, searching to find the right words. Lucy bit her lip to stay patient. He was doing well.

'Pisos can be, can mean 'layers', not only 'floors'.'

'Floors? Like Siete Suelos, seven floors? They were inside, er…estaban dentro, surely?'

'No, out here. I believe 'suelos', it is a later naming.'

'Sorry, Diego, I'm confused.'

'Bib-al-gudur was its name, you know. Tower of the Wells. But the name Tower Seven Floors, I think is a mystery, no? No people ever found seven floors, only two, so why the name?'

'But, what you are saying is that there were seven steps out here leading from the tower to the wall of the graveyard?'

'Yes, maybe they confuse the two words. Piso y paso.'

'Diego, oh my god. It's not a reference to the floors, it's a reference to the steps! Fuck me!'

'Sorry, señora?' He looked slightly shocked.

'I'm just excited, Diego. You are a genius.' She prodded his chest with her finger.

'A *bloody* genius.'

'Why is it a matter?'

'Oh that might have to wait. But believe me, matter it does.'

After a quarter of an hour scraping grass and weeds away from the surface it was clear that this was indeed a step and in Lucy's mind, it was the seventh step; one of seven steps, she calculated, given its width, that led down from the tower.

'Can we find out if anything lies beneath this step, Diego?'

'Yes, I can help with that. Wait here, please. I will five minutes only be.'

Ten minutes later, he was back carrying an instrument that brought a smile to Lucy's face.

'Diego, I may have to hire you at some point in the future. Thank you, thank you, thank you!'

Diego smiled and held out a geo-radar, a German made OKM Future i 160. Not the most expensive by any means but a very accurate hand help device for detecting amongst other things, spaces underground.

'Could you work it for me? Along the step and at its base, down in the pit?'

'Yes, certainly.'

Diego seemed to be having the time of his life and a more eager help, Lucy could not have wished for.

Lucy decided to stop jumping ahead of herself by striking up a conversation, whilst he tested out the battery.

'Do you have a girlfriend? Una novia?'

His grin was wide and long. 'No, señora, no una novia, but I have un novio. I'm gay.'

'You are a handsome guy, Diego. Your partner is lucky having you.' He grinned back at her, a little shy.

'You?'

'Er, no. None of either, though it would be una novia too, if I did.'

Diego smiled at her. This guy was so easy to be with. Not like some of the guys she knew. So gentle and a big heart.

'OK, let's see.' He gave Lucy the geo-radar to hold while he jumped into the pit. She handed it back and he switched it on. Lucy knelt to watch the small screen over his shoulder.

Neither of them could believe the result.

'Oh Jesus, Diego. Oh my god. There's something down there.'

Lucy never felt more alive than when she was close to a discovery, however small or large. She was tingling all over.

'I think. I would say it is more than a space. And the measurements, mas o menos, it is possibly a chamber, maybe, I think, a burial chamber.'

Lucy sat on the ground and wrapped her arms round her knees.

'Diego, I need you to not say anything, nada, about this. Not yet.'

'OK, Señora. No problem. But, it is not strange, no? This is a cemetery after all.'

'Well, for me, it is where it is on this site that makes it special.'

'What are you looking for exactly?'

'If I told you, you wouldn't believe me, trust me.'

'We could look in?'

'Look in? What? How?'

'We could maybe move this lintel. There may be steps, they are going down below, down into the chamber.'

'That is going to take some shifting, Diego, unless you're an Olympic weightlifter.'

'Yes, no problem. I can get some, er, some…'

'Equipment?'

'Si, yes, equipment, we can have it open in, er maybe, an hour.'

'I don't have that much time sadly.'

'I am ok with my boss; I ask a favour. Ask to give you one more hour.'

'You think he will be okay with that, really?'

'Yes, he is not only my boss. He is my boyfriend too!'

Lucy lay back and grinned at the sky. 'You are full of surprises, amigo.'

She watched as he clambered out of the pit.

'I will be twenty minutes. You wait here?'

'Yes, I'll be fine here. I'll have time to think. Make some notes. Can you pass a message on to my friend, Alvaro? Tell him to come back with you if he can.'

Diego nodded and headed off.

Lucy sat down again on the edge of the pit, feeling rather puzzled. She wondered what Diego was up to. She looked back over her shoulder to the doorway. Whatever equipment he thinks he's getting won't just be hanging around in a store cupboard. Moving that lintel would need time and care. And manpower and lots of paperwork from the local authority.

So, what's your plan, Diego? The only conclusion she could logically come to was that he was going to tell Victor. No doubt Diego would be back soon with Victor in tow. Wanting to know what was really going on. She realised her cynicism was unpleasant but she had lost a lot of trust in people recently.

The sky was clouding over and shafts of sunlight broke through only occasionally like a flickering torch shining through a forest of trees. Something was not right. It was too easy. Why this owl, here? Why one owl? Lucy's mind tumbled the words over and over. Seven floors. Seven steps.

She jumped back into the pit and in that split instant a glint of a stray beam of sun hit something several meters away catching Lucy's eyes for a nanosecond. But it was enough. She looked briefly at the owl again, then she saw it—the right wing was outstretched—as if pointing.

She hauled herself up, grazing her knees as she did so. She stared at the place where the glint of light had come from. Half stumbling, half running she quickly covered the distance, ignoring the pain of the cuts. A grate at the foot of the wall of the Tower of the Seven Floors. A water inlet? There were inlets all-round the Palace that had once brought water into the building from the nearby river. But here? In a graveyard? It didn't make sense.

She stooped and pulled away weeds that had encircled the grate half obscuring it from sight. The grating was loose and as she yanked at it, it gave slightly and a gap opened up. Then she saw it. In the bottom corner of the iron work, an engraving of an owl. This had to be a trail. Lucy had now gone into autopilot. The moment was taking over. This had to be it.

Her pale cotton shorts were now not so pale, covered in dust and dirt. She tucked her black t-shirt in, tied her ponytail up in a tight bunch and put her bag across her shoulder, tying the handles together to stop it slipping off. She took a look back at the doorway. No one there, yet. Then she began to ease herself through the narrow gap beneath the grate. Let's hope it's not a long way down. Please. She prayed as she always did, but it was more a desire not to be wrong than a plea for any divine intervention. Suddenly, a large lump of the ground gave way beneath her and she slipped down quickly stopping herself just in time before her head cracked against the foot of the grating. 'Fuck! That hurt.'

Her back sang out in pain. She clung on tight with her hands to the grating and lowered herself a little further to see how far down she had to go. Her hands were hurting like hell. She thought her toes touched solid ground. She hoped it was solid. She could hang on no longer.

She let go and, with a squeal, disappeared from view.

Chapter 26

Gomez's day was slipping from bad to very bad. It had not begun well either. Several cock-ups in communication had led to police not being in the right place at the right time and, although a few small groups had been stopped at the train station, the majority had come by coach or by car and had been missed. An unpleasant stand-off had ensued at the station and Gomez was of the distinct impression now that it had been staged as a decoy.

Too many officers had been sucked into the clash. Flares had been thrown, fencing torn down and used as shields as well as to hurl at the police who held back on any aggression, simply forming a blockade at the entrance to the station. But the rioters, most wearing face masks or balaclavas, seemed content to stay their hurling insults and jibes as well as bits of metal work and masonry. No effort was made to break through.

Then Gomez had learned that a mob of some 50 or so skinheads had assembled in Plaza de Trinidad shouting support for the Voz party who were holding their election hustings in the nearby Plaza Bib-Rambla. Police had arrived just in time to block the route to Plaza Nueva where PRUNE were holding their peaceful rally to raise the profile of the Muslim community.

Reports so far from his observers there, suggested nothing controversial was being said and it was mostly being ignored by passers-by, though it had drawn a small crowd of locals who were listening or signing a petition of some sort.

However, by 11 a.m. windows were being smashed in the Plaza Trinidad and some passers-by had been attacked or hit by missiles; sadly, the injured were all Muslims who had clearly been in the wrong place at the wrong time. One elderly resident needed stitches and some Muslim youths had now turned up to voice their opposition to the far-right chants.

The police were having a hard time keeping the groups apart. Gomez could not see how these thugs could possibly be seen to be doing the cause of Voz any good, but when he had messaged their representative to ask for someone to come down to Trinidad to talk to them, she had replied that people were simply fed up with immigrants and this was the result of successive governments doing nothing to halt the influx, that the people had had enough and were bound to take matters into their own hands. Gomez had no time to point out before she cut him off that most of these people were not from Granada and according to reports, some not even from Spain.

When Gomez arrived on the scene, after having realised the station affray was going nowhere, he stood behind a police van and watched the protesters through binoculars. One guy, a rather tall skinhead with various tattoos on his forehead and neck was spouting forth in a mixture of Spanish and German. He got Rueda on the police radio.

'José, are you nearer than me, can you see the guy with the megaphone.'

'That guy we have already put a name to, boss. That's our friend Jurgen Schneider.'

'Fuck, of course. I can't believe he's surfaced in day light. He's got several international arrest warrants out for him. And here he is, putting two fingers up.'

'I know. And we can't just go in and take him. It would be a blood bath and he knows it.'

'If he is here, then he must know he has an escape route. Eyes on him at all times. I want all routes in and out of Plaza Trinidad blocked as best we can.'

'Most already are, boss. But this is a powder keg. I have a nasty feeling they're going to make a move towards the PRUNE gathering.'

Gomez was just wondering how worse this could get when a group of skinheads and men in masks made a break and ran at the Muslim teens hurling rocks and what looked like large marbles over the heads of the police toward them. Several went down with head wounds and panic ensued. The police at the front charged forward with batons and shields and fights broke out at random points.

'Jesus, Mary and Joseph, what a fucking mess,' thought Gomez.

Arrests started to be made and several of the thugs were dragged off to waiting police vans.

Then suddenly, most of the remaining group formed a ring round Schneider and he raised the megaphone, this time focussing his words on the police and those watching.

'The time has come people of Granada to wake up to what is happening to your beautiful city. Foreigners and terrorists are infiltrating your world, taking your jobs and polluting your atmosphere. These Muslim scum will take over everything if you do not make a stand.'

The noise around began to grow again.

Gomez radioed Rueda. 'Can't we stop this bastard, José?'

'How?'

Jurgen Schneider continued to rant on, invoking the memory of Franco and even Isabella and Ferdinand. Gomez began to think he was sounding a little like Hitler, as he railed and his voice got higher and more angry. Each comment was punctuated by cheers from his supporters and sadly, thought Gomez, even by some from one or two of those listening, though maybe Voz supporters had come over to hear what was going on.

He knew that there were pockets everywhere of closet Francoists; those of the old guard still alive who wanted a return to days of suppression that they just saw as restoring order as well as their desire to rid the country of those seen by them as degenerates and deviants. Which, thought Gomez, was anyone who simply wanted freedom of expression, be it through religion or sexuality. These people wanted to take Spain back to the dark days of 1939.

Well, they're not doing it here, thought Gomez.

'Rueda, can you hear me. Start sending in snatch squads and pick them off one by one. We need to get Schneider.'

'Loud and clear, boss.'

The next few minutes were mayhem. Schneider's group had gone on the offensive and were now attacking the police as they rushed them. Stones and other missiles were thrown. An officer went down as he was hit by what looked like a club or baseball bat. His helmet had come off and blood spattered the pavement. A lot of the onlookers had by now run away and the young Muslim boys had been encouraged to move back and let the police sort it out.

The space was too confined for tear gas, but Rueda had called in a van with a water cannon.

As the spiral of whooshing water hit the front wave of protesters, the police began to swiftly move in and grab those who fell, dragging them off in handcuffs.

The rest began running in all directions, heading for any gap or side street or shop entrance they could get to. Gomez realised he could no longer see Jurgen Schneider.

'José, where the fuck is Schneider?'

'No idea. He's made a break for it somehow.'

'Find him!'

Only a minute had passed when Gomez got another call from Rueda.

'Boss, I've just spoken to one of our guys at the PRUNE rally, a group of protesters is heading towards them. Doesn't look good.'

'Who the hell are they? More of the same?'

'Not sure, I'm heading over there now.'

'Keep in touch, radio me as soon as you've assessed the situation.'

Half an hour passed. The tension had eased in Plaza Trinidad and the police had things more under control. Arrests had been made and many of the far-right protesters had scattered. The place looked a mess, chairs and tables from cafeterias and restaurants were strewn everywhere, broken windows here and there appeared to gaze blankly and with surprise at the chaos. Cans and bottles rolled around the Plaza like drunks on their way home. Nothing from Rueda yet.

Gomez took an officer with him and headed over to Plaza Nueva.

'Sir, by the way, did you get the message from HQ?'

'Hold on Mahrez. Tell me in a moment.'

The streets in between suddenly seemed eerily quiet but as they approached the site of the PRUNE meeting Gomez could taste the tension in the air. Their way into the square though appeared to be blocked. A large group stood staring at him, filling the street. On lookers? They certainly didn't appear to be rioters that was for sure.

Rueda buzzed in. 'Are you seeing this, boss?'

'I can see zilch at the moment. I've turned up Calle Elvira and it's blocked.'

'You won't believe this but I haven't seen anything like it. I'm in the middle of the Plaza by the PRUNE party stand. A small group, I'd say maybe 15 or 20 of those skinheads from Plaza Nueva got here somehow and they were clearly hell bent on spoiling the PRUNE party, but they can't get near them. And it's not 'cos of us.'

'Well?'

'Well, because we are all currently protected by a human shield of shopkeepers, grandads, teenagers, ladies of all degrees of social standing and even kids. Dogs in there too. And not many of them are Muslim either.'

'How come there's no shouting? I can't really hear anything'

'The only noise is from the mob on Placeta de San Gil. Throwing insults and chanting occasionally but the crowd are just giving them the silent treatment, just staring. But they have successfully blocked every entrance to the square, boss.

The locals have turned out in support of their Muslim neighbours. It's incredible.'

'Could be dangerous too.' Despite his fears though, Gomez could not have been more amazed and proud of these people.

'I'll double back up Calle Reyes Catolicos and go round the back to Placeta San Gil. Can you direct some police officers to meet me there?'

'Sure thing but be careful.'

The crowd stared back at him and several smiled but Gomez decided not to say anything. This was their city and clearly they had decided to protect it and more importantly, each other. It went against all his training, but this was mob rule he could live with for the moment.

The backstreet journey round to Placeta San Gil took him past the rear of several houses and shops, mostly restaurants as the mixture of smells clearly bore witness.

Suddenly, what sounded like firecrackers exploding not far away ripped the air.

Then to his utter disbelief a riderless police horse came careering round the corner towards them. His fellow officer tried to grab the reins and was dragged several metres before letting go and falling to the ground cursing. Two officers appeared shouting if he'd seen anyone.

'That bastard, the German guy, he shot Valverde.'

Valverde was one of the few mounted police they had in Granada. Gomez knew him well and only last year attended his wedding. He could only be in his early 30s. He couldn't believe it.

'He ran this way.'

'He must have got here just before us then; he hasn't passed us.'

'Christ he could be anywhere.'

Gomez got on his radio and pulled in units to search the buildings along the street.

'What the fuck did he shoot him for?

'He'd got hold of one of the Muslim teenagers in the blockade and was giving him a beating. The other people then went to help as Valverde arrived on the scene. Then the German tries to run past him. Valverde caught him on the shoulder with his truncheon. He drops to the ground, pulls out a pistol and shoots several times. Valverde fell backwards off his horse as it reared up.'

'Is he dead?'

'He's not in a good shape but he was being attended to as we ran after the guy.'

'You sure it was Jurgen Schneider?'

'Fitted your description.'

'He's clearly a fucking maniac. I want him caught. I don't care in what state.'

Gomez let Rueda know what was happening. The locals he learned had now turned on the mob and they were dispersing quickly, as they were simply outnumbered.

Then he got a call from an officer at the far end of the street.

'We think he's holed up in a bar. Casa Lola. We have eyes on all entrances. Someone said they saw him go in.'

'I'm on my way.'

His partner, Mahrez, was limping after his tussle with the horse.

'You OK, Mahrez?'

'Yes, I'm fine, boss. Shaken but fine.'

'Sorry, you said earlier something about a message?'

'Yes, Rodriguez has been trying to get hold of you. Something about a woman called Lucy Hawksmoor. Said it was urgent but you're not answering your phone. I explained the situation here and he asked if you could phone him when you can.'

'Really? Long ago?'

'Just before we came here.'

'I'll call now. You go ahead. I'll catch up.'

'Happy to wait.'

'Go, they'll need you.'

He turned his phone back on. Two rings and Rodriguez picked up.

'Last thing you possibly want to hear at the moment, but you did ask to be informed if we got anything about this Lucy Hawksmoor's movements.'

'Not now Matias, this can wait.'

'Not sure it can. A guy called, wait a mo… yes, a guy called Alvaro Castilla called in, asking for you. He's up at the Alhambra doing some work there and says he saw someone trying to attack this Hawksmoor lady.'

'Is she OK?'

'Yeah, she's fine but this Alvaro is concerned that someone wants to do her harm. We sent guys up there. Most of the Nacional are with you so we pulled in a Guardia Civil car off the highway.'

'Good, thank you.'

'But what's odd is he said she'd gone home in a taxi. Call me Mr Sixth Sense but I wasn't convinced. Especially when he said I didn't need to send anyone round to check on her.'

Gomez could just imagine Matias adjusting his red Gucci glasses.

He was desperate for him to get to the point. 'Which means you did check up on her.'

'Bingo! And she wasn't there. So, I called Señor Castilla back, just now in fact and he sounded not great. Sounded upset but denied it when I asked, wouldn't say what they had been up to or were doing there either. Said it was coincidence. He was visiting a colleague. Blah Blah. There's nothing official logged with the Local Authority, apart from one Victor Morata who is registered to do research there but neither she nor Castilla are on the approved list with his group.'

'Really! Now that is interesting.'

'There's more. I have bad news and bad news. Which do you want first, boss?'

'For fuck's sake, Rodriguez, we are in the middle of a major incident here including mob violence and a manhunt and you're playing games with me. Just cut the crap and tell me what's happening.'

There was an audible gulp.

'Apologies. Point taken. So, we have had word from the GEO that when they raided Jilani's home after his death, they found an encrypted laptop which they've accessed and amongst the photos on it is one of Gloria Sarmiyento Ruiz and she's wearing a suicide vest. So now, of course, they want to talk to her but she's done a runner.'

'Gloria, the friend of Lucy Hawksmoor? Well, well.'

Gomez had never got round to making his own enquiries as he had promised Lucy and now he regretted it.

'And the last piece—GEO also let us know an hour ago that they have INTEL on Ximena Martinez and that she may be in Granada too and that she has been having Lucy watched. They didn't give their source but when do they ever.'

'I need to let Señor Hawksmoor know. You try her mobile. I'll forward her number. Find out what the Guardia Civil guys at the Alhambra are up to—tell them if they find Hawksmoor they need to pull her in for her own safety. I need to sort this mess out here first. I'll be in touch soon. Wait till I call you. And thank you.'

He hung up.

Mahrez met him at the top of the street and within half an hour police had swarmed through the building.

But they found nothing. No sign at all. But they knew he'd been there. The unconscious body of the owner tied up in an upstairs toilet was enough to decide that, plus the open skylight that he must have climbed up to and out onto the roof. And away.

Gomez knew this was bad. Very bad.

Chapter 27

'Who enters my chambers finds my treasures, my pomegranate, my myrrh, my cinnamon, my nectar.'

Ibn-Gabirol

Alvaro stood in the centre of the graveyard and looked around. The place seemed eerie in the late morning gloom.

'Well, where is she?'

'She, she was just here. She said she'd wait.' Diego looked worried. 'I need to tell Victor. He will not like it that she is looking round on her own. If anything happens, he will get in trouble. Did he say where he was going?'

'To meet someone apparently. Another guest to show round the work he's doing. And I doubt you'll be in trouble. You can blame me. So, why did you come back by the way? Just to get me? Or were you going to tell Victor something? Something about Lucy's search?'

'No, not at all. I came to get you. She asked for you. But when Victor gets back from wherever he is, of course I have to tell him something. What we did. I work for him, señor, not you or the lady.'

'Give her twenty minutes, she'll appear. Maybe she followed you back and is looking round the Tower itself.'

'Yes, OK, maybe. I will go look there for her. Wait here. Please.'

Alvaro sighed and rubbed the small of his back. He detested being so tall. As he'd grown older the pains had got worse, not that his job had helped, craning his neck to read script high on ceilings on tiptoes in a cherry picker. Oddly, he had never been great with heights either. He wanted the quiet life really, so what the hell he thought am I doing here? And where on god's earth have you gone Lucy Hawksmoor?

He surveyed the site slowly, like a shepherd looking for a lost sheep. Diego had shown him the owl in the pit and explained what she had said about the seven steps. Now he was trying to think like Lucy. What had she deduced? He refrained from jumping into the pit, he doubted he'd get out again. He walked to the base of the tower and followed the line of the wall north. Then he saw it. The grate. Low down, partially covered with weeds but at its foot a gaping hole, not big, but big enough he surmised for a slim, determined 28-year-old woman to pass through. But why would she go through here? A water passage? Then he whispered it out loud as he thought it through.

Alvaro moved away and to the far side of the ground to look back at the wall. There was only one other inlet he could see and it was beyond the wall of the grave site. He walked over, clambering across the rubble of what was once a high wall and looked closely at the grate there. It looked different but couldn't figure out why. Like when you look at those puzzles, he thought–two pictures seemingly identical and you had to spot the differences. And there was one. It had to be. He counted the bars, eight. He moved back to the graveyard grating as quickly as he could. His back was giving him serious aggravation now. His sciatica was clearly kicking back in as well down his left leg.

'Incredible,' he said aloud. 'Seven bars. Seven everywhere surrounding the tower of the Seven Floors. Seven steps.' He knelt down and peered through. Then he saw the owl motif, almost like a stamp in the iron work. Intricate. Not obvious at all. But an owl. He peered back to the pit. Alvaro had a feeling that at one time there would have been a trail of some kind. A trail of owls leading here, because way back when there would have been tomb stones here, small dividing walls, other obstacles now crumbled to dust, blown up or just simply moved.

Alvaro smiled. Are you really down there, Lucy Hawksmoor?

Quietly he did his best to hide the gap with a few rocks and some weeds.

As he stood up a voice took him by surprise.

'Found something interesting, Señor?'

Diego was watching him from the other side of the pit.

'No, sadly not.'

Diego walked over to him looking out of breath and sweating like a hog. 'I cannot find Victor. Please could you come and help me. I am worried.'

'Of course. On my way. No sign of Lucy Hawksmoor either?'

'No, no sign.'

Alvaro headed for the archway that would lead them back to the entrance.

Diego stared at the grate at his feet for a moment. No, surely not, he thought. Then he turned and followed Alvaro out.

****

Lucy had taken a little while to get her eyes adjusted to the dark. She checked her bag and felt around for her Maglite torch. The beam swept around and welcomed her into the inner world of the palace walls. She was standing on a ledge of what looked like a channel that led down a gentle slope, but the roof seemed higher than she imagined it should be for a water inlet.

She would have to stoop to walk but at least she wouldn't have to crawl—not something she ever liked doing since the time early on in her career, when on a field trip she nearly got trapped in a cave system near Zaragoza while searching for a cache of gold coins thought to have been hidden from the invading Berbers. There were no coins and nearly no Lucy Hawksmoor. She still bore the scar, now hidden by her hairline, from the deep cut she got whilst being rescued. She always touched it when she needed reminding not to do anything stupid or dangerous or both. She touched it now.

'Oh well, what's the worst that can happen?'

She heard voices back in the graveyard coming closer, which made her mind up for her.

Until she had left the grating a few meters behind she walked in the dark then switched her torch back on. She had gone maybe 10 meters when suddenly she came upon a large pit.

She couldn't believe what she was looking at. Down in the pit stood an aljibe—a type of water tank used by the Moors to store clean water. Lucy had written a piece for a travel magazine several years before on the 25 aljibes dotted around the Albaicin. She knew there were a couple just inside the palace walls too, but one down here? Maybe, thought Lucy, this was built just for the Bib-al-Gudur, the original name for the gate above, the Gate of the Wells.

Maybe there were more down here. It was built of brick and looked like a small house with an arched entrance. But by the look of the decay around it and the smell, no one had ventured down here for a very, very long time. Gingerly, Lucy walked down the narrow steps into the pit. She could hear scuttling close by, no doubt rats making way for her. She knew something was odd. The placing of this here didn't seem to make sense.

'Come on think, Lucy,' she whispered into the dark. The Christian conquerors never really understood how the water system of the Alhambra worked which was one of the reasons it quickly fell into disrepair. They never tampered with any of the aljibes which was why they survived, probably they imagined that destroying them would hasten the water drying up. And they were often miniature works of art, the Moors did nothing by halves.

Lucy's mind was beginning to rush forward as she shone her torch over the building that stood not much taller than her.

What better place to hide something, than in a place the Christians thought was for another purpose. That is if they ever even got down here. Which she was beginning to doubt—the whole place smelt and felt unvisited, unloved. The front was seemingly well blocked off as it should be though there should have been some kind of door there to gain access if need be, if, of course, it was a water tank.

There was not a lot of space around it so she slowly skirted the rectangular edifice looking for any clues. Then as she rounded the corner at the rear her light caught an engraving.

Another owl. Low down, on a lintel similar to the one in the pit in the graveyard. Clearly various creatures of the dark had had a go at the grouting, but as she looked over the rear wall, she could see the outline that told her that here had once been a small door.

Lucy bent down to the owl and above it there was a hole where something had clearly burrowed in, probably a long time ago given the state of the moss around it. It didn't look like human intervention. After a few minutes she had widened the hole enough to shine her torch through and allow her to peer at what lay within. But not with the naked eye. She'd see zero.

She pulled out of her bag a handheld endoscope. A small piece of kit, not that expensive but it had over the years proved its weight in gold in the way of archaeological finds. She fed the start of the 5-metre length camera tube in through the gap and switched on the 4-inch LED screen.

At first nothing much seemed visible, then she realised she needed to pull back a little. And when she did, her heart skipped several beats and her mouth went arid dry.

It was a tomb. A tomb she felt she had seen before. Not as high as a Christian tabletop tomb, almost more like a stone sarcophagus, but there, lying on the top, was the clear outline of a woman's body, her arms down by her side, hands up turned as if in prayer. The folds of her dress were obvious and yet almost too real to be stone. But weirdly and this spooked Lucy slightly, no face and not much of a torso—almost as if it had been left unfinished.

Who the hell are you, thought Lucy?

As she manoeuvred the scope, she realised that around the tomb were chests. They looked as if they were made out of leather or perhaps it was lacquered wood–hard to tell from distance–but as her pulse began to sprint she could clearly make out that they had not been touched or interfered with for a very, very long time. If ever.

Lucy was just about to switch the machine off and decide what to do next when she realised she was not alone. Faintly in the distance, coming down the tunnel she could hear soft footfall. Someone trying to not be heard.

Someone who knew she was down here.

Someone who was looking for her. And not, Lucy sensed someone who wished her well.

She packed the scope away and shone her torches thin beam around her. No way out, which in that moment struck her as peculiar because if her calculations were right, given where the steps were when Diego registered the chamber there should be more than just this space. She waited with her back against the rear of the aljibe that wasn't an aljibe–the uninvited guest would have to choose one side to come down. Lucy was trying to keep calm but her stomach was in multiple knots. A torch beam struck the wall on her left and Lucy gave out a little gasp.

Then a voice she instantly recognised spoke quietly into the dark; one she had hoped she would never have to listen to ever again.

'Hello, Lucy Hawksmoor.'

Ximena Martinez, the leader of Casa Social, the woman who had threatened her at her lecture in Madrid. Lucy couldn't believe it. How the fuck did she find me here?

'I know you're there, Lucy. You obviously chose not to listen to my advice. People who interfere in things they do not understand often come to an unfortunate end I find. And your end will be more appropriate than most I guess. Entombed with your work.'

Lucy couldn't summon up any words. She had no idea what to say or whether to say anything at all. Her mouth was as dry as the dust she stood on. This was not a world she was used to. She was no female Indiana Jones and didn't want to be. Right now she just wanted to be back in Cordoba with her cat and a cold beer.

'Are you coming out or shall I come to you. Or I could just go back and block the grate up I guess. Leave you alone here with your thoughts. A pity you didn't find anything other than this aljibe. Though I don't want to give you another chance to find anything else, I'm afraid. Time has run out for you, Lucy Hawksmoor. You have chosen the wrong people to support.'

'Why are you doing this? It's crazy. You think killing me will matter one bit in the grand scheme of things? I'm just a professor of history for fuck's sake.'

'Not just, Lucy. You know something. You've found something. Someone might be down here, someone of no consequence to us. But someone nonetheless who should, if he *is* here, be left here.'

Lucy could feel the sweat run down the nape of her neck. This was not good. How had things got to this?

'I don't know what you're on about.'

'Now you insult me. We have followed your interest in the last king of the Moors. We have had you followed, watched you and your friend, Gloria. And we have seen the picture of the piece of paper that was on her phone. We do not know what it means, but we know it's significant to your search. Since seeing it you have been doing lots of delving. All interesting but also dangerous.'

Jesus Christ thought Lucy. Not good, not good at all.

Lucy didn't want to beg, but the situation here was making her feel very scared. A fear like she had never experienced before.

'Look, I'll give up the search. Just let me go. I don't think you're a killer, Ximena.'

'I never thought I was either but then you wake up. I have orders and I'm afraid I have to follow them. And I will be happy to have you as my first kill. Especially as you are also a lesbian and I hate lesbians. All queers are scum, just like Muslims and Jews.'

'Well, you know what, fuck you!'

Lucy decided in blind panic to take her chances. She started to turn the corner towards Ximena's torch beam and it caught her for a fleeting second, then a gunshot followed a split second later, cannoning off the rock by Lucy's head. She had no time to think now. Ximena ran down the side but Lucy had already headed back along the far side of the aljibe. Lucy heard her curse, then scream in pain as she tripped over something. She turned near the tunnel entrance for a split second to look and saw a handgun spinning along towards her along the ground. She wasn't going to go back for it. She got to the grate and blue sky stared down at her; then she realised she hadn't figured out how she was going to get back up.

The sound of Ximena crawling toward her made her mind up for her. She took one step back then scrabbled up as high as she could, missed her foothold and slid back again, almost losing a shoe in the process. She tried again and this time managed to get one hand on the lower bars of the grate. Her knees were scraped and sore. Then she sensed movement behind her.

'Stop there or I'll fucking shoot you dead.'

At that moment a hand clung to her wrist and another voice spoke to her—this time one she thought she would never hear again.

'I've got you. Give me your other hand.' Lucy did as she was told and despite the pain in her back, wrists and hands she found she was half pulling herself and half being dragged up though the space below the grating. Though she was expecting to be shot any second, the will to survive had taken over, there was no going back. Her upper body was half out then she heard it, the click of the handgun.

It jammed.

The banshee like cry that followed was terrifying and Lucy felt a rush of fear scourge her spine.

'You queer whore bitch, I'm coming for you!'

Then Lucy was out.

She was helped over to a nearby wall and sat leaning against it, eyes closed, breathing hard.

When Lucy opened her eyes, there, kneeling before her was Gloria, hair tied back, sweat glistening on the amber skin of her brow and a warm smile that Lucy had missed.

She put out her arms. Lucy sat up and fell into them, hugging her tightly.

'Are we safe?'

'She isn't going to get out of there anytime soon and anyway, the police will be here any minute no doubt.'

'You didn't get to the demo then?'

Gloria released Lucy and let her sit back against the wall. She bowed her head.

'I was never going. I had other places I had to be. But then, only minutes after we drove away, I spotted Martinez sitting on a café terrace on her phone. It was too coincidental. I asked to be let out. My friend was angry but understood. Said he would come back for me later. Maybe he will. We'll see. I had to see what she was up to. After a while she headed off and I followed, watched her meet Victor Morata at the doorway and shake hands then disappear inside.'

'Oh my god, she knows him? So how did you get in?'

'Through a side entrance, my cousin let me in.'

Lucy was now confused. 'Your cousin? No, wait a minute, not Diego?'

Gloria smiled. 'I have a lot of cousins. I told him you were coming here today and to watch out for you if he could.'

'You are one dark horse, Miss Sarmiyento.'

Diego at that moment was placing a rock in front of the gap beneath the grate. Muffled sounds of swearing and various insults were escaping from below.

'That should hold her for a while. Not that she looks as if she can even stand at the moment. Come Gloria, time to go. The police are on their way.'

Lucy pulled herself upright and they stared at each other.

'You're going again? Why? What's up, Gloria. Tell me what's going on. Are the police after you?'

Gloria inclined her head, not wanting to make eye contact.

'What for?'

'It's all in the letter, Lucy. I have to go. I have no choice but I know I want to see you again someday. If you still want to see me, that is.'

'Of course, I do.'

Then, for a split second, Lucy thought Gloria was about to kiss her. She closed her eyes. She could sense her lips so close.

'Gloria!'

Diego pulled her away.

Lucy stared after her as they ran through the arched doorway. Her heart was beating fast and she suddenly felt like crying but she didn't know why. Her feelings were a mess. She sat back down again and tried to give herself a good talking to. That was how Gomez found her.

An hour later, Lucy was trying to get her head around all that had happened and trying to figure out what to do next. The Inspector had explained what had happened in Granada centre. How the locals of all description had stood against the far right mob and protected their Muslim neighbours. How Jurgen Schneider had escaped but was later shot dead at a roadblock to the north of the city, trying to escape on a stolen motorbike.

The intel he had received that Martinez was following Lucy, and about the guy who had tried to snatch her bag who had no doubt been working for her. And what had happened to Alvaro and Victor. The latter had apparently been duped by Martinez, thinking she was a journalist interested in his restoration work. Stolen credentials. She locked him in his office. Not before beating him with the butt of a pistol to make him tell her where Lucy had gone.

'And Alvaro? Please tell me he's OK.'

'He's fine. He's had to go to hospital for stitches. She hit him over the head with something but fortunately this Diego guy found him, stemmed the bleeding and hid him safely till we got here. We found him in a cupboard near the room where Victor was.'

'And Ximena Martinez ended up coming more quietly than we expected. She was not in a good way. She'd twisted her ankle very badly and was concussed after hitting her head in a fall.'

'I'm afraid I'm not too bothered about her condition. Just glad you got her. Though why her, why not send one of her cronies after me?'

'She claims she had had no choice but to kill you herself. Says she was being blackmailed somehow. She wouldn't go into detail. But she was more compliant than I'd expected, I kind of believe her; it's never been her style to be directly violent, but these small groups of far-right morons are now prey to the larger more dangerous far right groups spreading through Europe. Its dog eat dog, even if the dog is one of yours. But having her in custody is at least a victory of sorts. Never thought we'd get her on anything and then she suddenly does this.'

'She's deranged, Inspector and believe me, she wanted to kill me down there. She's only saying all that as an excuse.'

'No doubt you're right. Maybe because she knew Schneider was dead she felt safer telling me something.'

He opened a bottle of water and handed it to Lucy.

'Are you going to tell me what the two of you were doing in a water tunnel?'

Lucy smiled. 'In time, Inspector, in time.'

'OK and what about how you got out of the tunnel? My men said they had to use a grappling rope to get out.'

'I guess that's because someone wasn't trying to kill them. The desire to stay alive gave me strength I didn't know I had.'

'Indeed. Quite the spider girl.'

Lucy stared at him.

'I'm sorry. Not a time for jokes. Bad taste.'

Lucy noticed he'd actually gone red again. Jesus, she thought, he really has got a crush on me.

'It is but I forgive you.'

'I'll need you to come to the station, Lucy. Give us a brief statement and then we can discuss your friend Gloria. We need to find her.'

'I don't know anything, I'm afraid.'

'Well, when you come, I'll tell you what we know and why we want to speak to her. You need to hear it from me but now isn't the time. First you need to go home and sort yourself out. A car will take you to your room, wait and then bring you back to the station.'

'No need. I'll make my own way. I'll be fine.'

Chapter 28

It was late afternoon by the time Lucy was sitting in a quiet, dark corner of the Ras Café bar on Carrera del Darro with a beer and a few olives. The letter from Gloria lay on the table in front of her. She closed her eyes and thought back to what had happened at the Alhambra.

What she found, what might still be there.

The police hadn't batted an eyelid about what Lucy was doing down by the aljibe. Gomez had been his usual gentlemanly self, in the end insisting on driving her home himself. There was a lot she had to do. She knew she had to speak to Alvaro soon. She'd ring him after she'd spoken again to the police. Figure out what to do next.

And so to Gloria. Lucy's feelings for her over the past weeks had swung from liking her to mistrusting her, then to worrying about her and then to that kiss. Well, almost. Was it just a moment of relief or of madness or did she really feel something for her? And why would Gloria have kissed her?

Lucy slit open the envelope and took out the piece of folded A4 paper. She took a long sip of beer and read.

'Mi querida amiga,

I have so much to say to you, about how I feel, about my wishes for the future, but I want to save it until we have more than just a fleeting moment together. We have been through a lot in a short time and I know you have not always trusted me, yet you did me the honour of believing at least in the piece of red paper and the message it brought us from the past. And you are going to follow it through to the end, I know. I see your passion for the past and indeed for the truth in every fibre of your body. I am so proud of you, Lucy. I wish I could be as good a person as you. But I have to go away for a while. I have not always been what you see today. I have let my father down and my own self through stupidity and naivety. I am a better person now though. I really believe it and meeting you has made me realise there is something positive to live for.

When I first came to you, I thought I was truly doing what all guardians of the silver pouch had wanted to do for centuries—find someone to give it to who would understand it and do with it what needed to be done to bring the truth from the darkness of the past into the light. But I had, as you now know, got mixed up with some bad people. Believe me, Lucy, when I say I have been trying my best to be the daughter my father wants me to be, to be someone he is proud of. But when my mother left home, I made his life difficult at times and over recent years I went with the wrong crowd.

I felt so committed to the cause of PRUNE and to help our people regain their pride and standing in the community and the country. I made friends who were exciting and vibrant like Reda. But then things changed when Jilani came along. He was so persuasive and magnetic in his speeches. I was warned several times by others that they thought he was trying to radicalise the youth of the party. It was when Reda started to change that I realised too late that the man was dangerous. One night we had been drinking, something neither Reda nor I had done much before. Jilani was encouraging us and then he made Reda put on a mock suicide vest, for a joke he said. And he took pictures of him wearing it and shouting and laughing. And, to my eternal shame, I allowed Reda to put it on me. And Jilani photographed me in it.

The next morning, he showed them to me, along with several obscene pictures he had taken whilst I was asleep. He threatened to show them to my father if I did not do as he asked. I know it would have killed my father to see them. And so, one of the things he wanted was for me to meet you. He had read all about you, told me about you, showed me videos of you lecturing. I lied when I said I had been following your work for years. Jilani had. He knew you were looking for Boabdil's last resting place and he saw in you a vehicle to find the truth about Boabdil and what he believed was the secret contained in the pouch.

Yes, he knew my father had the pouch, one night I had boasted about it to Reda and some others when I had stupidly been smoking some marijuana and Reda told Jilani. None of us knew what the pouch contained and I, of course, refused to show it to him.

Anyway, he got me to convince my father that I should take it to you. I will never know now, of course, what he wanted from it. But I think he was hoping maybe that the pouch contained the location of a supposed hidden Nasrid treasure chest, a myth that has lasted since Boabdil left—that he had hidden gold and jewels somewhere in the palace for when, as he believed, the Moors would one day return and reclaim the Alhambra and Granada.

Jilani was always talking to the party about the importance of financing and the need to 'grow the power of the party' as he put it. He was mad and at times he spoke as if he was somehow the heir to Boabdil. I know now too that he had killed before; he told me and he also said he would never be taken alive. I never really believed him but his attitude towards Reda's death was so horrible, he almost wanted to use it as a reason to hit back at the non-Muslims.

So, I have to go away because I fear the police will not believe me. I know they have the photos. Officer Carrasco, called me to warn me. She seems to care and wants to help. They need a scapegoat, I fear, for losing one of their officers when Jilani blew himself up. I am convinced it was Jilani who had my father's house raided looking for the pouch because Carrasco also told me that since finding the photos the police went back to search the house and they say they found a gun, drugs and some explosives hidden in a wardrobe in my bedroom. Jilani's men must have planted them there in case he ever needed anything extra to hold against me. My poor father must be so upset and angry. I cannot bring myself to speak to him, but the letter you have for him explains everything.

If you feel you could, please put in a good word for me with Inspector Gomez. Maybe that is asking too much. I don't really deserve it.

So, there you have it. You have now many reasons to hate me and to never trust me again. But I have changed, Lucy. I only want peace for our people and peace for myself. I want you to find Boabdil and do what you think best. I am not a criminal.

And one more thing—perhaps the most important—the main reason I have to go, I have to give you space because I think I am in love with you. I have never had these feelings before and I need to take time to think them through. And to give you time too. If I stayed and told you this to your face, I do not think I could bear the rejection if you said you hated me and never wanted to see me again.

I wish you well with your search. I will find you at some point in the future. And by then I will know what I want and I hope when we do meet, you too will know what you want. I will know by your face, no words will be necessary, so do not worry that I will make life difficult for you. You are a special person, Lucy E. Hawksmoor. Go with peace and may Allah watch over you.

Gloria x

Lucy sat back, tears filling her eyes. So many emotions flooded over her. She knew she should be angry but she also knew it was going to be hard to stay mad at Gloria Sarmiyento Ruiz for very long. Then she cried more than she had done in a very long time.

Chapter 29

Cordoba-One Month Later

Lucy and Alvaro sat opposite each other at a corner table in the small walled terrace at El Rincon. No one else was around, despite the November weather being a pleasant 18 degrees and the sun cutting a sharp figure in the cloudless blue above. A bottle of water and a bottle of Albariño stood between them, as well as a few plates of untouched tapas. Alvaro had been so good and helpful over the preceding weeks.

He looked worn out as he sat in his crumpled blue cotton jacket and open necked shirt, unusual for him to be so casual but Lucy had noticed how he had visibly relaxed more and more since she had known him. He sat almost slouched, as ever trying to hide his height, elbows resting on the arms of his chair, hands steepled together beneath his chin, eyes closed. His hair seemed to have gained a few more wisps of silver but his moustache had clearly been treated to a trim and was less wild than it had been in Granada. He had several stitches, but the wound had healed quickly. Lucy had a real soft spot for him; he just seemed to 'get' her and, despite being 30 years older, was fun to be with as well as being patient and kind and very loyal.

Lucy sipped her wine and reflected on what had happened since Gloria took off. And she wondered once again where she was now. She'd had no word, not even a simple text saying she was OK. Inspector Gomez had explained a little more about why they were pursuing her and it had not done a lot for Lucy's confidence in Gloria's character or motives but she had decided to try and think the best of her. She so wanted Gomez to be wrong.

According to him, the GEO had not only found the pictures on Jilani's laptop as she had described, but also they had found a detonator near the teteria in Granada. It could have been used to trigger the explosion of Jilani's suicide vest. They would never know now but they found Gloria's DNA on it. Had she been

211

the back up if his vest didn't go off? Had she detonated it anyway to get rid of him? Or, as Lucy was hoping, had someone planted her DNA on it?

As long as Gloria was in hiding, the finger of guilt was very much pointing at her. Lucy had done her bit, backing Gloria up, saying she didn't have it in her. But Gomez argued, politely, that Gloria had every motive to want Jilani dead. Sadly, it looked that way but still, Lucy wanted to hear it from Gloria.

She was worried, confused and angry all at the same time. None of it seemed to make sense to her but Lucy had realised she had, for everyone's sake to focus on their find at the Alhambra, as that was what this ultimately was all linked to.

It turned out that Ximena had tripped over the lip of a trap door. Lucy with the help of Alvaro and Victor got permission to go back and investigate. Victor did not, as she had thought, in any way wish to stand in her way. Indeed, his input got things moving way faster than normal. He also said that if she needed any of his support or advice regarding any findings to just ask.

When, with help from one of Victor's team, she and Alvaro got the trap door open it led down exactly seven steps to an alcove, then on turning a tight corner a further seven steps down into a hidden chamber. In there they found clear evidence that this had once been used as a habitation, though not a very pleasant one. Jars, drinking vessels, a large wooden table heavily beset with rot, oil lamps, as well as tools and various weapons dating back to the late 1400s were littered all around.

Then, to their amazement, the puzzle of how this room was accessed once long ago became clear. A tunnel led out from the chamber and Lucy made her way along as far as she could, Alvaro was too tall and didn't want to risk stooping any lower than necessary given the state of his back. From the direction of the tunnel, she could deduce that it ran towards the river known to the Moors as Hadarro, now morphed over time to the Darro. But then she encountered serious evidence of cave ins and the way became too narrow and dangerous without specialised equipment. She thought that could wait. Survival instinct kicked in and she had headed back.

On reappearing she found that Alvaro had been busy and had discovered a small leather-bound book inside a roll of what appeared to be cow hide. He said nothing, just pointed to the cover on which was etched a Hand of Fatima, with 7 fingers. Lucy felt cold hands on her neck and she turned sharply but it was simply an errant draft from the tunnel. Well, she hoped it was.

In the quiet and half-light, they stared for a moment; they both knew that this was the key to their quest but they would have to wait to open it under laboratory conditions to ensure it was intact. She could tell that Alvaro was clearly, quietly, in a state of what passed for him as excitement. She had not seen him so speechless.

They both knew there and then that they had found a hiding place of some sort. This was no addition to the palace used post 1492 by Isabella or Ferdinand. Alvaro had answered Lucy's query about the trap door and steps. Why was it necessary with the long tunnel to the riverbank? Alvaro had explained that it was most likely another escape route in the unlikely event that the tunnel was discovered. Possibly also as a get out if it ever flooded. And Boabdil had had to lay a trail somewhere nearby so not only you but others could find a way in if needed from close by.

Alvaro was certain that Boabdil had expected to be found at some point in the future. Though perhaps when he thought about it, given the additional symbol on the red paper in the pouch, it had most likely been La Mora of Ubeda who laid the owl trail.

And then there was the tomb. They would have to return to gain access and find out exactly who was buried within or, if indeed, if there was any one there at all. Lucy had added a healthy dash of pessimism to their conversation about it, mainly in order not to raise her own hopes. It tended to be useful in most aspects of her life. But she knew who she hoped would be in the tomb. It had to be Moraima.

Alvaro tapped the table lightly with his fingers and Lucy was back in the present.

She realised Alvaro was staring at her.

He gestured toward the envelope that lay on the table, unopened since it had come back from the University. The translation of the book he had found. He and a good friend, another multi-Arabic linguist, had worked on it for several days. It had been written in a curious mixture of Ḥassāniyyah Arabic, Arabized Amazigh, a language used by the Berbers, Latin and aljamiado.

The book had few pages, but they were all of red paper. Lucy had been unable to sleep waiting for this moment.

'So, are we now both calm enough to read this?'

'After you, Alvaro. Read it to me.'

'Absolutely not. This is your moment. You deserve to read it. I will listen closely, ensure it reads as well as we hope it will. And I don't think we should wait any longer.'

'Just give him a few more moments. I said he deserved to be here when it was read.'

At that moment, she heard the voice of Maria, welcoming someone and thirty seconds later, Faris Sarmiyento appeared. He had visibly aged since hearing about Gloria, but nonetheless he had agreed to be there. He smiled warmly and gave Lucy a gentle hug.

'Thank you both for inviting me. I feel very honoured.'

Alvaro smiled. 'Well, let's all say a quick prayer to the gods and ask Lucy to read. See what you both think.'

Maria had agreed to close the restaurant for an hour to give them privacy. She would clearly still do anything for Lucy Hawksmoor.

In the silence of the afternoon, Lucy began to read:

These are the true and faithful words of Abu Abdallah Muhammad Bin Ali, Muhammad, the last and forever faithful Nasrid Sultan of Granada, as told to Al -Mulih, his loyal servant and Vizier in the Year of Allah 905 (translator's note—1499 CE) of the Hijri Calendar.

Let it be known here and for all time to those who come after and those who read these words that I, Abu Abdallah Bin Ali kept my promise and did not desert Granada nor Al Andalus.

It has been foretold to me that one day the world will know what truly took place and that what I have passed on to my friend, mentor and spiritual guide, La Mora of Ubeda, will come into the possession of one who will take the blindfold off the eyes of history.

My desire before Allah is that I am now speaking to that person.

Lucy paused for a moment and looked up to the sky. This already was staggering. She swallowed hard, took a deep breath and continued:

To my beautiful wife, Moraima, who blessed me with her love, care and patience for longer than I deserved and by whose side I long to be, I made a vow on the day she left my world, that one day we would lie side by side in the Alhambra. It was not a promise I ever thought I could keep. But I had grown stronger in my knowledge of my worth and self than my younger years. As a youth imitating others, I failed to find myself. I looked inside and discovered I only knew my name. But since the day I rode away from the palace seven years ago I found myself. And with the help and wise counsel of my mother I was guided to the road I should take. And so another left these shores in my guise, my uncle, El Zagal, accompanied by my brave mother. He finally got his heart's desire and was welcomed as the last Sultan onto the shores of Africa in Melilla. I have had word that he prospers in Fez. No one questioned his haggard looks.

With Allah watching over us and with the help of my good and faithful friends, Moraima's mortal remains were carried here to the Red Palace and the terrible vultures of Isabella did not see us enter. For we took the route of an ancient tunnel unknown to the Christians, yet remembered by my mother, built over 200 years ago by Sultan Ibn al-Ahmar, as a means of escape, leading from the River Hadarro under the walls to chambers below Bib-al-Gudur.

In one such chamber we now sit. Moraima is buried within an aljibe. My wish was to have a likeness of her carved in stone but our mason has now disappeared through fear or death I know not. Perhaps it was a sign that Allah knew she was too sacred to have any image of her remain in this world.

I have passed many of the years since, reading the Qur'an and in prayer. Waiting for a sign. I have come and gone only several times each year, to see the sky, breathe sweet air and recently to meet those good people with whom we plan to bring rebellion to the Catholic King and Queen.

The time has come and I must ride out to bring down the vultures and strike at their heart. They have gone against their word. The treaty we agreed to the year before I left for the Alpujarras has been torn asunder. They now force my people to convert to the Catholic faith. With violence if necessary. Allah has spoken to me. I must act.

To you who read this, know that I hold no hatred in my heart for anyone. I intended to die here and I know I do not have long, but now when promises are broken and I hear of the burning of the blessed Qur'an and my people turned away from their mosques, I must meet fire with fire. Moraima will understand and wait for me.

Allah will guide me back here. I know it is not a war we can win, but we can harm them, let them know they are wrong to do this, that we will not standby as cowards and dogs and fall subservient before their god and rituals.

May Allah shine his light on you across the years. I know not when this will be read but I have looked into the future and with the guidance of La Mora, I have felt your presence, my dear reader, and know that you will be true in your quest for the truth.

Reach out and let the dead hold your hand.

We will guide you along the right path my friend.

(Here on the original follows the signature of the Sultan known as Boabdil)

عشر الثاني محمد الله عبد أبو

Lucy did not know how much more she could take, she had shed several tears during the reading, though feared if she stopped, she would really break down. Faris and Alvaro had both encouraged her along the way and she was so glad they were there with her. Lucy then looked at the brief translator's note—*Here follows words written seemingly later by the same hand, that of Al-Mulih:*

She read it a second time, aloud and then continued.

I have returned from a meeting this past night by the banks of the River Genil with one who knows and has seen all that has occurred since my lord departed to raise battle. It has been two months now since the rebellion broke; nothing more than skirmishes at first within the city but now more serious fighting bloods the land and has spread to the foothills of the Sierra Nevada. I know not what will transpire but I have had no word from my lord and master. I pray each day to Allah for his safe return.

It is now with heavy heart that I fear the worse. The year is close to turning and winter wears his full armour.

(Translators note: The final entry which follows appears to have also been written by Al Mulih but it is clearly a far less neat or precise script, so hard to say with absolute certainty that it by the same hand, though likely.)

News comes to me today that splinters my world, my lord and master has fallen in battle. The enemy did not take him. I am told his body has been taken away to a cave near the village of Capileira. Whether he will return here to lie by his wife's side is at the present time uncertain. But you who read my words must know that I have to leave. I have to search for him.

My final words for now are farewell and may Allah watch over you, Allah 'Akbar.

The three of them sat in silence for several moments. Alvaro spoke first. 'You realise we should all be popping open champagne right now and screaming from the rooftops.'

Lucy smiled softly. 'I know, but somehow, this makes it all so real, more than anything I have ever been involved with. And I just feel so sad. Not that we didn't find him, but that he didn't get his wish to be buried next to Moraima. I knew it was her in that tomb. Jesus. What a story.'

Faris leant over and put his hand gently on Lucy's shoulder.

'But he would not be sad. In fact, I am certain he is not sad because you have brought him into the light. What you have found changes history, Lucy. I for one am so proud of you.'

'Even after all that has happened to Gloria because of all this?'

'Yes, for I know my daughter and not for one second can I believe any of what the police say. She would be proud.' He changed tense quickly. 'Will be proud also of what you have done. I wish she was here.'

'Me too.'

Alvaro sipped his wine and sat up straight, always a sign that he was about to get serious.

'I too am proud of you, Lucy, but now is the time to tread carefully. This discovery will do more than change history, it could set off all kinds of changes, not all necessarily for the good.'

Faris looked upset. 'Are you suggesting we do nothing? Keep all this to ourselves?'

'No, not for one moment. But we need to think it through and we need to do more research and analysis down in the chambers we discovered. When this is launched to the Spanish public and to the world, it will cause a tidal wave of interest and we need to have all the facts, all the proof. No stone must be left unturned.

The authorities are under no allusions either. Those who do know and thankfully they are not many, they have now granted us a year to investigate down there further. They also want this delivered in the most positive light and at exactly the right time, whatever that may mean. The Alhambra is already one of the biggest tourist magnets in the world, over two and a half million people visit it every year and the authorities know that this news will also turn it into a place of pilgrimage. And that will bring gigantic logistical problems too. What we are doing comes with a huge responsibility. And, though you need no reminding, sadly not everyone will be overjoyed at this discovery.'

Lucy looked over at Faris.

'He's right. This is going to be huge and for the sake of Boabdil as much as anything, we need to get it right.' She paused and then looked at them both.

'You know it's strange. At times I was unsure why I was pursuing this. I can't say that I was ever really convinced that we would make such a find. But now, slowly, the consequences of it all are sinking in. Really sinking in.'

She poured a glass of wine for her and Alvaro and ordered a glass of water for Faris who had gone very quiet.

'A toast. To Boabdil and to both of you, for all your support and friendship and much wisdom too.'

The atmosphere lifted and they all smiled.

'I have a feeling, gentlemen, that life is not going to be quite the same for some time.'

Faris stood up. 'And let me toast you, Lucy Hawksmoor. I am beyond proud and privileged to have been the keeper who saw the truth brought to light. And proud to know you and to see what you have done and no doubt what you will do in the near future. And to Gloria, for it was she who, for whatever reason, convinced me you were the one. I know she lied to you and brought you into danger. But deep down she is a true and honest girl.'

'Faris, it's OK, no need to worry. I know.'

'One more thing, Lucy, whilst I am on my feet. Do not give up on Boabdil.'

Alvaro looked up at him with a puzzled gaze.

Lucy knew what he meant. 'I have no intention of doing so. But I have to share something with you both, though you may think me stark raving mad.' She paused. 'Well, I have felt at several moments over the past weeks that someone was looking for me, someone I couldn't see, someone from another time. And I have had odd dreams. Alvaro, I didn't tell you before but I saw that exact same tomb in the aljibe in one of them, with a woman in blue lying on top of it. And now, reading this, he is talking to me, as if he knows I would find him. It is scary, but somehow, Christ I can't believe I'm saying this, but I believe it. I wouldn't share this with many others I promise but I had to say these words out loud, just so it is more real to me. I'm jabbering now, sorry.'

She took another sip of wine.

'Don't be, Lucy. I think I can speak for both Faris and I, when I say neither of us think you're mad.'

Faris smiled warmly. 'No and he still wants to be found. Boabdil wants to be returned to his wife's side. And he wants you to find him. Of this, I am certain. Until he is, perhaps no one will truly believe what these words say.'

Lucy sighed. 'Exactly. I've lost sleep over this. Perhaps we need to wait until we have found his remains. Somewhere up near Capileira.'

Alvaro shook his head. 'You are right I believe, but that is a huge ask to find his body in those mountains. How would you even set about it?'

Lucy looked at them both with a glint in her eyes.

'Gentlemen, I will find him, with both your help and with Boabdil's.' She raised her glass again.

'And I accept the challenge, Boabdil. I *will* let the dead take my hand and guide me.'

And Alvaro ordered champagne and together they sat and talked for many hours. About all that had passed since that day when Lucy first met Gloria in the Caixa Forum. And all that lay ahead of them.

Epilogue

Christmas was in the air and Lucy still retained her love of the period that once excited her so much as a child. She had no religious views at all but that did not stop her enjoying the build-up, the magic and mystery of the festive period. All being well, her family was flying out the next day, the 23rd to spend it with her, even her mother. They would celebrate Spanish style and she had all the food and drink ready.

Then the doorbell rang. Two minutes later, Inspector Gomez walked in.

'Hope you don't mind, Lucy, but I have left the door downstairs propped open. My driver is just parking up and will be here any moment.'

'That's fine. I'm a little wary of why you're here though, Inspector. It's a long way to come just to bring a Christmas card. Should I be worried?'

At that moment, a slim, dark haired girl in tight black trousers, black t-shirt and leather jacket walked in through the door, a police badge clipped to her jeans pocket. Lucy was lost momentarily for words.

'Ah, Lucy, let me introduce Officer Carrasco, my driver.'

'Pleased to meet you, Miss Hawksmoor,'

'Call me Lucy please, everyone else does, otherwise I sound like an ageing professor.'

'Fine, thank you. Call me Marta.'

Lucy made coffee and once they were sat down, Gomez began.

'I wanted to tell you what I have to say in person, not over the phone or by e-mail. And we both had time off, so, that made it easier.'

'Have you found Gloria?'

'We have had no word of her whereabouts. But the car she left in, a red Seat Ibiza was found abandoned near the airport in Madrid. But we do not believe she has left the country, we would have known. However, I am here chiefly to warn you that yesterday, Ximena Martinez escaped from custody. She was being escorted to a different facility, when the car she was in was hijacked and she took off. Sadly, we believe one of our officers was in on it. It was all too easy and he has now disappeared also. His partner was left with a bullet in his spine and he is in a critical condition.'

'Shit. And are you worried now she might come after me?'

'Not imminently, we have reason to believe she may have left the country, possibly crossed the border into France. There is a warrant out for her arrest but, well, before she left she had been seeing a doctor, supposedly for depression, but two days ago she started rambling about you and your work and what she wanted to do to you. That was just before she attacked the doctor, a female who I have to say in many ways bears a likeness to you, hair colour, age, height etc. She left her in a bad way. That was why she was being moved. Perhaps it was all part of the plan but the doctor has told us that Martinez made it very clear she was going to look for you, er, 'ruin your face, ruin your job, ruin your search' in her exact words.'

'Jesus! That's not a great Christmas present, Inspector. What do you suggest I do?'

'Be very, very vigilant. Maybe move apartments in the New Year. And in January, Officer Carrasco here, Marta, will be acting as your bodyguard for a month or two, with your permission. She is technically on leave, but she is adamant that she wants to do something to get back at the people who took the life of a colleague and nearly took hers.'

'I'm fine now, my hearing is not what it was but the scars in my side are healed and I may never have babies, but hey that's OK with me.'

Lucy stared at her. Of course, this was the officer Gloria mentioned.

'I'm sorry about what happened, but I'm sure I'll be fine.'

Gomez cut in. 'Lucy, let it be seen as a gesture that we care about the work you are doing. I have been told by a higher authority more or less what it is and I have been instructed to give you every assistance possible, including plain clothes, police guards at the work site in the Alhambra whenever it recommences. Carrasco is insurance for me. That I am doing my job.'

Carrasco leant forward; Lucy couldn't take her eyes off her.

'Lucy, I will not be intrusive in any way. You will not know I'm there. But also, I'm even happy to help as an assistant if you wish. I am a quick learner and I speak Arabic. I have a lot of connections that might prove useful in Granada and elsewhere amongst the Muslim population. Please, think about it.'

This reminded Lucy so much of her first meeting with Gloria it was scary.

'I will, yes, of course.'

They stood up to go.

'Oh and any news of Diego?'

Carrasco and Gomez exchanged a brief glance that Lucy spotted.

'Well?'

'After helping Gloria escape, we apprehended him. But we had no cause to detain him. We had no concrete proof that he had in fact been with her. He certainly didn't go in the car to Madrid. He was on his way to see Victor Morata, his boyfriend, when he was set upon and beaten to within an inch of his life. He is recovering in hospital but he's not in a good way. I did not want to alarm you, but we believe from his description that he was set upon by known members of Casa Social. They had tried to get him to tell them about what work you had been doing in the Alhambra.'

Lucy had to sit down. 'Oh, god no. Victor must be beside himself. Poor Diego.'

'I am happy to reassure you that the hospital say he will be fine.' He stood up. 'We can see ourselves out, Lucy. Be careful.'

'I will. My family will be here.'

'Good and have a peaceful Christmas. Please think about our offer.'

Gomez walked out.

Carrasco was about to follow but paused in the doorway then turned.

'Oh, sorry, I forgot.' She took a small package out of her jacket pocket. 'The postman handed this to me on my way up to give to you.' She popped it on the table.

'I really hope you will let me work with you. Look out for you. It would be an honour.' She left a card with her phone number on top of the package.

They exchanged smiles.

'That would be nice. I'll be in touch, Marta.'

Once all was quiet. Lucy sat on her sofa, her favourite orange wrap thrown around her shoulders with Jasper purring by her side and the package on her knee. The post mark was Zaragoza.

She couldn't think of anyone she knew that well there who would send her a present.

'Come on Jasper, let's see what it is.'

She opened it. There was a small purple velvet pouch inside and a card with 'Hand Made Jewellery by Silvia Ortega Zamorano' printed on it.

On the flip side in a small neat hand was written a short verse:

'I tried to give you up and
Live without the pain of longing
I tried to be empty of all passion for you -
I failed.'
Feliz Navidad

She opened the pouch and onto her lap fell a beautiful silver Hand of Fatima on a fine silver chain.

Lucy held it up in front of her. The piece was exquisitely made. She couldn't believe it.

Then, suddenly, she noticed something else about the hand.

It had seven fingers.

Lucy laughed as she cried and placed it round her neck.

Now there were two people she had to find.

I would like to thank first and foremost the renowned historian, Dr Elizabeth Drayson, whose magnificent book *The Moor's Last Stand* inspired me to write this novel. Also, many thanks to my friend, Annie Mihell, whose reading and critique at an early stage spurred me on. I also want to say a huge thank you to my amazing children for always being so supportive and understanding. My gratitude also goes out to my publishers for their patience, support and encouragement.

Finally, to the people of Spain, for whom this story is written. The land of my heart and now my home, and especially to the wonderful citizens of Madrid, Granada and Cordoba who have given me so much inspiration, warmth and friendship.

Further Reading

The Moor's Last Stand by Elizabeth Drayson
Destiny Disrupted by Tamim Ansary
Arabs: A 3,000-Year History of Peoples, Tribes and Empires
by Tim Mckintosh-Smith

I also recommend reading the online newsletter openDemocracy
(openDemocarcy.net) for up-to-date unbiased reporting on the actions of
the far right across Europe.